He was being sweet.

And that confused Val. She was used to knowing her emotions and acting on her instincts. But nothing was safe where Con was concerned.

She fought an urge to run her fingertips over his chin. His mouth was sharply defined, the top lip disciplined, the lower one fascinatingly full.

"Keep looking at me, and one of us is going to get ideas."

Her blood drummed in her ears. Ideas. Oh, yes. Oh, heavens. She usually trusted her feelings. But these were so new, she no longer trusted herself.

"Would that be bad?" she asked.

"Not bad," he rasped out. "I'm willing to bet we'd be pretty damn good, in fact. But it wouldn't be smart."

Dear Reader,

Happy New Year! Silhouette Intimate Moments is starting the year off with a bang—not to mention six great books. Why not begin with the latest of THE PROTECTORS, Beverly Barton's miniseries about men no woman can resist? In *Murdock's Last Stand,* a well-muscled mercenary meets his match in a woman who suddenly has him thinking of forever.

Alicia Scott returns with *Marrying Mike... Again,* an intense reunion story featuring a couple who are both police officers with old hurts to heal before their happy ending. Try Terese Ramin's *A Drive-By Wedding* when you're in the mood for suspense, an undercover agent hero, an irresistible child and a carjacked heroine who ends up glad to go along for the ride. Already known for her compelling storytelling abilities, Eileen Wilks lives up to her reputation with *Midnight Promises,* a marriage-of-convenience story unlike any other you've ever read. Virginia Kantra brings you the next of the irresistible MacNeills in *The Comeback of Con MacNeill,* and Kate Stevenson returns after a long time away, with *Witness... and Wife?*

All six books live up to Intimate Moments' reputation for excitement and passion mixed together in just the right proportions, so I hope you enjoy them all.

Yours,

Leslie J. Wainger
Executive Senior Editor

Please address questions and book requests to:
Silhouette Reader Service
U.S.: 3010 Walden Ave., P.O. Box 1325, Buffalo, NY 14269
Canadian: P.O. Box 609, Fort Erie, Ont. L2A 5X3

THE COMEBACK OF
CON MacNEILL

VIRGINIA KANTRA

Silhouette®

INTIMATE™MOMENTS®

Published by Silhouette Books

America's Publisher of Contemporary Romance

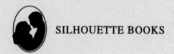 SILHOUETTE BOOKS

ISBN 0-373-07983-4

THE COMEBACK OF CON MacNEILL

Copyright © 2000 by Virginia Kantra Ritchey

Visit us at www.romance.net

Printed in U.S.A.

Books by Virginia Kantra

Silhouette Intimate Moments

The Reforming of Matthew Dunn #894
The Passion of Patrick MacNeill #906
The Comeback of Con MacNeill #983

VIRGINIA KANTRA

credits her enthusiasm for strong heroes and courageous heroines to a childhood spent devouring fairy tales. After graduating from Northwestern University with honors in English, she shared her love of books as a children's story-teller. She still visits classrooms on Valentine's Day dressed as the Queen of Hearts.

When her youngest child started school, Virginia fulfilled her dream of writing full-time. Her first book, *The Reforming of Matthew Dunn,* won RWA's Golden Heart Award for Best Romantic Suspense, received the Holt Medallion and was nominated by *Romantic Times Magazine* as Best First Series Romance in 1998. Her second book, *The Passion of Patrick MacNeill,* was a Golden Heart finalist and Maggie Award winner, a *Romantic Times Magazine* Top Pick and a winner of a W.I.S.H. Award.

Virginia is married to her college sweetheart, a musician disguised as an executive. They live in Raleigh, North Carolina, with three children, two cats, a dog and various blue-tailed lizards that live under the siding of their home. Her favorite thing to make for dinner is reservations.

To Michael—
There are no books without you.

and

To my editor, Mary-Theresa Hussey,
who always sees something to like
and always finds some way to make it better.

Special thanks to Pam Baustian and Judith Stanton,
to Lieutenant Gary Blankenship of the
Chatham County Sheriff's Office,
and to Marvin and Carla Swirsky of Zest Café
in Raleigh.

Chapter 1

Con MacNeill rubbed sweat from his chest. This Carolina town was too damn hot for a Boston boy.

He leaned against the wall of the First Baptist Church, seeking shade and the cool prickle of brick against his back. Main Street, North Carolina, was not his scene at all. But with Lynn's wedding scheduled for three weeks from today, even Boston had begun to feel uncomfortably warm. Too many parties. Too many phone calls from mock or mutual friends eager to pry or express sympathy. He was better out of it. All of it. The offer from Edward Cutler couldn't have come at a better time.

Nothing like a new challenge to get a man over being fired.

Con crossed his arms against his chest, shutting down the flare of frustration. Define the problem, he reminded himself. That was the way he operated. Solve the problem.

He surveyed the street, spanned by a banner that proclaimed the town of Cutler's Seventh Annual Super Summer Sidewalk Sale. From the church parking lot to the county courthouse steps, racks of out-of-season clothes competed with bins of plastic trinkets. Halfway down the block, Arlene's Country Café supplied coffee and doughnuts to passing patrons, while the rival establishment on the opposite corner handed out clear plastic cups of…Lord knew what.

Con narrowed his eyes at the freshly painted green-and-white sign over the door: Wild Thymes. Cute. Very cute. As he watched, a vendor leaned forward from beneath the cool canvas awning to offer an elderly customer a plastic fork and a smile.

Sunlight dropped across her face. Her tawny hair blazed, stirred by a hot breeze. For that one moment, sun and wind combined to create a vision of light and movement that burned like summer sparkling on lake waters. For that one moment, the woman leaning across the plank counter was Woman, divine and incarnate. Wild yearning uncurled in Con's Celtic heart. Awe breathed through his Catholic soul. She was Eve before the Fall. She was Niamh of the Golden Hair, legendary love of Oisin. She was the Lady on the White Horse in his mother's stories.

Desire hit him, hard and low. And striking harder, unrecognized and unwelcome, possibility assailed him like the sea.

Then the breeze dropped. The woman turned her head to talk to someone over her shoulder. Green shade drabbed the golden hair and dimmed the radiant face, leaving only a waitress, chatting up a customer.

Holy saints and martyrs.

Con forced himself to relax against the brick wall at his back. She was just an ordinary pretty girl in jeans and a gauzy shirt and a glint of silver jewelry. Less Venus, he thought, his mind recoiling in panicked reaction, than a poster child for Haight-Ashbury. She looked like she smoked dope or at least ate sprouts.

He started to feel better. He could only have imagined that one moment of blinding beauty. He must have imagined his over-the-top reaction. His brothers would laugh them-selves sick at the picture of cool, logical Con losing it over some sweet Southern thing in barely there gauze. Lynn, at least, had been a rational choice for an ambitious deal-maker with no social background.

Con scowled. He had a new business to occupy his mind and a new client to focus his thoughts. What he'd experi-enced was a normal male response toward a passably attrac-tive female, that was all.

Simple male appreciation. Sure.

He caught himself watching for that fall of brown-and-gold hair again, just to prove it to himself, and snorted in disgust. Pushing away from the shadow of the church, he strolled along the baking sidewalk, conscious of heads turn-ing to follow his progress. A woman nudged her neighbor. A trio of old men broke off their conversation to stare him past the hardware store.

Under his sweat-dampened shirt, his shoulders squared. Okay, sometime during puberty he'd caught on to the fact that MacNeill men attracted their fair share of feminine glances. More than their fair share, in his younger brother Sean's case. But this wary inspection felt different. Wryly, Con wondered if they still hung carpetbaggers in Nowhere, North Carolina.

On the sidewalk ahead of him a couple of boys had dragged out a card table and a cardboard sign. Lemonaid, it proclaimed, the word misspelled but boldly lettered. Base-ball Cards. The setup reminded Con of a time twenty years ago when he and his big brother Patrick hawked Kool-Aid from the bottom of the driveway in Quincy. God bless free enterprise. He stopped by the table, digging in the back pocket of his jeans for his wallet.

"How much?"

The boys gawked at him as if he'd just asked to buy a jug of moonshine.

"For the lemonade," he clarified. "How much?"

One of the boys, older or quicker to scent a profit, pushed his baseball cap back on his head to evaluate his mark. "Uh…fifty cen'."

The kid next to him made a strangled noise and was kicked under the table.

Con suppressed a grin. "That's kind of expensive."

"It's hot. We can sell lots of lemonade."

"It's good lemonade," the younger kid chimed in help- fully.

"Is it? All right." Con laid a dollar on the table. "Give me a big glass, then."

The older kid stuffed the bill away and then poured, slop- ping liquid on the table. "Here."

Con accepted the sticky cup cautiously. "Thanks."

He turned, lifting the cup to his lips…and found himself staring over the rim straight into the wide gray eyes of the tawny-haired goddess, behind him in line.

A trio of silver hoops glittered from one of her earlobes; a feather on a hook dangled from the other, lending her face a lopsided appeal. Her hair waved in heavy snakes of brown and gold, inviting him to imagine how it would look spilling over his pillow. Tickling his chest.

Con sucked in a breath. What the hell was the matter with him? He was a business consultant, not a randy teenage boy.

His turn, so close, had startled her. Her mouth parted in surprise. Recovering, she stepped back and smiled, revealing quick creases at the corners of her eyes. So, she was older than she looked from half a block away. The spurt of relief he felt annoyed him.

Define the problem, he reminded himself. He had a job to do. Obviously, Blondie here worked at the restaurant Ed- ward Cutler had hired him to advise. Here was an oppor- tunity to start interviewing the staff.

"Can I buy you a drink?" he offered.

Val felt the exploding attraction like a bitten peppercorn, hot and unwelcome. Her mouth watered. The man had the lean, disciplined face of a scholar and the hard, muscled body of a gym jock. His eyes, meeting hers, were bright and cold as sapphires.

Not her type, she decided instantly. He was too tall, too broad and much too full of himself.

"Thank you, no."

Her eyes were on a level with his big, broad chest. He was still in her way.

"Pardon me," she said politely to his sternum, and then made the mistake of looking up into those cold blue eyes. They smiled at her with such unexpected humor, such seductive complicity, that her insides went as gooey as melted chocolate. She stepped around him, uncomfortably aware of his size. His heat. His torso in that snug white T-shirt.

Forget the torso, she ordered herself, and smiled across the card table at Jimmy Jackson.

"Hey, Jimmy. How's business?"

Jimmy twisted his baseball cap around and grinned bashfully. "Great. You want a lemonade?"

"I sure do," Val said. She needed something to cool off. She felt like that frustrated spinster in *The Long Hot Summer,* sipping lemonade to quench her desires. "How much?"

"Uh…" Inexplicably, the boy's gaze flicked over her shoulder to the big man standing behind her. "Twenty-five cents."

The man laughed. Val ignored him. She gave Jimmy a quarter and her best smile and accepted a foam cup in return.

"Mmm. This is good. You planning on putting me out of business?"

"Naw. This is kid stuff. My dad says I should go into computers when I grow up like him."

Val couldn't help it. Her smile froze. "Don't do it. Follow your dream, Jimmy."

"He's what, ten?" the man behind her asked. "More

likely to dream about major league ball than selling lemonade.''

Despite herself, Val laughed. "Much more likely," she agreed.

That blue gaze snagged hers as she turned. Attraction thumped her midsection. Oh, my. Flushing, she looked away, down the street. Oh, dear. Was that Rob Cross parading from the bank, blond hair gleaming, warm and welcome—in most circles—as a pastry tray?

"Pardon me," she murmured again, and stepped off the curb. "Thanks for the drink, Jimmy."

The torso fell easily into step beside her. "The kid charged me fifty cents."

Like she would stoop to flirting with a man who practiced pickup lines over lemonade. But the humorous grievance in his tone drew her response. "Not from around these parts, are you?"

"I take it it shows?" His voice was pure Yankee—New England, maybe?—with a cool assurance that raised her hackles faintly.

She bit the inside of her cheek. That was definitely Rob, stopping to chat with the trio of regulars holding down the bench in front of the hardware store. He was a popular guy. He remembered your daughter's name and your son's soccer team and your mother's arthritis. Everybody in Cutler liked Rob.

Except Val.

She quickened her walk, dodging a rack of pale blue and lavender polyester, disconcerted by the way the stranger kept pace at her elbow. "Yes, it does. Would you excuse me?"

"Do you make a practice of stiffing strangers in this town?"

"Not at all. Jimmy gives me a discount. As a professional courtesy."

They'd reached the restaurant. Her unsought companion rocked back on his heels, hands thrust casually in his back pockets as he surveyed the entrance. Val satisfied herself with a quick glance around.

Perfect, she thought. Perfect and hers.

A standing chalkboard in the doorway announced the day's specials. White caladium and red impatiens spilled from a terra-cotta planter. Around the big picture window, Ann had stenciled bunches of herbs with joyous care. Ann herself tended the makeshift counter they'd set up on the sidewalk, her hands folded over her pretty green-and-white apron, and that guarded look she wore too often on her face.

Everything about Ann was quiet and neat and understated, Val thought with appreciation, from her smooth brown hair to her soft tan flats. Even in this heat, she wore a full-length slip, its straps visible through her white camp shirt, tucked into the waistband of her khaki skirt.

"Annie, Rob's on his way here," Val said quietly. "Was he expecting you at the bank? Do you want to call it quits for the day?"

"Oh, I... Yes, I'd better." Ann's hands reached behind her for her apron strings.

"You both work here?" the torso asked.

Why didn't the man just go away? "Yes."

"Nice place?"

Val angled her chin, mildly affronted by the question.

"Do you like the working conditions?" he amended.

She thought of her twelve-hour days battling purveyors over freshness and price, kitchen help who didn't report to work, repairmen who never seemed to come when they were needed. The unforeseen operating costs. The struggle to make the day's deposits cover the unexpected expenses. The blessed, blessed independence.

"Yes," she said again.

His mouth, with its full lower lip, quirked up. "That's it? No sales pitch?"

"Are you a food critic?"

"No."

She shrugged. "Well, then."

"But I could be a customer."

"I doubt it."

His dark brows lifted in surprise. "Why the hell not?"

Momentarily distracted, she permitted her gaze to drift down the well-developed pectorals and muscled forearms of a man who pressed weights and loaded proteins. "Wild Thymes features a vegetarian menu. Our clientele are students who want sandwiches and seniors who want soups and ladies who lunch. No offense, but you look like you hunt your kill and eat it charred."

She thought—maybe she hoped—he might laugh. Instead, the lean, handsome face shuttered up and the humor died from his eyes.

"Yeah, one look and you've got me figured, don't you, Dixie?"

Val flushed under the relentless sun and his cold scorn. Whatever her mother's failures, Sylvia Cutler hadn't raised her daughter to be rude with impunity.

"The name's Cutler. Val Cutler. And I'm sorry. I just assumed there wouldn't be a lot here likely to appeal to you."

He looked at her strangely, but Val barely noticed. Rob was almost to the corner.

She turned to smile reassurance at Ann and plucked a plastic cup from the makeshift counter. Maybe if she fed this large, inconvenient stranger, he would leave? "Please. Have a sample."

Warily, the man accepted her peace offering. "What is it?"

"Tabbouleh." She handed him a fork. "Bulgur wheat, parsley, peppers, tomatoes and mint."

Before he could comment, before he could taste, Rob spoke from behind her.

"Poisoning the customers, Val?" He chuckled at his own joke.

The customer in question narrowed his blue eyes. Val felt her face, her jaw, her entire body stiffen. She turned around slowly.

"Gee, not yet," she drawled. "Maybe I need to put more insecticide in the salad dressing. What do you think?"

They both pretended to laugh. Behind the counter, Ann twisted her hands until her diamond wedding set cut into her fingers.

Rob spared a glance for his colorless little wife. "Running late today, baby?"

Ann answered in a flat voice that had none of her husband's charm. "Just a little. I left Mitchell at your mother's."

"That's right. She phoned me. I thought you were dropping by the bank."

"Well, I…"

"We're open late today," Val interjected. At the other end of the counter, the dark-haired giant watched them, eyes sharp and cool in his politely disinterested face. Impossible to guess how much he could hear. "Because of the fair. You don't mind, do you?"

"Mind? Why would I mind? You certainly can use the help. Free help, that is."

He spoke so smoothly it took a moment for the offensiveness of his words to sink in.

Val bit her lip. "You know I've offered to pay Ann."

"I know you can't afford her. Fortunately, I can." He leaned confidingly against the counter. "I've got to tell you, Val, you're overdrawn at the bank again. Your quarterly tax check just bounced."

The giant faded from Val's peripheral vision. Panic twisted inside her like a knife. "It can't have. I've made deposits every day this week."

"Sorry. It wasn't quite enough to cover it," Rob informed her. And as vice president of the proof department, he was in a position to know. "Did you keep records?"

"My deposit slips."

She'd never been that good with figures, and they both knew it. Which was why she took her receipts to the bank to be tallied.

"Well, bring them in. We'll see what we can do." His brown eyes brightened with malice, although his tone stayed suitably grave. "I'm sure your daddy can help you out."

Damn him, he was enjoying this. Val swallowed her resentment, refusing to feed him one trace of her disturbance.

Whisking crumbs from the makeshift counter, she said coolly, "That won't be necessary, thanks."

But she was dreadfully afraid she was wrong.

"I should go," Ann said, laying down her apron. "I promised Mitchell I'd take him to the library."

Rob frowned. "You coddle that boy. It's summertime. Turn him loose outside, that's what he really needs."

"I promised," Ann repeated dully.

"And we know how seriously *my wife* takes her word, don't we?" He placed his hand on the back of Ann's neck in a seeming caress.

Ann didn't flinch from the hand beneath her hair—didn't, in fact, make any move at all—but Val's gut tightened.

"I don't think there's ever been any doubt about Ann's honesty," she said sharply. "Or her loyalty, unfortunately."

"Thanks for the sample."

The clipped northern accent dropped like hail in the heated atmosphere. Val started at the interruption.

Her Yankee customer strolled forward, smiled politely at Ann and set his plastic cup, still half-full, on the counter.

"How did you like it?" Val asked.

He hesitated. "Interesting."

"Well, thank you for that ringing endorsement," she said dryly.

He shrugged, his hard, cool eyes touching her. "It's just not to my taste. Like you said, there's not a lot here likely to appeal to me. No offense,'' he said, as she had to him, and the heat whipped into her face.

He walked away. Val watched him go.

Rob straightened, smiling. ''Guess I'll be going, too.''

He drew Ann to him by her nape and kissed her cheek, a big, blond, handsome man flirting with his wife in public. It should have been charming. Val felt slightly sick.

''Have a fun time at the library, baby. Too bad you didn't get by the bank. I'll see you at home tonight.''

There was no reason the casual domestic endearment should ring like a threat. But as Val looked from Rob's handsome face to Ann's blank one, she wished futilely that Ann could be anywhere but in the big white house on Stonewall Drive when her husband came home that night.

Too bad Val couldn't convince Ann to take a job at Wild Thymes. Aunt Naomi had always maintained that a woman's financial independence made her strong and the men in her life respectful. But Rob had nixed that idea early on. It was one thing for his wife to help out an old school friend and quite another for her to work as a waitress.

Sighing, Val began to stack leftover samples of tabbouleh. Besides, the little amount she could pay Ann now wouldn't provide independence for a cockroach. Rob was right. The restaurant couldn't afford another employee. Couldn't even afford its taxes, apparently.

She needed money.

She pushed impatiently at her hair, curling around her face in the humidity. Like it or not, Monday morning she would have to present herself at the bank to learn the new terms the bank president was setting on his approval.

So much, she thought wryly, for financial independence.

Everything in Edward Cutler's office—the kilim carpet, the original oil paintings, even the vaultlike temperature—advertised wealth. Evidently, the banker wanted everyone to know that he could buy the best.

And the best, it seemed, included Con.

Sold, one hotshot Yankee venture capitalist, for three weeks' salary and a decent business recommendation.

Sudden anger scooped Con's gut, leaving an aching hollow.

He sucked in a careful breath, filling the void with oxygen. Anger was unproductive. Define the problem. Solve the problem. That was all this stopgap job was about.

He leaned back in his chair, deliberately matching Cutler's casual pose. "Look, I can do what you want. But my time will cost almost as much as the actual loan. Don't you think before committing to this project I should meet with your daughter to define her objectives?"

Edward Cutler laid his manicured fingers together tip to tip. "No. My daughter isn't hiring you. I am."

The heck you say, Con thought, narrowing his eyes at the tanned and tailored executive. No matter how much Con needed Edward Cutler's business, no matter how eager he was to be out of Boston for the next month, he didn't relish dealing with a matched set of some uppercrust family's baggage.

"So, from your perspective, what is the problem?"

"Look, MacNeill, I'll be blunt. My daughter is not a competent businesswoman. She turned down the chance at college. She spent four years at some cooking school in New York and then worked at various restaurants for a while after that. As a waitress, I believe, and a hostess and something called a sous chef? Have I got that right?"

Con nodded, working to match the banker's description with the tawny-haired girl from Saturday's street fair. Too bad it fit. The last thing he needed complicating this job was some inconvenient attraction to the goddess of sprouts and tofu.

"And what do you want from me?"

"I want you to take over," Edward said frankly. "I want you to make her restaurant a success. Now that she's come to her senses and come home, I'm not having my daughter called a failure in my town.''

What he wanted was impossible to guarantee. Con was good. He'd had to be, and no damn dismissal could be allowed to shake his confidence. But there were factors here outside his control.

He chose his words carefully, forced to choose between honesty and antagonizing an important client. ''I'll do my best. But you have to realize going in that the failure rate for restaurants in the first three years is close to ninety percent.''

Edward's face frosted. ''I'm taking a chance on you, MacNeill, because I like you. Not everyone would have pulled a small bank like mine in on that development in Raleigh last year, or on the Atlanta merger. But our former relationship doesn't blind me to the fact that your recent business judgment has been called into question.''

From frosty, the atmosphere turned crystalline cold and cracked like ice on a pond. Con felt his footing shift, felt the treacherous waters seep through. Cutler knew. And plainly the banker was prepared to use what he knew to leverage their deal.

Con swallowed his anger. ''Whatever you've heard, I stand by my decisions. And my record.''

''And I appreciate that,'' Cutler assured him with false geniality. ''But I won't appreciate it if you fail me on this.''

Through his teeth, Con said, ''I'm not in the habit of failure.''

There was a tap on the door, and Cutler's secretary stuck her styled silver head inside. ''Miss Cutler is here.''

''Of course, of course. Send her in.'' The banker leveled a look at Con. ''Just as long as we understand each other.''

Con understood him only too well. But before he could say so, before he could say anything, Edward Cutler's daughter stalked into the room in heavy dark shoes, wearing something short and green that fluttered at the tops of her long, pale thighs.

It was the stall proprietor, all right, looking like the Lady of the Lake after a night on the street. Her extravagant hair flowed halfway down her back. Silver studded her ears and dangled to her shoulders.

Beside him, Cutler stiffened with annoyance at the girl's unconventional business attire. Con tried to summon a matching disapproval, but his body had other ideas.

Oh, yeah.

His body approved.

"Con MacNeill." The banker introduced them. "My daughter, Valerian Darcy Cutler."

Con narrowed his eyes, striving for his customary professional detachment. "We've met."

Chapter 2

Well, shoot. What was the torso doing in her father's office?

Val's nerves already simmered. MacNeill's solid, unexpected presence just turned up the heat. She hated coming to the bank. She hated asking her father for money even more. In a frivolous attempt to bolster her spirits, she'd chosen the most defiantly un-Junior League dress in her closet. Judging from Edward Cutler's spasm of distaste, she'd only managed to annoy him.

Val suppressed a sigh. She'd always been good at that.

She offered MacNeill her hand. As they shook, his assessing gaze flicked over the gauzy green dress before returning politely to her face. Was that amusement at the back of those cool blue eyes? He raised one eyebrow, ever so slightly, and her cheeks heated.

She retrieved her hand. "Nice to see you again," she lied. "Why is he here?" she asked her father.

Edward frowned at her directness. "Mr. MacNeill is

MacNeill Business Solutions from Boston. I thought his presence this morning would be helpful.''

Val surveyed the two executives sandwiching the desk. Matching slices of white bread she thought, in pinstriped suits and power ties. She was outnumbered and outgunned, and the meeting hadn't even started.

"Helpful," she repeated. "You bet."

She was almost certain this time that the blue eyes laughed at her as they all sat down. In appreciation? Or ridicule?

She smoothed her short skirt over her thighs and then looked squarely at her father. Since she had to be here, they might as well get this over with. Edward Cutler would, as always, hear just what he wanted to hear and say precisely what he wanted to say. Bashful refinement would get her nowhere.

"I thought we were discussing my loan application today," she said bluntly.

"We will. But these things take time, punkin. I was just telling MacNeill here that—"

She could just imagine what he'd told MacNeill. It was galling enough to approach her father for money without having her familial and professional shortcomings trotted out for this cool, shrewd stranger.

"Yes or no?" she interrupted.

"Now, Val, I told you, you want money, you don't have to go through all this rigmarole with the bank. I can make you a loan."

"Maybe I like the bank's terms better."

Edward Cutler's thin smile flickered. "Maybe you haven't heard the bank's terms yet."

Val folded her hands to keep them steady. "I'm listening."

"A restaurant isn't a good financial risk. There are reasons you've been turned down by every other bank in a radius of three counties. Now, I didn't say anything when you decided to open—''

Val grinned. ''As I remember, you said plenty.''

Con found it hard not to like the grin. He bet this one had been a handful growing up. Heck, she'd be a nice handful now.

Edward waved away his daughter's remark. ''But since you've seen reason and come home—''

''I came back because Aunt Naomi left me the house.''

The bank president stiffened. ''To live in. Not to turn into some ill-conceived eatery destined to fail.''

''To live in,'' the girl agreed quietly, her hands tightening in her lap. ''And to turn into whatever I chose.''

''You haven't succeeded yet,'' Edward retorted.

She smiled and quoted the old man's words back at him. ''These things take time, Daddy. I will.''

''Not without my money, you won't.''

''I don't want your money. I'm applying for a bank loan, same as anybody else.''

''Then you'll accept my conditions,'' Edward declared triumphantly. ''Same as anybody else.''

Set and match, Con thought. But the girl wasn't ready to concede defeat yet.

She lifted smooth, dark eyebrows, a compelling contrast to her brown-and-gold hair. ''So, what are your conditions?''

Edward nodded across the desk. ''MacNeill, here. He's the biggest condition.''

''Pardon me?'' the girl said.

''You take him on as your financial adviser. He approves all expenditures, makes all the business decisions for the restaurant. Or you don't get your loan.''

She actually gaped before she got control of her jaw and closed her pretty mouth. She looked like she'd been sucker punched, Con thought, not unsympathetically. Edward's blunt delivery left Con a little winded himself.

But Cutler's daughter bounced back like a fighter off the ropes.

"You must be joking," she said flatly.

"No. I'm not throwing good money after bad. If you want the bank loan, you'll take him with it."

Her scornful glance swept from Con's suit to his highly polished shoes. "And just what does he know about running a restaurant?"

Con's sympathy faded. He didn't have to sit by while another person took swings at his professional competence.

"What do you know about running a business?" he returned evenly. "It could be an education for both of us."

"No."

Edward shrugged. "Your choice. The bank's money under his control, or—" he watched his daughter carefully "—my money under mine."

This pair didn't need a business consultant, Con thought in near disgust. They needed a lawyer. Hell, they needed a family therapist. But he needed them, needed this job. He had bills to pay, and he wanted Edward Cutler's recommendation even more than cash.

He leaned forward out of the deep leather chair. "Look, Miss Cutler... I've got a Harvard degree and ten years' experience. I advise small businesses, I put together plans for them, I help them secure funding and ensure they're on solid-enough financial footing to succeed. If you've got a cash flow problem, odds are I can help you."

He honestly thought she might be—not grateful, exactly, but—impressed. But the restaurant owner was made of stronger stuff than Con had given her credit for. "How nice," she murmured. "Do you wash dishes, too?"

"Only if you need me to," he replied.

Startled, she looked at him, really looked at him, for the first time since they'd sat down. Slowly, those clear gray depths warmed and filled with amusement. Her pale pink mouth curved in a wry smile. Con's breath rushed to his throat and lodged there.

Edward drummed his fingers on his desk. "My other offer still stands, punkin."

The girl didn't blink at the repeated use of the demeaning pet name. Maybe she was used to it. It set Con's teeth on edge.

She stood, surprisingly dignified in her flirty skirt and clunky heels. Con did the same, keeping his hands quiet at his sides, although the tension in the room had him balancing on the balls of his feet like a boxer.

Val Cutler tugged thoughtfully on one of her long silver earrings. "So, my real choice is between the devil I do know, or the qualified devil I don't, is that it?"

"Unless there's a door number three nobody's told me about," Con agreed, straight-faced.

Edward stiffened.

His daughter laughed, and the sound loosed something warm in the center of Con's chest.

"We open for lunch at eleven," she told him. "Why don't you stop by around ten tomorrow and I'll give you the tour?"

"Ten o'clock," Con confirmed.

"You call your mother," Edward said. "She's waiting to hear from you."

"Yes, Daddy."

Con watched her exit with small, firm steps, her short skirt riding those curvy hips and flirting with the tops of her thighs. She looked even better in the Lady of the Lake getup than she had in jeans.

He was out of his head to even notice such a thing. His interest in her was business, he reminded himself. Strictly business.

In the back of his mind, he could hear his brothers laughing.

* * *

Oil sizzled. The range fan whirred. Dishes clattered as George, the latest of a long line of dishwashers, unloaded the big machine. Val was knee-deep in worry and up to her elbows in flour. Straightening from the marble board, she pressed the back of her wrists to her temples as if she could squeeze her headache away.

Ann hadn't returned any calls in two days. The produce truck was due in—Val glanced at the big kitchen wall clock—less than forty minutes, and her purveyor wanted to be paid. William Foster of Foster's Goods and Teas had already informed her he wouldn't make another delivery on account. Payroll checks were supposed to be cut on Thursday, and Val didn't have the money for that, either.

She had the bank loan, she reminded herself, drawing in a deep breath of humid air. She just didn't have authorization to use it.

She flattened a circle of pizza dough and slapped it on a baking tray. No, the man with the means was that broad-shouldered, narrow-minded, meat-and-potatoes Irishman from Boston. And as long as he was paying the piper, he could insist that she dance to his tune.

Val punched another lump of dough. For most of her turbulent childhood and stormy adolescence, she'd struggled with the peculiar restrictions of growing up female and Cutler in the Cutlers' town. Aunt Naomi's legacy had seemed the perfect opportunity to return to Cutler on her own adult terms. Wild Thymes was the creative expression of Val's best self—quirky, sociable, accepting of all comers... everything her family was not. And yet here she was facing the same old issues of money and control, of what her father could do for her, what he could buy for her, what he demanded from her in return.

She drew another centering breath and bent over the board, folding and kneading the bread between her hands, seeking comfort and release in the satiny-smooth dough and the smell of yeast.

"I take it the tour starts here?"

She recognized the dark voice, the cool tone. Her pulse pounded in her temples. She turned, already fighting a sense of disadvantage. "Mr. MacNeill."

"Con," he corrected her. The word rang between them like the kiss of swords.

She was struck all over again by his sheer size. He loomed in the narrow work alley, one shoulder canted to avoid the saucepans hanging into the aisle, a slim black briefcase in his hand. A patterned navy tie hung straight from his collar, but she noted with reluctant approval that today at least he'd left the suit at home. He wore khaki pants and a crisp blue oxford-cloth shirt that intensified his eyes and skimmed the solid length of his abdomen. She bet he did crunches. By the stove, her chief cook, blond, bearded Steven, straightened jealously.

"You've got flour on your nose," MacNeill added.

She swiped at it. "How did you get in?"

He raised his eyebrows and set down the briefcase. "I did knock. Your front door was open."

Val flushed and brushed again at her face. Her fingers were sticky with dough. "Sorry. It's just that the entrance is supposed to be locked before eleven o'clock."

"Here," MacNeill said suddenly.

Stepping forward, he withdrew an immaculate handkerchief from his hip pocket. With brisk efficiency, he tipped her chin and cleaned her face. His touch was dispassionate, his fingertips unexpectedly callused. The folded square was warm from his body and smelled of cedar. Val, trapped between the counter and his body, felt her heartbeat quicken.

The blue eyes narrowed. "Better."

He was too close. Too large. And way, way too attractive.

She jerked her head away from his thumb steadying her chin. "You could have handed it to me," she said crossly. "I'm perfectly capable of wiping my own face."

"Sure. When you can see it."

His easy confidence ruffled her. But the man—annoying as it was to admit it—was right.

"This hasn't started quite the way I was hoping. I planned on meeting you in my office."

He propped a shoulder against the steel storage shelves, angling to get a better view of the countertop. "Fine by me. Today I'd rather get a general feel for how you work, anyway. What are you making?"

"Pizza crusts." He was making her nervous. She shaped another round with quick, neat pats, settling herself with the familiar routine. "It's a popular item. We serve nearly twenty a day."

"Smells good."

"That's the cinnamon rolls, actually." She glanced over her shoulder to the square oven at the end of the work aisle. "They'll be out in a minute."

Just for a moment, the sharp, assured consultant looked like a big, hungry boy who'd wandered into his mother's kitchen.

On impulse, she asked, "Would you like one?"

Surprise crossed his face before he nodded. "Thanks."

Val rubbed her hands together over the floured board. Maneuvering around him, she grabbed an oven mitt. The pans were heavy. She set them on top of the oven and cranked the temperature up to five hundred degrees to cook the pizzas. With practiced movements, she turned out the sticky rolls onto racks. MacNeill stayed out of her way. To reward him, she selected the two largest cinnamon buns and dropped them on a plate.

"Anything else?" She smiled at him.

Con's sexual response was instant and unwelcome. Holy saints. Val Cutler stood before him in jeans and a soiled cook's apron, and he reacted as if she were naked. Above the line of the bib, he could make out the name of her restaurant, stenciled over her breast. She was flushed and

messy, her braided hair springing loose around her face, a
faint sheen of sweat above that full upper lip.

He wanted her mouth.

Dammit, the woman wasn't even his type. He preferred
them sleek and smooth and elegant. And right now, he'd
prefer no distractions at all. He needed Edward Cutler's recommendation more than he wanted his daughter.

"Something to drink?" he suggested levelly.

"Iced tea?"

His mother Bridget sometimes drank tea, Irish Breakfast
steeped strong enough to stain the cup. The MacNeill men
all drank coffee. The one time Con had tried the Southern
brew—at a rest stop outside Petersburg, where he'd been
forced to pour more oil into his thirsty car—it had coated
his teeth like flavored corn syrup.

"The sweet stuff?" he asked cautiously.

"No. I use a herbal blend. Raspberry, mostly."

Worse and worse.

"Fine. I'll give it a shot."

She busied herself with a glass and ice. "Here you go.
Thirty-five gallons brewed fresh every morning."

He could see the marks of her warm fingers against the
cold, cloudy glass. To test himself, to test her, he deliberately brushed her hand as he took it from her. Her fingers
were slim and wet.

She gave him a freezing look. Con grinned at his own
conceit. Apparently his libido was safe with her, after all.
He followed her through the swinging double doors to the
dining room.

Wicker baskets and salt-glazed North Carolina pottery
adorned the creamy yellow walls. The mismatched tables
had been stripped and painted with fruits and vegetables.
Everything looked fresh and bright and attractive. Val Cutler
might not know much about bookkeeping, but she understood ambience.

With neat, competent movements, she laid a place at one

of the small tables set along the side. Daisies stuck out of a bright blue bottle in the center. The cinnamon rolls steamed seductively on a white china plate. Inhaling, Con felt his shoulders start to loosen up.

Define the problem, he reminded himself. Establish a rapport with the client. He chose a seat on the bench running along the wall, in command of the room. "Join me?"

"I really ought to get back to help Steve—my cook. We open in half an hour."

"He can't manage a few minutes longer without you?"

At his questioning of her staff's ability, she stiffened. "He can manage."

"Then you can join me."

Slowly, she sank onto the ladder-back chair. Even in her floured apron, she managed to look like a queen granting audience to a peasant. Con might have admired her composure if it hadn't challenged his own.

He directed his attention to his plate. "These look very good," he complimented her. "Have you ever considered opening for breakfast?"

Her well-bred face with its incongruous earbobs assumed an expression of polite dismissal. "I've considered it. Unfortunately, I don't think we'd get enough foot traffic to make it worthwhile."

"What about dinner?"

She leaned back defensively in her chair. "You haven't been here long enough to know, Mr. MacNeill, but this town pretty much rolls up the sidewalks at five o'clock. If anyone wants dinner, they go across the street to Arlene's Café for pork barbecue and chicken-fried steak."

He paused in the act of lifting a roll to his mouth. "That suggests that a dinner market exists. You could compete. Add meat to your menu."

She straightened. Her chair thumped as the front legs hit the floor. "Let's get one thing straight right away. I may have been forced to accept you as my accountant—"

"Financial adviser."

"Whatever." She waved the distinction away. "But as far as I'm concerned you're just a glorified bean counter. I won't have you interfering in my kitchen."

He raised his eyebrows. "You cook 'em, I count 'em?" he murmured.

Instant humor danced in her eyes like the sunlight on the gray seas off of Ireland. An undercurrent more dangerous than lust suddenly threatened his balance.

"Something like that," she said.

To distract his unruly body, he took a bite of the fragrant roll in his hand. It was wonderful. Hot and sweet. Soft and sticky. Delicious.

He cleared his throat. "You know, there's no reason this has to be an adversarial relationship. I'm here to do a job, that's all."

"I agree. As long as your job doesn't interfere with mine."

"You'll hardly notice I'm here."

Her gaze skittered over the height and breadth of him, from his shoulders rising above the narrow padded bench to his feet sticking out from under the table.

When she looked back up at his face, her eyes were bright with amusement. "Now, why do I have difficulty believing that?"

Con's blood surged. His jaw tightened. He had a sudden vision of laying her down across the table in front of him like an exotic dish for his delectation. He wanted to free her hair to spill over the edge. He wanted to part her firm, round thighs and push inside her soft, warm body. He wanted to take that pale mouth with its full upper lip and watch those gray eyes darken in passion.

Con set down the roll slowly. As a plan of action, it had a lot of appeal. As an approach to a woman he barely knew and was hired to analyze and advise, it probably lacked something. Subtlety, maybe. Sense.

His appetite for this woman unnerved him. Maybe this kind of reaction was appropriate for Patrick, blissfully happy with his new wife. It was only to be expected from Sean, whose appreciation for anything female was well-known and often indulged. But Con, the middle brother, the cool, logical one, had always let reason rule his selection of partners.

There was nothing *reasonable* about this attraction at all.

Chapter 3

Blond, bearded Steven, his ponytail secured in a hair net, stuck his head out of the kitchen. "Val, we need you back here."

Val exhaled in relief at the interruption. Her cheeks felt warm and her palms were clammy. She'd like to blame it on the heat of the kitchen, but the bald truth was her father's hired gun raised her temperature. And not only because Con MacNeill was trying to interfere in the running of her restaurant. She expected that. She was prepared for it. Unfortunately, he also challenged her to engage him on some deeper, more personal, man-woman level. And that she was determined to avoid. In the war between the sexes, Aunt Naomi always said, women lost even when they won.

On the other hand, Val didn't want her orderly retreat to look like a rout. "In a minute, Steven."

"We haven't got a minute," he said, aggrieved.

MacNeill stiffened at the blond cook's tone.

Shoot. They were due to open in twenty minutes. She couldn't afford to have Steven in a huff.

"A second, then," Val said equably. "Come meet Con MacNeill. Con, this is Steven Gray, my head chef."

"And you're Edward Cutler's pit bull," Steven said.

Cold temper lit Con's sapphire blue eyes. "That's a hell of a tableside manner you've got, Gray."

The blond beard jutted aggressively. "So what?"

"So, I'm just wondering. They let you out in the dining room much?"

Loyalty—and the need to keep Steven from quitting— smothered Val's spurt of laughter. Wild Thymes was her place. Hers. She'd created a haven of warmth and acceptance here in deliberate contrast to the stiff hostility that permeated her parents' house. She wouldn't stand for her chief cook and her financial adviser facing off like a couple of bull seals on a contested strand of beach.

"Steven is a very talented cook. We can't spare him from the kitchen. Which is where I should be now, too." She smiled in dismissal. "I'll be right there, Steve."

"The gazpacho isn't ready."

She tipped up her chin, looked down her nose. She wouldn't be pressured by his pouting any more than she'd be swayed by her father's manipulation. "I said I'll take care of it."

"Right."

He stalked away. The double doors swung shut behind him.

"You've got a personnel problem," Con observed.

"Besides you, you mean?" she retorted.

He regarded her steadily with that cool, blue, superior gaze that made her see red.

She twitched her braid with annoyance. "All right, yes, I do. So do most restaurants. I still don't want you interfering with my staff. We're shorthanded all the time. Steven's been with me since we opened. I can't lose him, and I won't antagonize him. So next time you're tempted to make comments, I suggest you wait until you have all the facts."

''The fact is, you shouldn't have to put up with that kind of attitude from hired staff.''

She shrugged. ''That's your opinion. And if I want that, I'll ask for it.''

''I get paid to offer my opinion.''

''Not by me.'' She pushed away from the table and stood, simmering. ''Enjoy your breakfast.''

She hoped he choked on it. Or at least added an unwanted ounce to his ridged and perfect abs.

Con MacNeill was a Grade A, inspected-and-approved, prime macho pain in the butt. But not, she noted reluctantly half an hour later, a difficult customer. In that, at least, he was different from her father.

She watched him smiling and joking with her two wait-resses, sulky seventeen-year-old Jenny and amiable Doralee. Jenny put her shoulders back to show off her two little bos-oms. Doralee chuckled and said something in reply. Con's rich laughter rolled across the dining room, making other women shift in their seats, crossing their legs or patting their hair.

Maybe she should stick him in the window to attract new business, Val thought wryly, and then pressed her lips to-gether.

She did not want him here.

He was a dark blot against her butter-hued walls, an alien invader in her cheerful, feminine retreat. Every time she passed his table on her way through to the kitchen, the fine hair on her arms and the back of her neck rose. She tried to tell herself dislike caused the reaction, or caution, but she had never been good at fooling herself.

He got to her.

Val bit her inner cheek. So, what did that prove, except that she was normal?

An attractive man—a man like Con—probably got to a lot of women. It was part of his allure, and part of his dan-ger.

Val had wasted the first half of her life struggling with the limits of her parents' and the town's expectations. Breaking free had been more painful than she liked to remember. Now that she was home to stay, she wasn't risking her wobbly autonomy with some hard-jawed, sharp-eyed financial adviser forced on her by her father.

As if Val needed another cautionary lesson in the misery that love could lead to, Ann walked through the door. Relief swamped Val at the sight of her friend and then coalesced into a tight knot of anger in the center of her chest. Ann shuffled like a marionette, her movements stiff and unfinished.

There was more than one means for a man to get to a woman, Val reflected bitterly. Apparently Rob had gotten to Annie again in the worst possible way.

An old, remembered helplessness froze Val for a moment. And then rage returned, warming and welcome. She handed menus to two young mothers out lunching with their babies and hurried to greet her friend.

"How are you?" she asked, hugging her with care.

She heard Ann's harsh intake of breath as she inadvertently touched someplace that hurt. Her shoulder? A rib?

"Honey, I'm sorry."

"I'm okay," Ann assured her.

Val snorted.

"No, really, I'm fine." Ann's smile was strained, her eyes weary.

"Did you go to the hospital this time? See a doctor?"

"Oh, no. I just had a little accident. I'm okay."

Experience had taught Val that if she pushed Ann would withdraw even further. But the words came out, anyway. "Ann, you don't have to put up with this. There are shelters, programs—" Val broke off as Ann began to shake her head.

"I can't leave him."

Him. Rob. Cutler's golden boy. He dressed well. He smelled good. His people knew your people, and your people still talked about the time star quarterback Rob Cross took tiny Cutler's football team all the way to the state championships.

Frustration choked Val. Swallowing, she said as gently as she could, "Counseling? Maybe if you talked to your pastor…?"

"I can't do that. Rob's on the church board."

Yeah, and he beat his wife. "Annie…"

"I should go."

"*No.* No, I'm done." Val sighed. "Can I get you anything? Ice packs? Aspirin?"

Ann's smile was so grateful it almost broke Val's heart. "How about something to do?"

"Is that…wise?"

"Probably not. But I need it."

"Whatever you want." Val handed her the sheaf of menus. "The dining room's all yours."

She found plenty of opportunities to make trips in from the kitchen, though, alert to Ann's interactions with the customers, watchful that her friend didn't spend too long on her feet.

Every trip took Val past Con MacNeill. In spite of his aborted restaurant tour, he apparently found plenty to keep himself occupied. Once his plate was cleared away, he sipped from his glass. At some point, she noted, he'd exchanged the raspberry tea for plain water. Occasionally he wrote things down in strong black writing on a long yellow pad.

He stopped Ann to ask her a question. Val felt her hackles rise like a cornered possum's and hurried across the dining room.

But when she reached them, Ann didn't appear in need of rescue. Her thin face animated, she actually smiled at Con before hurrying away.

"Well!" Val exhaled. "What did you say to her?"

Dark brows lifted. "I thanked her for bringing me a menu."

Tugging a cloth from her apron pocket, Val proceeded to wipe off his table. "I told you I didn't want you interfering with the staff."

Con tipped his head back to regard her from beneath lowered lids, his mouth a straight line. "I don't believe I was."

Val grinned. "Mmm. Well, you've charmed the socks off Doralee. And if Jenny comes by any more often to fill your water glass, she's going to wear a track in the linoleum."

The blue eyes widened. And there it was again, that spark of humor, that arc of understanding, that flared between them as brightly and suddenly as an electrical connection. Her breath caught.

"You've got very attentive service," Con said blandly.

"And you, of course, did nothing to encourage them," she teased.

"Not a thing." With the sole of one shoe, he pushed out the chair opposite him, silently inviting her to stay.

She sat. Somehow, she needed to find a way to work with this man. She needed his signature on her checks, at least.

"So, what's the matter with your hostess?" Con asked.

Val blinked. She hadn't expected him to notice anything wrong with Ann. No one else did. No one cared, except for her.

Carefully, trying to preserve Ann's privacy and whatever dignity she had left, Val said, "She's not feeling too well today."

"Not feeling well, my foot. Somebody knocked her around."

Her face must have betrayed her surprise.

Con's smile showed the edges of his teeth. "I was a boxer in high school. I recognize the signs. That lady's ribs are hurting. Will she let you help?"

Shame and frustration made her abrupt. "No."

"Tough," he said sympathetically. "She lose a lot of time for sick leave?"

Val straightened. "Are you about to tell me that I can't afford to pay for absentee help?"

"Nope."

"Good." She relaxed a little in her chair. "Besides, Ann isn't actually an employee. She just comes in to help out."

He nodded and made a note on his yellow pad. "You ever consider offering her a salary?"

Val put up her chin at the implication she might be taking advantage of Ann's friendship. "I need money to do that. Besides, she won't take it. Rob doesn't want his wife to work."

"That settles that, then."

"You think a woman shouldn't work without her husband's permission?"

"I think it's real unlikely a battered woman would take the chance," he responded coolly. "Next time you're tempted to make comments, you might wait until you've heard me out."

She heard the echo of her own rebuke and flushed. "You're good."

"That's what I'm trying to prove," he said smoothly.

An edge to his voice snagged her attention. He was determined to prove something, all right. But what? And to whom? Val sorted through the threads of her own experience for one that might produce a corresponding pull in him.

"Only child?" she guessed.

If he felt a tug, he didn't let on. "Middle."

"'We're Number Two, We Try Harder'?"

He looked back at her steadily, giving nothing away.

She tried again. "You mentioned brothers?"

"Two."

She toyed thoughtfully with her earring, a long loop of blue and silver beads. In her experience, most men expanded at any opportunity to tell a sympathetic woman all about themselves. Con MacNeill, she was discovering, was not most men. His very reluctance to hand out bits and pieces of himself roused her interest and challenged her own reserve.

"And what do they do?"

"What is this? Twenty questions?"

"Something like that," she admitted. "Since I'm being forced to work with you, I'd like to know something about you. You already know all about me."

"Not quite all," he drawled.

A shock of pure sexual energy arced between them. Val fought the connection as it crackled and sparkled all the way down to her toes. Good heavens.

"So, are you animal, vegetable or mineral?"

She thought she saw a glint of appreciation in his eyes. "Let's make a deal," he offered, leaning his elbows on the table. "I tell you about my family, and you show me your books."

Val gnawed the inside of her lower lip. She was going to have to show him the books eventually, anyway. She might as well get something out of it. "Deal. Mother and father?"

He settled back against the padded seat, debating, she thought, how much to tell her. "Mom's a trauma nurse, Quincy Community Hospital. Dad's a career marine. Sergeant major, retired."

Interesting. Edward Cutler usually chose pedigreed associates. But the military background fit. Con had that decisive, commanding air. Bossy, Val corrected herself.

"And did you ever...?"

"Enlist? No. Patrick followed Dad into the Corps. He left after his son was born. He's a charter pilot now over in Jefferson. Married a doctor in the burn unit there. Nice lady."

So he didn't have a prejudice against working women. She should find that reassuring. "And the other one?"

"Sean. He works construction, mostly. He's good with his hands."

It all sounded very macho. Val tried to reconcile the blue-collar brothers with Harvard and her father's bank. She couldn't.

"Your parents must have been proud of you, the first one to go to college and all."

A muscle jumped in his cheek. "Yes."

She sighed. Deal or no deal, they were obviously not going to have a cozy conversation about family expectations. "What brings you down to the Carolinas?"

"Your father offered me a job."

"There are jobs in Boston."

He shrugged. "I wanted to get out of town for a while."

"Why?"

The hard, cool eyes touched her briefly. "Personal reasons."

"That's enlightening. Are all the MacNeills as talkative as you?"

Absurd pleasure warmed her when a corner of his mouth quirked up in a smile. "That's us," he agreed. "Chatty as hell. Can I see your books now?"

She glanced around the emptying dining room. Unfortunately, nothing was going on that would claim her attention. Ann was making nice to some ladies in coordinated short sets and diamond tennis bracelets who were lingering over lunch, Doralee was bussing tables, Jenny was in the kitchen.

Con leaned forward again. "Look, I can't approve withdrawals against your loan until I have some overall picture of expenses. The sooner I get a crack at the budget, the sooner you get your money."

Shoot. As much as she resented admitting it, he was right. Reluctantly, Val stood. "We'll have to go to my office."

Con pushed open the door for her before she could get it herself. She snatched up his water glass and marched through ahead of him. Nodding to Steven on her way through the kitchen, she deposited the used glass with the pile waiting to be loaded into the dishwasher.

"This way," she said, skirting a stack of cartons piled in the hall. "Through here."

Space was at a premium in a restaurant. Every square foot used by the back of the house took away profitable seating from the dining room. Val's office was small and cramped and flooded with bills, receipts, menus, recipes, newspaper clippings and order forms. Her desk was swamped. Her files overflowed. Her bulletin board was buried under schedules, and the pile on her chair had spilled over to the floor.

She glared at MacNeill, daring him to say something.

He turned around slowly in the middle of the room. "Interesting decor."

She didn't think for one minute that he was referring to the MOMA poster over her desk or the whimsical ceramic pig that held her pencils.

She tossed her head. "I don't have a lot of time to spend back here. My first priority's always been the kitchen."

"And your customers." He nodded as if he understood.

"Exactly." She relaxed slightly, coming forward to perch on an exposed corner of her desk. "I guess when I opened I figured that if I served good food in an attractive location, the books would see to themselves."

"Well, now you've got me to see to them. Where do you want me to set up?"

His dismissive tone stirred her resentment. She didn't want him sitting at her desk. Maybe she didn't spend much time there herself, but she felt that holding on to the desk would remind them all, MacNeill and her father and herself, that Wild Thymes was still hers—an outlet for her creativity, an expression of her independence, a haven for every friend in need she had.

Jammed into the corner of the office, an old typing table teetered under its load of papers.

"There," she said impulsively.

One dark eyebrow flicked up.

"It will look better after I clear it," she said.

"That would certainly help," Con agreed impassively.

Val escaped to fetch an empty carton from the hall, fighting an unwelcome spurt of guilt at the thought of his long legs crammed under that puny table. His comfort was not her responsibility. She'd certainly never asked for Mr. Business Solutions to invade her office and her life.

But she hesitated in the doorway, holding the box protectively in front of her, troubled by an unexpected pang. "Or you could work in the dining room."

Con turned, a sliding stack of folders in his arms. "Maybe I will, some mornings. But your records are in here. Which reminds me…I'd like anything you've got that documents the way you do business. Accounting records, purchase orders, tax records, that sort of thing. Normally I'd also ask for some kind of statement of purpose or market strategy, but—"

She cocked her head to one side. "You mean, like a business plan?"

He didn't apologize, but he smiled, exposing big, white, even teeth. *The better to eat you with, my dear.*

"You have one?"

"Of course I have one. I needed it to get the original loan. I'm not completely ignorant of standard business practices."

Of course. Con cursed his quick assumption. Where the hell was his usual detachment?

He eyed the woman framed in the doorway, her exuberant hair and mismatched earrings a contrast to her capable hands and cameo face. She was like an asymmetric equation, he thought, the two sides of her personality existing in uneasy equilibrium.

He'd always liked his sums to come out even. But just because Val Cutler upset his sense of balance and whetted his appetite was no excuse for his drawing sloppy conclusions about her business.

"I'll take a look at it," he said.

"I can hardly wait."

He had to turn away to hide his grin.

But half an hour later, all impulse to smile had faded completely. The restaurant's records were a mess. In an attempt to keep track of her finances, Val had labeled numerous folders and envelopes to save things in. Peering inside yet another stuffed and dated file, Con felt the muscle in his jaw start to twitch. Apparently, she saved everything. How could he begin to advise her when he couldn't figure out how much she spent or what she owed?

But Edward Cutler wasn't paying him to write his daughter off as hopeless. Grimly, Con loosened his tie, rolled up his sleeves and got to work.

Val stopped in her office door, appalled. "What on earth do you think you're doing?"

She'd had to give out two free lunches today because the Misses Minniton were disappointed that the vegetable lasagna they'd ordered didn't include ground beef. Her produce purveyor had threatened not to come back unless she paid up her account immediately. She'd bussed tables, baked and seasoned potatoes for tomorrow's quesadillas, dusted the moldings in the dining room and scrubbed pots. She was dirty and tired. Her back hurt.

And now her office looked like it had been hit by a bomb. Or an efficiency expert.

Con looked up briefly from the stack on his lap and then pitched something—a cooking magazine, she saw as the cover flashed by—at a carton at her feet. Similar cartons, apparently dragged in from the hall, lined the walls and dotted the floor. "Cleaning."

She pounced on the magazine and hugged it to her chest along with the zippered bag that held the day's take. "You can't just throw that away. There are recipes in here."

He paused. "Have you used any of them?"

"No, but—"

"Have you changed your menu at all since you opened?"

"I change at least a few items every week to take advantage of seasonal produce," she retorted.

"Using recipes from this magazine?"

"No. But I was planning to go through them when I had the time."

"Trust me. You don't have time." And he tossed another magazine on the pile.

Val restrained herself from flinching. Or screaming. She wasn't going to make a fool of herself wrestling for every issue. She stepped forward cautiously into her office, noting scraps and stacks of paper half-filling other boxes. "What else are you throwing away?"

"Anything over three months old that hasn't received or doesn't require follow-up. All duplicates of reports, regulations or information. Any interesting articles you've collected in the mistaken belief that you'll read them later." He reached behind him to put a slim sheaf of papers on the tiny typing table. "That's all."

"*All?*" Val repeated, her voice strident. She took a deep breath, hoping to relax her vocal cords. Hoping to relax.

"All so far," he amended.

Well, shoot. She should have suspected that any-old-corner-will-do-for-me routine of his was an act. She'd never known a man who didn't mark the boundaries of his territory.

"All right," she said carefully. "I admit my office needs organizing—"

"Your office needs gasoline and a match."

Unexpectedly, she laughed, surprising them both. He looked so frustrated, sitting there, his long legs drawn up to avoid the piles around him, his tie askew. He looked hot. And almost human. And very, very attractive.

Never mind attractive. He was invading her space.

"You know, your attitude could use a little adjustment," she offered.

He narrowed those stunning blue eyes at her. "What?"

Val perched on the edge of her desk, dropping the bag behind her, swinging her sneakers back and forth. He didn't intimidate her. She wouldn't let him.

"You're a consultant, right? So, aren't we supposed to, like, consult? Shouldn't you ask me before you waltz into my office and start tossing things out?"

His lean, clever face shuttered up. "I need to organize before I start work on your books."

"All right. I'm not a dummy. I understand that. But if we talked about it ahead of time, maybe I could help you find what you need. Or maybe I have personal stuff I don't want you getting into. Just ask me, okay?"

Con's shoulders squared defensively. The Lady of the Lake was not his client. Edward Cutler was, and Cutler had specifically instructed him to take charge, to take over. Con was comfortable with that. He was used to going his own way. At Millennium, his ability to make tough calls had earned him big bucks and an office with a view of Federal Street.

Of course, one of those calls had also gotten him fired. Which was one reason why he was in self-imposed exile in Hicksville, North Carolina, getting lectured by the goddess of sprouts and tofu.

She watched him expectantly, gray eyes glowing in her porcelain-perfect face. He could have resisted cajoling. He would have brushed off anger. But he wasn't proof against her reasonable appeal.

"You could be right," he admitted stiffly. "I haven't been a consultant very long."

Her smile broke over her face like sunshine. He felt amply rewarded for his concession…and that made him question his judgment. Was he responding to her argument? Or to her?

She hopped from her desk. "Well, that's settled, then. I'm off to the bank."

"Why?"

She held up a gray zippered bag. "Daily deposit," she explained. "My purveyors are begging—demanding, really—to be paid."

Con frowned. "Shouldn't you enter your numbers before you leave?"

"I'll do it when I get back."

Her airy reply set off his internal alarm system. "I can do it for you. What's your take?"

She gave a short, embarrassed laugh. "I, um, have the bank add up the deposit. To avoid errors."

"Banks make errors, too," he informed her. "Give me your receipts. I'll total them for you."

In Val's experience, offers of help came with strings attached.

"No, thank you," she said politely. "The teller does it."

He held out his strong, broad palm. "Not anymore."

In spite of that calm tone, she recognized his resolve.

She dangled the bag between them. "What makes you think I'm just going to hand this over to you?"

He raised one eyebrow. "Maybe the fact that you need me to countersign those checks to your vendors? Unless you have enough money in that bag to pay them all yourself."

Fury flushed her cheeks. So, Con MacNeill's earlier concession, like his apparent agreeableness regarding his desk, had just been a ploy to put her off her guard. Plainly, this Yankee carpetbagger was determined to do everything he could to show her up, to interfere in her business and prove her unequal to the task of running her own restaurant.

Shoot, darn, dang and triple blast him.

Silently, she handed over the bag.

Chapter 4

Something didn't add up.

Con hunched over the laptop balanced on his thighs, stabbing at the closely spaced keys. Maybe it was Val Cutler's arithmetic. Maybe, in his massive overhaul of her office, he'd missed something, or misplaced something. Val's presence was a compelling distraction, and her scattershot approach to bookkeeping made piecing together a clear financial picture of her business a challenge. But after three days of shoveling out her office, it seemed to Con that Wild Thymes was doing a brisk-enough turnover for its owner to be making some money.

So where the hell did it go?

Con frowned, glancing toward the doorway. Val had excused herself several hours ago to deal with the lunchtime crowd, but traces of her crammed the tiny room. A canvas tote printed with dancing tomatoes swung from the back of her chair. A mug shaped like a pig smirked at him from the top of a towering stack of papers. All his efforts over the last few days still hadn't cleared that desk. He might as well be back sharing a room with his kid brother Sean. There was even a naked lady posed on the museum poster above the desk's cluttered surface, reclining with perfect confidence in the jungle while lions peered from the brilliant foliage surrounding her.

Damn, it was hot in here. If Con closed his eyes, he could almost smell Val's scent lingering in the humid air, a floating combination of spices and vanilla, tempting as cookies and milk to a hungry teenage boy.

His cell phone twittered. Con felt behind him with one hand, silently cursing the interruption and the lack of space.

"MacNeill."

"Heavens, Mack, you sound like a bear."

Even through the hissing connection, Con identified the light superiority he'd once mistaken for class, the casual unkindness he'd once confused with humor. He hadn't forgiven himself yet for that outstanding failure in judgment.

"Hello, Lynn," he said coldly. "I thought I told you not to call me at this number."

"Well, and I wouldn't, if I had any other way to reach you. Are you even checking your voice mail?"

"Regularly," he assured her. "What do you want?"

Her well-bred voice crept up a breathless half octave, Katharine Hepburn imitating Marilyn Monroe. "I heard from Josh Wainbridge you'd applied for financial vice president at Northern Ventucom."

Con tightened his grip on the flimsy handset, squelching his instinctive anger at her prying. What was the saying? Money talked. And in Boston, rumor ran wild wherever the elite gathered: in boardrooms and bedrooms, over tee holes and teacups. Apparently even leaving town hadn't discouraged the gossips. Outsider Con had shrugged off the jealous speculation that accompanied his rise. He would endure the malicious whispers that followed his fall.

"Word travels fast."

"Josh says you're sure to be called for an interview."

Satisfaction, fierce and sweet, almost robbed Con of his breath. "So?"

"Well, I was wondering..." The coyness in his ex-fiancée's voice made him profoundly uneasy. "If you're going to be back in town, anyway... Are you coming to our little celebration next week?"

It took Con a second to make the leap from job prospects to matrimonial plans. Even then, he couldn't quite grasp what Lynn was asking. Or rather, why.

"The bachelor party?"

She sighed, as if forced to explain to a small and backward child. "Not a bachelor party, Mack. Some men don't feel the need to indulge in puerile experimentation with alcohol and lap dancers just because they're contemplating marriage."

He turned away from the open doorway, bending his legs to keep his computer from sliding off his lap. "Depends who you're contemplating marriage with, I guess."

When he was engaged to Lynn, his own brothers had wanted to throw him a wake.

She must not have remembered. "Are you coming? Next Friday?"

"No."

"But it will look so odd if you don't. You and Todd used to be such friends."

"It will look pretty odd if I do," Con said levelly. "Seeing as you and I used to be engaged."

"But that's the whole idea. I want everyone to see there are no hard feelings."

She wanted everyone to see, all right. Appearances meant everything to Lynn. Nothing would give her more pleasure than to show off her ex-lover and her future husband at a party of two hundred or so of their closest mutual friends. Con didn't love her anymore—hell, maybe his brother Sean was right, maybe he'd never loved her—but he'd rather stand naked at noon on Boston Common than expose his supposed feelings for his former colleagues' amusement. Not to mention their speculation about his job prospects.

I heard from Josh Wainbridge… Pride squared his shoulders.

"Sorry. I'm on a job down here, Lynn. Even if I fly up for the day, I can't take time to socialize."

"Oh, Mack." Her voice softened. "I forgot how painful all this must be for you. I'm so sorry, darling."

If it made her feel better to imagine he was hiding his wounded heart, fine. As long as he didn't have to endure another evening of casual digs and not-so-casual inquiries into what had happened to his meteorlike career at Millennium.

"Yeah, well, I'll stagger on somehow," he said dryly. "Give old Todd my best."

He sat like stone through Lynn's protracted and patronizing farewell—he bet it never once occurred to her that he paid for calls made to his cell phone—before ending the connection. He flipped the phone shut. Twisting around on his straight-backed, short-legged seat, he saw Val Cutler standing in the doorway with a plate in her hands and her gray eyes wide with sympathetic interest.

Hell.

"I was just, um…"

"Eavesdropping?" he suggested, since for once she seemed at a loss for words.

Her lips pressed together. "Bringing you a sandwich."

His irritation at being caught with his professional pants down faded. How much could she have heard, after all? And she'd brought him lunch. "Thanks. What is it?"

She tilted her perfect chin at him. "I'll tell you after you've tried it."

And that, he thought, would teach him not to growl at her.

"Okay. Thanks. Put it…" He looked around.

"I think I can find a space." She waited a two-beat pause. "Now."

He grinned. So she was still steamed at him for cleaning her office. He could handle her annoyance. It made a welcome change after Lynn's false sympathy. Swiveling, he set his computer on the tabletop behind him and then held out his hand for the plate. "I'll take it."

She gave it to him before taking up her perch on the desk, directly in front of the naked lady and watchful lions. Deliberately, Con turned his attention to his plate. If she wanted to watch him eat, that was her affair.

He picked up the sandwich. Reassured by the sight of melted cheese and the scent of charcoal grilling, he took a bite.

She waited a moment for his reaction. When he didn't say anything—his mouth was full—she shrugged and offered, "Grilled summer squash and portobello mushroom with Monterey Jack on sunflower bread."

Con swallowed. "It's good."

A rose blush swept from her jawline to the hair springing loose at her temples. He watched its spread, fascinated by her apparent pleasure at his simple compliment. Something trembled between them, tangible as hunger, insubstantial as smoke.

He cleared his throat.

She looked away. "If you need time off, we can get along fine for a few days without you."

So she'd overheard…something. Even irritated, Con found it hard not to admire her challenge. And impossible not to respond.

"A few days like forever?" he asked dryly.

Val met his eyes evenly, not denying it.

"What is it about me that gets your goat, Dixie?"

"Besides your apparent failure to remember my name?" He grinned.

Val smiled back cautiously. Maybe if she were very direct

with him he would back off and let her have her way? It wasn't as if he had any real stake in the place.

"You're probably aware that my father and I don't see eye to eye on my running this place."

"Yeah, I picked up on that."

"Well, my needing this loan is like a great big I-told-you-so for him. Only he gets to keep telling me so, telling me how to run my business. Or rather, you do."

"Have you considered that he's only trying to help?"

Old memories, old resentments, flashed through Val's mind and tightened her chest. Her father's hands, pushing hers aside on a fishing pole. Her father's pencil, striking through the laboriously copied problems of her math homework. Her father's voice, rising over her frustration: *Punkin, I'm only trying to help. You're not very good at this.*

"Oh, yes. He's always tried to help."

"Some people would count themselves lucky to have family in a position to give them a hand. It's natural for parents to want what's right for their kids."

Val tossed her head, making her silver hoops tinkle defiantly.

"Well, wasn't I lucky, then? I had the right clothes, the right friends, the right schools, the right manners.... And if I wouldn't marry the right husband they had all picked out for me, it must be because I was spoiled and ungrateful and lacking in mature judgment."

She caught his quick, assessing glance at her fingers, curled around the lip of the desk. No rings. She never wore rings in the kitchen. She wondered about this girl—Lynn— he "used to be engaged to," the one he apparently wasn't going to see.

He picked up the other half of his sandwich. "So, what happened to Mr. Right?"

Nine years later Val could still feel that ballooning sense of panic, as if the expanding press of her parents' expectations could actually squeeze the air from her chest. She took a deep breath.

"Oh, he went on to share his fabulous career with another lucky girl, and I ran away to New York." It was hard, even after all these years, to keep the bitterness from her voice.

Con raised both eyebrows. "Alone?"

She grinned. "Not on the back of somebody's Harley, if that's what you're asking. My aunt Naomi helped me. My father's oldest sister. I don't know which one of us made Daddy madder." She shrugged, trying to dislodge an old pain from her shoulders. "Me, I guess. For leaving."

"But you came back."

"Almost a year ago. When she died."

"And left you this place."

Val nodded in confirmation.

"No kids of her own?"

"Nope. There were men, I think. Not anyone from around here, though. She had her horses and her books. She played the organ at church. She was, I think, the most self-sufficient person I've known." Val met Con's eyes directly. "And the happiest."

It was a line scratched in the dirt of the playground. A warning and a dare.

Without hesitation, Con crossed it. "Most people can use some help from time to time. That doesn't make them weak."

She lifted her chin. "No? And what does it make me, if I let you march in here, into my place, and start issuing orders?"

"Smart?" he suggested.

Unwillingly, Val laughed, torn between appreciation and annoyance.

He set his plate on the floor, out of the way of his big, polished brown shoes, and reached behind him for his laptop computer.

"I've been meaning to ask… What made you decide to turn that space by the counter over to retail sales?"

She floundered briefly. "The marinades and spices and things?"

He nodded, blue eyes watchful. She guessed he hadn't become a corporate shark by losing sight of his objectives. Or was she his prey? Had her personal confessions, like blood in the water, somehow drawn this new attack?

"Well…I thought it would be nice to give people waiting to be seated something to look at, something to buy. Besides, there's no other place locally to get specialty items like that miso paste or the basmati rice."

"Have you ever done a breakdown by item to see which are your best sellers?"

"No. I do a quarterly inventory."

He tapped one finger against a folder on the corner of his little table. "Got it here. Ever done a comparison by square foot on the profits of your retail space versus your restaurant space?"

"I…no."

"Okay." He typed something into his computer.

Despite his casual acceptance, she still felt him circling just beyond her reach. "Is that what you're doing? Comparing the take from the shop and the restaurant?"

"As much as I can. I don't have all the information yet, but I'd say at your present business volume, you ought to be showing more profit."

If it was a strike, it missed its target. Val flicked her braid impatiently over her shoulder. "I hardly need a fancy Boston business consultant to tell me that."

"Aunt Val?" a boyish voice asked hesitantly.

Val's focus dissolved at the interruption. She turned her head. Mitchell Cross skulked in the doorway, his eight-year-old frame tall for his age and thin. Too thin, like his mother's.

Val clamped a lid on her simmering annoyance and smiled. "Hey, Mitchell."

"Hello," he mumbled politely, the way he'd been taught. He dropped his head to regard her from under his lashes, his shoulders slightly hunched.

Val felt a familiar pang at her heart at Mitchell's cautious response. Mindful of her own special relationship with Naomi, she'd tried hard to bond with her godson in spite of her antipathy to his father. He was Annie's son. She'd seen the boy almost every day for the past year. And still he acted as if she might turn suddenly and bite him.

Con's chair creaked as he shifted his too-big body on the too-small seat. She ignored him, making another effort to reach Mitchell.

"What have you got there?"

Stiffly, he proffered a sheet of paper. "Mom did that drawing you wanted. For next week's menu? And she told me to bring you the key."

"Thanks, honey." Mindful of Con's quizzical gaze, she stopped herself from ruffling the boy's short, fair hair. Mitchell didn't like to be touched, anyway. "Can you hang it up for me?"

"Sure."

He sidled forward into the room, digging the key from the pocket of his neat khaki shorts. Con pulled in his long legs to let the boy pass. As Mitchell stood on tiptoe to reach the hook above the filing cabinet, the man steadied him with one hand on his elbow.

"Good job," he said quietly.

Val was taken aback when Mitchell actually smiled shyly in response. "Thanks, Mr. MacNeill."

Con jerked his head toward the sheet of paper in Val's hand. "That your mom's drawing?"

"Uh-huh."

"Can I see it?"

He could have asked her for a look at the menu, Val

thought. She would have shown it to him. Eventually. But she allowed Mitchell to take the typed sheet covered with Ann's delicate line drawings and hand it to Con, unwillingly intrigued by their interaction.

His dark brows rose. "Very nice," he said. "Your mom does good work."

Mitchell looked at the floor. "I guess. Thanks."

Val liked that Con praised Ann to her son. Rob absorbed most of the adulation in town, like a fire sucking oxygen from a room.

And then Con frowned and looked up from the menu. "Where are you getting your cheese from? The feta and provolone?"

Her goodwill faded. Apparently nothing deflected the business consultant for long, not even a needy boy. "Poplar Farms. They have the best prices."

"I know. I've called other distributors."

She twitched her braid over her shoulder. "Checking up on me?"

He met her gaze without apology. "Yes. The money has to be going somewhere."

Mitchell scuffed his new hightops along the linoleum floor, bored with their adult conversation but too polite to say so.

Con handed the new menu back to Val. "You find that book I told you about?" he asked the boy. "The castles one?"

"Yeah." His throat moved as he swallowed. "It was cool." His next words rushed out, as if he'd been saving them up and couldn't contain them any longer. "Did you know they used to throw dead cows over the walls in a siege to make people sick?"

Con nodded. "Or lime, to burn them. Or severed heads."

"To gross them out. Yeah." Mitchell's grin was blinding. He caught himself, self-consciously ducking his head be-

tween his shoulders as if his enthusiasm might attract unwelcome attention. "I gotta go. Bye."

"See you around," Con replied.

Val blinked. "Well." She didn't know what to say. She
was bewildered by Con's perception, his evident interest in
her bony, unassuming godson. And astonished by Mitchell's
brief response. "I didn't know you'd met Mitchell."

Con shrugged casually. "He's been in a few times."

"He talks to you."

"Some."

"About dead cows?"

Another shrug. "I tried basketball, but he's more interested in knights and castles."

"Real he-man talk."

"Something like that."

"I didn't know." She was still struggling to grasp how
this Yankee stranger had broken through where all her patient efforts had failed.

"Maybe he figured you weren't into dead cows," Con
said dryly. "You being a vegetarian and all."

Val summoned a weak smile, determined not to show how
Mitchell's rejection hurt her. So what if Con had gotten
closer to the boy in a few days than she had managed in the
past year? The important thing was that Mitchell had found
a friendly adult to talk with.

Con leaned forward on his chair, his expression earnest.
"Hey. I'm just somebody new to pal around with. The
blood-and-gore stuff…it's a guy thing."

His attempted reassurance eased the hollow feeling in the
center of her chest. He was being…sweet. Not just kind to
Mitchell, but nice to her. Val blinked fiercely. Well, shoot.
It was just possible that she could like him.

And that confused her.

Val was used to knowing her emotions and acting on her
instincts. Her survival had once depended on it. But she

wondered now if either would be safe—or even possible—where Con MacNeill was concerned.

His movement forward had put his chest warm and close to her knees, his head just below hers. She pressed her thighs together, fighting a ridiculous urge to run her fingertips over his closely shaven jaw, his long and stubborn chin. She could see the shadow of his beard just under his skin. What would it feel like? Against his darkened jaw, his mouth was sharply defined, the top lip disciplined, the lower one fascinatingly full. She wanted to rub her fingers over his jaw and test the textures of that mouth.

It quirked. "Dixie?"

"Mmm?"

"You keep looking at me like that, one or the other of us is going to get ideas."

Her blood drummed in her ears. Ideas. Oh, yes. Oh, heavens. She usually trusted her feelings. But these feelings were so new, so contradictory and so contrary to her best interests, she no longer trusted herself.

"Would that be bad?" she asked.

The cold blue eyes ignited so suddenly they exhausted all the oxygen in the room. Her breathing hitched.

"Not bad," he rasped. "I'm willing to bet we'd be pretty damn good, in fact. But it wouldn't be smart."

Val exhaled slowly. No. Not smart at all. "We can have ideas without acting on them."

He laughed shortly. "Maybe."

She lifted her chin. "What's that supposed to mean?"

"It means don't send out signals, sweetheart, unless you want me to get the message. I'm not slow on the uptake, and I'm used to going after what I want."

His confidence shook her. She admired honesty, but she wasn't ready for a man who was even more direct than she was. "I wasn't sending out signals."

"Right."

"I certainly would never get involved with a man I did

business with, or one who had any kind of association with my father.''

He shrugged. ''Whatever you say.''

She hadn't convinced him. She was having trouble convincing herself. ''I'm not even interested in you,'' she insisted.

His eyes narrowed. ''No?''

''Not in the slightest,'' she lied rashly.

''Okay,'' he said.

And then he leaned forward a little farther in his chair, cupped the back of her head with his hand and brought her mouth down to his.

Not hard. His lips were firm and warm and knowledgeable. They pressed and hovered and pressed again, deliberately, experimentally, getting the angle and the pressure just right. He teased her with his taste, complex and inviting. When he withdrew, she ran her tongue over her own lips to catch his flavor. He made a sound deep in his throat and slanted his mouth to give her more. She accepted it greedily, opening, then seeking.

Under her rising hunger, wonder swelled, ephemeral and shining as a child's soap bubble. Sensation shivered through her. Her curled hands left the cool edge of the desk and sought the hard curve of his shoulders, the column of his throat. As they kissed, harder, deeper, wider, her fingers burrowed beneath his loosened collar, discovering warm skin and rough hair. In the hollow below his strong jaw, his pulse hammered under her touch, and hers leapt in response.

Her mind fogged. Her lungs constricted as she bent, as she fed. He gave her his breath, smoky from his mouth, warm from his lungs. She was hot. She was cold. Her nipples tightened under the soft cotton barriers of her bra, her T-shirt, her apron. She wished there wasn't so much clothing between them. She wished there wasn't so much space. She wanted to drag him out of his chair and up against her, hard, so she could feel his broad chest against her aching breasts, his muscled thighs hard against her thighs.

He held her off. His fingers tightened in the hair at her nape as he stood. For a second, as his chest rose and fell with his breath and her heart pounded, she thought he would haul her into his arms. And then his grip released, and his arm fell away.

Con stepped back, regarding her with satisfaction and intent, lazy sensuality. "Tell yourself you're not interested, if you want to, Dixie. But don't tell me."

Chapter 5

He must have been out of his mind. Nuts. Wacko.

Con tightened his grip on the Jaguar's steering wheel. Pixilated, his mother would call it. What his brothers would say didn't bear thinking of.

He guided the sedan down Cutler's main drag, trying to make sense of the incident in Val's office yesterday. It wasn't like him to think with the bulge behind his button-fly. Sean was the impulsive brother, Patrick the man of deep emotion. He, Con, was the cool and rational one.

But Val Cutler had blown his cool.

The street was nearly empty of traffic under the hot morning sun. Spotting a space at the curb right in front of Wild Thymes, Con pulled in.

He expelled a frustrated breath. Even the memory of Val's hot mouth made his body respond in irrational, if predictable, ways. His blood heated. His chest got tight. When he'd kissed her, he'd been seized by the crazy desire to cushion her head against his shoulder and murmur rash promises into her scented hair.

There was no logical explanation for it. No excuse except maybe temporary insanity.

He did not get involved with clients. He did not intend to jeopardize a potentially lucrative contact by playing Cutler Family Feud. And no way was he pursuing a relationship with some Dixie debutante in need of an attitude adjustment.

He jammed on the clutch, ignoring the car's deep groan. Even if Val would let him.

Con sat for a moment with the key still in the ignition, battling unaccustomed regret. Fact was, he wasn't proud of his caustic comment following that absorbing kiss. The heat of his own response had caught him off guard. Jolted by the unruly lurch of his heart, the unanticipated ache of his loins, he'd spoken as much from self-defense as pride.

And Val, damn his conceit to hell, had gone as pale as his plate. He'd been briefly, savagely glad he could get to her the way she got to him, and then ashamed. Bridget MacNeill had not raised her sons to score off women.

But then, this woman had taken a few good shots at goal herself. While the air around them sizzled, she'd tipped back her head and stared down her elegant little nose at him.

I wouldn't dream of telling you anything, Yankee, she'd said.

He'd admired her recovery. And he'd wanted to haul her right back into his arms and kiss her again.

She hadn't given him the chance. She'd hopped off her desk and marched from her office, leaving him with crumbs on his plate and a sharp-edged dissatisfaction.

For the rest of the day, she'd thrown herself into proving to both of them that the kiss was a mistake on her part and an aberration on his. She avoided the office. Con grimaced as he got out of the car, locking his doors. She avoided him. When their paths inevitably collided, her natural warmth frosted over like a beer glass in a bar.

Con told himself that suited him fine. He had work to do and goals to accomplish. He needed to wrap up this job and get back to Boston while he had half a chance to jump-start his stalled career. He didn't need the feelings Val aroused in him, feelings he could neither define nor solve.

Pausing on the front walk, he examined the restaurant's blackboard with the day's specials chalked in pink and green. Reading them, his mouth set. Today he was discussing the menu with Val whether she wanted to avoid him or not.

He tested the front door—unlocked again, he noted with disapproval—and negotiated his way through the quiet dining room. Val wasn't in the kitchen. Steven Gray looked up from seeding peppers long enough to scowl. The dishwasher guy stacked plates, the college girl—Rhoda? Ronnie?— shook flour into the chugging mixer. She called a greeting. Con smiled reflexively before striding down the narrow hall to Val's office.

He caught himself hurrying and deliberately slowed his pace. He wasn't eager to see her, he told himself. It was just that this dead-end town made him desperate for distraction. He missed his job. He missed Boston. Even fighting with Val Cutler seemed preferable to the mind-numbing boredom.

But when he entered her office, fighting was the last thing on his mind.

Val sat huddled over her desk, surrounded by the sheets of her bank statement and stacks of canceled checks. Her shoulders hunched. Her wrists pressed her temples.

His heart contracted in quick concern. Was she sick? Between her supporting hands, her face was pale and bleak as Niamh Golden-Hair's when Oisin deserted her for Ireland. And then she saw him.

Her head rose, and a corner of her full mouth quirked. "Oh, look, it's Mr. Business Solutions."

He wanted to shake her. He wanted to laugh. And neither action would do her a bit of good. Focus on the problem, he reminded himself.

Setting his briefcase on his inadequate little table, he asked calmly, "What's the matter?"

"Nothing. Not a thing," she enunciated. Reaching over her paper-strewn desk, she grabbed the restaurant's big duplicate checkbook and tossed it at him. "Here."

He caught it two-handed. Folding himself onto his stubby chair, he balanced the book on his lap. He pretended to scan it, all the while sneaking looks at her drawn, discouraged face.

And then he stopped. Frowned. "What is this?"

Her chin tilted defensively. "You have to co-sign the checks. Isn't that right? I can't spend the money without your okay?"

"That's right. And you haven't got it. You should be paying these bills out of operating expenses, not the loan account."

"I would," Val agreed promptly. "If I wanted the checks to bounce."

Con narrowed his eyes. "There's no money in the restaurant account?"

Her controlled flinch made him feel like Scrooge going after Tiny Tim with his crutch.

"Not according to the bank statement," she said.

He had to admire her cool. But at the moment it was damn inconvenient. How could he get to the bottom of whatever was troubling her if she wouldn't confide in him?

"Tell me about it."

"You want me to sob and throw myself on your manly chest, too?"

It sounded good to him. Which only proved he was a bigger fool than he'd previously thought. "Here's the way this consultant gig is supposed to work, Dixie. You define the problem. I solve the problem. What's your problem?"

"Well, according to Customer Service at the bank, my problem is that I'm skimming my accounts. According to my father, I'm too incompetent to manage even that. You pick.''

Her flippancy couldn't mask the misery in her eyes.

Con held out his hand. "Let me see your bank statement.''

"I've already been over it. I must have made a mistake. Miscalculated the deposits or something.''

He admired her staunch acceptance of responsibility. But even as his rational mind conceded the likelihood of her mistake, a rusty intuition protested her guilt. He didn't *want* to believe she was at fault.

"Let me see," he said again.

"What is it with you? Do you have to have everything in black and white? Can't you trust me to do anything?''

"If I didn't trust you, I'd take your word for it that you screwed up and let it go at that. I want to see the statement from the bank.''

Her gaze dropped to the papers on her desk. She started to slide them together. One of those damn envelopes she kept her receipts in spilled its contents, and her neat, narrow hands hovered over the mess before she lifted and opened them in a gesture of letting go. His heart lurched at the vulnerable gesture.

"Here," she said abruptly. "You might as well sit down. This is probably going to take a while.''

Con lifted his brows in surprise. As long as she'd relegated him to a tiny table in a corner of her room, Wild Thymes was still her sandbox. Was she finally yielding control of the playground?

"Probably," he agreed coolly. "Thanks.''

Val slid out of his way. She watched him take his seat— her seat—with an unsettling combination of resignation and resentment churning in her stomach. But then, he'd already familiarized himself with her inadequate bookkeeping system. How much lower could his opinion go?

She sat slowly, watching as he selected a pencil from the

ceramic pig on her desk. Today he'd unbuttoned and turned back his starched white cuffs to reveal strong-boned wrists and the rise of muscled forearms. Silky dark hair dusted the backs of his hands. Her breathing hitched.

Oh, no. So the man had nice hands. So what?

Her face, her whole body, burned as she recalled his laconic reaction to their one kiss. *Tell yourself you're not interested, if you want to, Dixie. But don't tell me.*

Had she sent mixed signals? She honestly didn't know. She was too used to seeing herself as others saw her, that was her problem. For twenty-eight years she'd defined herself as Sylvia Cutler's neat and shiny little girl or the high school quarterback's homecoming queen or Edward Cutler's runaway daughter.

It was this darn town.

It was coming home.

She'd sworn not to let herself be defined by someone else's expectations ever again. So if this Yankee had decided Val Cutler was some sex-starved socialite from a complicated Southern novel, she was just going to have to prove him wrong.

Unless… Her hand crept up to toy with her earring. Unless she really was attracted?

She studied the lean, clever profile bent over her books, aware of the little bump in her heart rate. Shoot. And here she'd been hoping her judgment had improved some since high school.

What did she know about this guy, after all? Her father had hired him to whip her back in line, she was sure of that. Yet for all of Con's irritating male assurance, he'd been gentle with Ann and patient with Mitchell. He hadn't yet taunted Val with her shortcomings. He hadn't disregarded her ideas or dismissed her presence.

But at that moment, he turned his head and asked, "Aren't you supposed to be in the kitchen?"

Val squinted at him. "I thought the line was 'barefoot and pregnant in the kitchen.'"

Instant humor leapt into those blue, blue eyes, but his mouth gave nothing away. "It's an appealing picture, Dixie, but actually I was looking at the time. Your chef usually starts bawling for help about now."

She looked at the wall clock. He was right. She was due in the kitchen.

Reluctantly, she stood. "I'll leave you to it, then."

"Fine."

He sounded distracted, already absorbed by the task in front of him. She might as well not be in the room. Fighting the urge to sulk, Val wiped her hands on her apron and went out to deal with the lunchtime crowd.

She blew back in three hours later, flushed from the stove and success. Maybe she had left Con in charge of her books and in possession of her office, but that didn't mean she had to let money—or the lack of it—dictate all her choices. Her new pasta salad had passed the dining room test with flying colors, and she'd convinced the Misses Minniton to give salsa corn chowder a try.

Besides, she thought with satisfaction, she had money now. Some, anyway.

She dropped the gray zippered bag full of the day's take splat in the middle of her suspiciously clear desk and smiled into Con MacNeill's surprised face.

"What's this?" he asked.

"Lunch money. I'm going down to the bank to make a deposit."

"Fine. Get me your receipts and I'll total them up."

She shoved a wandering strand of hair out of her face. She was not letting Mr. Business Solutions spoil her sense of accomplishment. "Is that still strictly necessary?"

"More necessary than ever." He smiled, showing the edges of his white, even teeth. A wolf grin. "I think you may not have made a mistake, after all."

Her heart stuttered in stupid hope. She was too old to believe he'd simply waved his magic pencil and slain all her dragons. "What are you talking about?"

"Here." Con pulled a sheet of the bank statement toward him, his long, blunt finger stabbing at printed columns. "And here. Your record of deposits. It's inconsistent."

Val sighed. "Well, it would be. We always do a greater volume of business on Tuesdays and Fridays."

"Yeah, but the total deposits should be consistent week to week. This week here?" He pointed. "Where you thought you'd made the deposit error? You're under by several hundred dollars. In fact, a lot of these totals are low, based on my projections of your profits."

"So, what you're saying is, I actually have money in addition to the loan?"

"I didn't say that. Without the register receipts, it's difficult to prove anything."

"My fault, right?"

He met her gaze evenly. "Like I said, it's too soon to tell who's at fault. Although more accurate record-keeping would certainly help us get to the bottom of this mess."

At least he wasn't condemning her right off the bat. It made a change. A pleasant one.

"So, what will you do?" she asked.

"I want a look at the bank's cash-in tickets. I scheduled a meeting for this afternoon with somebody in the proof department."

Val winced. "Rob Cross?"

"Yeah, I think that was his..." Something registered behind those blue eyes. "Ann's husband?"

"Yes."

"The guy who can't keep his fists to himself?"

"That's the one."

His teeth gleamed in his corporate shark smile. "This will be fun."

Well.

Val had always dreaded her quarterly bank visits. She hated Rob's smug assumption of superiority, the slick confidence he owed to his high school star status and his college education and his eight-hundred-dollar suits. She loathed the way he watched her over his desk, blandly discussing business, his brown eyes hot and knowing.

Maybe there were advantages to keeping a shark around. She smiled back. "Let me know if you draw blood."

Con's expression sobered. "I can't literally fight him, you know."

"Because he reports to my father?"

"Because I do. I can't march into a client's place of business and start throwing punches."

She was absurdly disappointed. "Oh, and of course Daddy will be thrilled when you march in and question his bank's deposit system," she mocked.

Con stiffened. "It's a reasonable request."

"Maybe. But if it makes me look good and it makes him look bad, he's not going to like it." She tilted her head. "In fact, if you make *Rob* look bad, my father's not going to like it. So you better figure out who you're really working for, MacNeill."

Her shot thumped home square in Con's pride.

"I work for myself," he answered through his teeth. "And right now I've accepted the job of hauling your restaurant's profits out of the basement. Which means we are overdue for a discussion of your menu."

Immediately, she went on the defensive. "There's nothing wrong with my menu."

"Not wrong," he corrected her. "Lacking. It would be nice to be able to get a real sandwich around here once in a while."

She arched a brow. "Instead of the free lunch you're getting now?"

Lord, she was a piece of work. And the Lord only knew why she appealed to him. He almost grinned. "No. As part of the free lunch I'm getting now. Beef. Turkey. Something I could recognize and sink my teeth into.''

"Well, you would recognize turkey," she said sweetly.

"This isn't personal, Dixie."

"It sounded personal to me."

"I'm talking about expanding your target market."

"No. You were talking about your lunch. I'm not changing my menu to suit you."

He stood up. "Fine. Suit yourself."

"I always do."

"But don't expect it to build your bottom line. And don't expect me to foot the bill."

Her eyes simmered with temper. "I don't expect squat from you, MacNeill."

If his goal was to drive some distance between them, he'd succeeded beyond his wildest designs. So why did he feel so empty inside?

"Then you won't be disappointed," he said. He picked up a sheaf of papers from the desk and stuffed it into his briefcase. "I've got a meeting at the bank."

Damned if she didn't get the last word, anyway.

"Don't hurry back," she said.

"Val, honey?" Ann's soft voice was filled with concern. "You all right?"

Up to her elbows in sudsy water, Val plunked another pot into the rinse tub and swished it around savagely. "Peachy."

Ann took another step forward, her narrow feet in their flat shoes making no sound at all on the linoleum floor. "You sure? You want a hand washing up?"

Val turned and regarded her friend with affection. "Bless you, Annie. No, I'm fine. Just feeling a little sorry for myself and ticked at men generally."

"Yes," Ann said. Val recoiled at the understanding in her eyes, green and brittle as broken glass.

"I didn't mean—"

Ann shook her head, as if to rob her own reply of significance. "I guess George going off early left you in a bind."

"Not George," Val grunted, dumping the big boiler kettle into the third tub to disinfect. Water sloshed to the floor. "It's MacNeill."

"Oh." Ann stepped back, out of the way of the spreading puddle. "What's he done?"

"Nothing."

She heard the bitter echo of her own words in her head. *I don't expect squat from you.* And MacNeill's mocking reply: *Then you won't be disappointed.*

"He wants me to change the menu."

Ann nodded. "And you don't want to."

"Actually, I'd been thinking about it," Val admitted. "I mean, when we opened, there was no way I could compete with the café's fried chicken and barbecue. I didn't want to. But if we could draw in more customers by adding something fresh and still healthy…"

"Seafood?" Ann suggested tentatively.

Val shrugged. "Possibly. Not if it's crammed down my throat, though."

Ann looked down and away, her lashes dark against her pale cheeks. In spite of the June temperatures outside, her tucked white blouse was buttoned to the neck. Val wondered if Ann buttoned up to pander to Rob's idea of modesty, or if the demure collar hid the marks of his fingers.

More secrets, she thought. Bile rose in her throat. Swallowing, she asked gently, "Annie, how are—"

"Don't ask." Ann moistened her lips. "Please? I'm so…"

"What?"

Hurt? Tired? Scared?

"Sick of lying," Ann whispered.

It was as close as Ann had come to admitting that her perfect life with her successful, handsome husband was falling apart, battered to bits by his fists.

Val let another pot slide into the water. She wiped her hands on her damp apron, anxious to give her friend a hug.

"Ann, if there's anything I can do, if you need a place to stay for a while, will you tell me?"

"I don't…I can't leave him."

Frustration knotted under her ribs. "I understand. But if you needed to get away—even just for a little while—you know you could come to me."

"Would you call the police?"

"Well, of course I—" Val caught herself at the flat look that entered Ann's eyes. "Only if you wanted me to. I won't make you do anything you aren't ready for."

Ann lifted her hands in oblique apology. "It's just…Chief Palmer's son…he was on the football team with Rob."

Val remembered Maddox Palmer, the policeman's son who was always in trouble. The intense center had protected quarterback Rob all the way to the state championships. Val was pretty sure Maddox left town the year before she did. But maybe that didn't make a difference in a town fueled by gossip and oiled by old loyalties. After all these years, maybe Ann was worried the Palmer family would still defend the team star.

"Okay. But you come, all right? Anytime you need to, and we'll take it from there."

The metal double doors that separated the kitchen from the dining room bumped open. Rob Cross, his blond hair boyishly disheveled, strolled through, smiling like a car salesman.

"Take what where?" he asked.

Val looked for some sign of his meeting with Con, but there wasn't a bite on him. Shoot. "Nothing, Rob."

"We were just talking," Ann said.

"Telling stories, baby?"

Val felt a spurt of dislike. "Why? Do you know any good ones?"

"Oh, yes. I know lots." His heavy gaze reminded her of

all he knew and remembered. Beside her, Ann hugged her elbows. "Fortunately, I'm the silent sort. Not everybody's so discreet. I'd suggest you tell that MacNeill fellow you don't need him poking around in your business."

"What did he tell you?"

Rob frowned. "I don't need to bother you with all the details. But he sure doesn't understand how we do business down here. He your accountant now?"

"Financial adviser," Val said. Stupid. What did it matter what his job title was? "And my father hired him."

"*Edward* hired him?"

She was surprised Rob didn't know. If Con reported to Edward Cutler, and Rob had come to warn her... What power game was her father playing? And who was on her side?

"Well, I'll have to talk to your father about that. Though this MacNeill fellow did catch one little bookkeeping error I was happy to take care of."

Rob patted his pockets absently, like a man searching for a smoke, and then held out a folded sheet of white paper.

Val regarded it as if it might metamorphose suddenly into a snake or a gun. "What is it?"

Rob chuckled. "You never did want anything that was good for you, did you, princess?"

She met his gaze flatly, deciding then and there that whatever her father was up to, Rob had never been on her side.

"Go ahead," he urged her. "Take it."

Val unfolded the paper cautiously. It was an adjusted bank statement for the restaurant's operating account, dated today. She skipped the long columns of amounts and references, going straight for the account summary information.

Her heart stopped. She had money.

She read the balance again, her heart beginning to slam against her ribs. She had money. She hadn't made a mistake. Her thoughts scattered in all directions like rainbow candies bouncing on the floor. Money enough to pay her bills and fix the clogged drain in the storage room. Money—maybe—to offer Ann part-time work.

The paper trembled in her grip. She clutched it tightly, as if her good fortune could somehow fly away, trying not to betray her relief and surprise in front of Rob. ''Nice of you to bring it by. Thanks.''

''I thought I'd save your tame accountant the trip.''

She wanted to protest that Con wasn't her anything. Certainly not tamed. But the evidence was in her hands. She had money. And whatever Rob might claim, she suspected she had Con MacNeill to thank for it.

The sharp Yankee businessman she thought she knew could have brought her the news himself, waving her adjusted statement like a trophy or brandishing it like a whip. Instead, Con had pressed the vice president in charge of the proof department into service as his errand boy.

To humiliate Rob? Val wondered. Or to send some kind of message to her? *Don't mess with me, I'm a consultant.* An absurd bubble of laughter rose in her throat. Oh, Lord, what could she possibly say to him now?

All too clearly, her last words rang in her ears. *Don't hurry back.*

Val winced.

Chapter 6

Not a damn thing to do in a one-bank town on a Sunday afternoon, Con reflected. At least in Boston the bars would be open.

He stood on the porch of Magnolia House Restaurant, watching two kids argue over a tricycle and a fat puppy stalk something through freshly mowed grass. Con scratched his jaw with one thumb. Maybe he shouldn't have turned down Patrick's invitation to Sunday dinner, after all.

Of all Con's close family, he was closest to his older brother Patrick. He genuinely liked his surgeon sister-in-law, a pretty woman with a mind as sharp as one of her scalpels. But since the firing, he was too aware he'd let his family down. He wasn't in the mood for Kate's perceptive questions or Patrick's unspoken sympathy. He wasn't sure he could stand all that newlywed domestic bliss stuff, either.

The bigger kid won the tricycle war, and the little one ran bawling into the house. A screen door slammed. The puppy caught a grasshopper and ate it. The whole scene felt familiar and uncomfortable, like outgrown hightops. Like the neighborhood he'd been so eager to escape, like the past he'd left behind.

He'd already made his duty calls before he left his motel, doing his best to respond reassuringly to his mother's questions and his father's silence. The new job was interesting, he told them. He'd actually gotten phone calls from two potential consulting clients, and he had a lead on a job in Boston. He'd see them Friday night after the interview.

Unless he didn't get the job, Con thought, in which case a bar somewhere had a hell of a lot more appeal than his mother's kitchen table. Con didn't relish facing another evening of his parents' unvoiced disappointment with their brilliant son's career.

It had been a relief to call his brother Sean, on the road with a construction crew in Fuquay Varina. Sean was still sleeping off his Saturday night, and cursed Con sleepily before hanging up.

His duty almost done, Con had driven twenty miles to attend a Catholic Sunday service and then backtracked into Cutler for food. The motel where he was staying ran more to vending machines than room service. Magnolia House, on the outskirts of town, was as high in salt and price as it was in charm. After fifteen minutes waiting for a coffee refill, Con had paid his tab and stalked out.

Val could make a killing in this town if she opened her place for breakfast.

In his mind, she lifted her chin, gray eyes glinting with challenge. *I'm not changing my menu to suit you.*

Fine by him. He didn't need her breakfast. He didn't need any part of her.

Restless and reluctant to return to his motel room, he'd read the paper on the veranda, watching a rumba line of blue-haired ladies shuffle in and out of the restaurant's doors. Now he stood, watching the puppy throw up on the sidewalk as if that were the high point of his day. Hell, maybe it was.

A white Honda Prelude, seven years old and powdered with red dust, rumbled onto the lazy street. Con watched idly as it slowed in front of the restaurant. The engine was cut. A car door slammed.

Into the sunshine swung Val Cutler. Long silver earrings tangled with the wild glory of her hair. A bright turquoise tank top shouted the attractions underneath. Her sandaled feet beat a parade rhythm on the concrete walk, and her smile glowed like carnival lights on the midway.

Well, well. Con grinned. Things were looking up. Whether or not he planned on a whirl, the circus had come to town.

Val squinted against the bright afternoon sunlight. The deep eaves and sheltering rail of Magnolia House created a backwater of shade. The splash of Con's white T-shirt swam in the cool recesses of the porch. Only the strong, smooth shape of his torso and the gleam of his teeth were clearly visible.

Like a shark's.

His voice emerged from the shadows. "What are you doing here?"

Val set one foot on the porch steps. So he was going to be difficult. No doubt it was annoyance that bumped up her heart rate, irritation that pumped heat to her cheeks.

"Looking for you."

He lifted an eyebrow. "You still use bloodhounds in the South?"

"The telephone, actually. I figured you'd either be here or at Arlene's, so I called and…" She was talking too much, she realized, mortified. "I came to invite you on a picnic."

He glided to the top of the steps and leaned against the supporting column of the porch. She had a very nice view of his chest.

"A picnic?" he repeated.

"Yes. You know, lemonade, watermelon, ants?"

He shifted a degree. "Yeah, I've heard of them. What happened to 'not interested'?"

Nerves jittered under her skin. She pushed impatiently at her hair. "Look, I'm not suggesting we roll around together on a blanket on the riverbank. It's just lunch, all right?"

He strolled down a step, so that her eyes were level with his chin. "Why?"

She didn't back down. "Why, what?"

"Why lunch?"

"Well, I...thought maybe I owed you a meal. Sort of as a thank-you for what you did on Friday."

His expression was unreadable. "My rates are usually a little higher than a sandwich."

"Then you're out of luck. That's my best offer."

"I'll take it." His blue eyes met hers directly, and her breath caught at the complicit humor in his gaze. A shiver of attraction ran up her spine. "Hey, I said I wasn't cheap. That doesn't mean I'm not easy."

Not easy, Val thought. Hard. Hard-muscled and tough-minded. Difficult for an easygoing Southern girl to understand and nearly impossible to resist.

She blushed. "Great," she said brightly. Too brightly. "Shall we go?"

He sauntered off the porch. Val preceded him down the short brick walk, conscious of his effortless, long-limbed gait behind her.

At the passenger door of her car, Con paused. "We could take my car."

Val smiled at him across the white roof baking in the sun. "But I know where we're going. And the cooler's in my trunk."

She observed his quick mental calculation before he shrugged and squeezed into her car. A lot of guys had trouble being driven by a woman, she thought. His knees bumped her dashboard. Although maybe this one simply needed more room than her little car could accommodate. She adjusted the front seat.

"What do you drive?" she asked, to test her theory.

"A 1972 Jaguar sedan." The year meant nothing to her, but she recognized *Jaguar*. He added, a shade defensively, "It's a very well-manufactured car. Mechanically, nothing can touch it."

Val grinned as she pulled away from the curb. "Well, you'd better hope nothing goes wrong with it while you're down here. Because no mechanic in Cutler *will* touch it."

She thought he stiffened, and then he laughed. "Tell me about it. Half the time I can't afford the repairs, anyway. I poured two quarts of oil down her throat from Philadelphia to Petersburg."

She glanced at him sideways. "Impulse buy?" she asked demurely.

"More like a girlfriend substitute."

"Excuse me?"

"High maintenance and heavy commitment," he explained.

She sniffed to cover her laughter. "It does seem like an irrational attachment for a logical, conservative consultant."

He shrugged. "It's a toy. You know, 'the guy who dies with the most toys wins'?"

A frisson of disquiet ran up the backs of her arms. "Oh, yes. I know. My father's a collector."

"What does he collect?"

"Anything he can put on display. New cars and clothes, old wine and silver." Deliberately, she kept her voice light to hide old hurts. "His wife. His daughter."

"Yeah, well, my collection never got that far."

She signaled her turn, sneaking another look at his hard profile. "Never married?"

"Nope."

She thought of that phone call she'd overheard in her office. "Engaged?"

"Once."

His stubborn privacy challenged her. She steered the car through a tunnel of trees down a winding drive dappled with sunshine. The crunch of gravel, the scent of earth and mold, rose through the open windows.

"And what happened to your fiancée?"

"Did I murder her, you mean?"

She bit her lip to cover her smile. "Well, did you?"

"No. She dumped me for somebody else. Some guy with a job and a pedigree. They're getting married pretty soon."

Sylvia Cutler always told her daughter that her prying would get her into trouble one day. "Oops. I'm sorry."

The canopy of trees parted to reveal the sky, and the drive opened into a parking lot.

"Don't be. I'm not."

"Oh, but you must be."

"Who says?"

Val spied a shaded spot under a cottonwood tree and turned into it. "Well, if you loved her…"

"Save the sympathy, Dixie. We didn't love each other. Not the way you mean."

"Then why get engaged?"

"I don't know. Why does anybody get engaged?"

She cut the engine. The sudden quiet reminded her they were alone. She swallowed past her constricted throat.

"Don't ask me. According to my aunt Naomi, a woman purchases the security of marriage with her name, her privacy and her career."

"Is that what you think?"

Uncomfortable with the turn of the conversation, Val shrugged, her hand still on the keys. "It sounded pretty plausible when I was seventeen. Tell me again why you were getting married?"

His brief grin gleamed in the shadowed interior of the car. "Because my ex-fiancée was a prize. And I like to win."

Val snorted. "And she accepted you because…?"

"I had some money and enough prospects to appeal to her. Plus, she may have figured that since she was lowering herself to marry me I'd be grateful enough to do as I was told."

"She didn't know you very well," Val observed.

"No. Maybe we both had our eyes opened."

Silence dragged between them. Inside the car, the air grew warm and close. Val sucked her lungs full of lulling, drugging heat, feeling the faint prickle of perspiration on her upper lip. The backs of her thighs stuck to her seat.

But then, she wasn't the only one affected. Con MacNeill's blue eyes looked anything but cold.

To break the rising tension, Val glanced out her window, scanning the empty parking lot. Where were the Sunday fishermen, the picnicking families? Even a few kids using the beach would be nice. She'd wanted neutral ground to make her peace with MacNeill. She hadn't counted on finding herself alone in a deserted area with a large man she'd known less than a week.

She cleared her throat. "What kind of prospects? What exactly did you do back in Boston?"

If Con observed her nervousness or understood its cause, he didn't remark on it. "I worked for a venture capitalist group." She must have looked blank, because he explained, "I obtained funding for smaller companies. Software firms, mostly."

"That sounds…"

"Boring?" he suggested.

She laughed and swung open her door, ignoring the faint suctioning sound as her legs unpeeled from the vinyl seat.

"Lucrative," she amended. "And you had the satisfaction of helping other businesses."

He came around to the back of the car to help her unload the trunk. "When I wasn't taking them over, yeah."

She hefted the cooler. "Gee, thanks for reminding me," she drawled.

He grinned and took it from her. "Anytime, Dixie. Get the blanket."

The trunk door slammed, loud against the stillness. Val was reminded again how isolated they were. She didn't take risks with men, not since that April night her senior year of high school. She bit the inside of her cheek.

Beside her, Con waited, his right arm corded with the weight of the heavy cooler. He was wearing a white T-shirt and jeans. The comb tracks still showed in his hair. Out of his buttoned shirts and pleated khakis, he looked even more like what he was, an attractive, dangerous male from a tougher town than Cutler, North Carolina.

And yet none of Val's feminine antennae quivered when she looked at him. Not with caution, anyway.

She nodded toward a break in the trees. "The path's over there."

"Lead the way."

The sandy track was rutted with rain and hedged with ferns and poison ivy. They emerged from the green cocoon onto the soft bank of the Six Forks River. Cattails, kudzu and leaning pines encircled an amphitheater of water and sand. Val shook out the quilt to create a ringside seat on the river and knelt beside the cooler.

"I hope you're hungry."

"Tempt me," he invited, dropping to the blanket beside her.

She glanced over at him, uncertain if she'd imagined the teasing insinuation in his voice. Lord have mercy, but *he* tempted *her*. His drying hair fell over his forehead, softening the aggressive angles of nose and jaw. His long body stretched out within reach of her hand. When did the man find time to work out? He was all muscle, from his powerful chest to his solid abdomen to his denim-covered thighs. She caught herself staring and hastily dropped her gaze. He had big feet, she noticed.

"Peppers, basil and mozzarella on whole wheat." She

cleared her throat, disliking the husky quality of her own voice. "Or there's tuna."

He raised his eyebrows. "Tuna?"

"Seafood isn't meat." She busied herself unpacking the cooler, aware she was offering him more than a sandwich. Would he gloat, as her father always gloated when she conceded a point? "Actually, I've been toying with the idea of trying out one or two fish entrées on the menu. Just to see how they do. Maybe some poultry."

"Turkey?" Con asked dryly.

Relief made her smile. "Maybe I can live with turkey."

His disciplined mouth curved. Heavens, he was attractive when he smiled. She wanted to tease him, to see his expression warm and his cool blue eyes ignite. She wanted to play with fire.

And because she knew that this time following her instincts could get her badly burned, she swallowed and looked away.

She wanted a drink. Something cool, to restore her composure. Her hands hovered over the picnic things before settling on the thermos jug of lemonade. "Can I pour you some?"

"Thanks." He leaned back on his elbows, watching her from beneath half-closed lids.

A freshening breeze rippled the water and set the cattails dancing. She felt the air lift the springing hair at her temples, but she still felt warm. Hot and close. Ice cubes rattled in the jug.

Con's large, warm hands closed around her slippery ones. He sat up, steadying the thermos and rescuing the plastic cup from her anxious grasp. Settling the lemonade on the grass beside the blanket, he twined his fingers with hers. Her breath stalled. The sight of his fingers parting and twisting with hers, her small, competent hand so completely engulfed by his, made her breasts feel full and her bones feel hollow.

The memory of her own words came back to mock her.

I'm not suggesting we roll around together on a blanket on the riverbank. She ought to pull away. She told herself she couldn't afford this complication, didn't want to explore this attraction.

"I'm getting ideas again, Dixie," he warned.

Heaven help her, so was she.

Her attention was fixed by that hard mouth, by the slight roughness bracketing the corners and the sensual curve of his lower lip. He drew on their joined hands, pulling her into his heat. Her body bent over his reclining one. She needed air. His breath slipped over her cheek and touched her mouth, and her lips parted to take him in.

He angled his head, kissing the tip of her chin instead. Surprised, she opened her eyes, and then closed them as his mouth cruised the curve of her jaw to the pulse point under her ear. Heat bolted through her. Con's sound of masculine satisfaction against her skin raised all the little hairs along the back of her neck and across her shoulders. She could feel the frantic beat of her heart under his lips and in their joined hands and lower, deeper, in her body.

Oh, no. Oh, my.

A smart woman lives to please herself, Aunt Naomi had said. But what if what pleased her was a tall, commanding Yankee with ice blue eyes and heated kisses?

"MacNeill."

He took advantage of his name on her mouth, giving her his breath, stealing hers. His tongue stroked and tangled with hers as he took the kiss deeper. She felt light-headed, drunk. Lack of oxygen, she told herself weakly. The pads of her fingers pressed into his hard shoulders.

"Con?"

He bent his head to her throat. From his came that sound again, that masculine rumble that could have been interrogation or assent. It vibrated along the sensitive cords of her neck, making her lips ache for the pressure he withheld from them.

Oh, the heck with it.

Rashly, she surrendered to instinct. She initiated their next kiss, straining against the grip of his hands, feeding greedily on his mouth. She wanted him. Her desire for him was boundless, almost mindless. She wanted his possession, the strength of his hands, the power of his body, on her, inside her. Her need for him was unprecedented and shocking and thrilling.

Was it this, this urgent call to complete and be completed, to claim and be claimed, that made a woman give herself over to her mate?

She went to Con's head like a shot of Irish whiskey. One hundred proof. He drowned in the flavor of her. The kick. The texture. Damn, she was fine.

And then she was pulling away, depriving him of her intoxicating fire. He bent to drink again, and she averted her face.

"Dixie…"

She shook her head.

"What? What is it?"

"It's…complicated."

Complicated? He was astonished how simple it was. He hadn't felt this mix of sweaty lust and wonder since he'd unhooked Rita Kelly's bra in the front seat of her father's Lincoln.

Easy, genius. He wasn't fourteen anymore. And the woman kneeling beside the well-stocked cooler was no Rita Kelly.

A little twist of Val's hair sprang free and blew across her cheek. Con resisted the urge to reach over and smooth it behind her ear.

"It seems pretty simple to me," he said coolly. "I want you, Val Cutler."

She flushed again at his plain speaking. "Inconvenient, then."

"Inconven— Hell." She was right. He couldn't afford to

get mixed up in the war for Southern independence she waged against her father. But that didn't seem to make one bit of difference to his hungry body. "Sex is inconvenient, Dixie girl."

She sat back on her heels. "I haven't agreed to have sex with you."

Her prim precision amused him, as if she were quoting from some college handbook of rules. As if they hadn't been grappling each other on her old-fashioned quilt a moment before.

"Yeah, and I haven't asked, but I kind of figured it was an outside possibility."

"Well, it's not." Shaking her hair back out of her face, she handed him a plastic-wrapped sandwich and a blue cloth napkin. Belle-to-the-bone, he thought, and suppressed a smile. "I hardly know you, for one thing. And there's a conflict of interest, for another."

There was a blush on her high cheekbones, a hollow under them. He'd have bet anything she was gnawing the inside of her cheek again. A new and troubling tenderness burst inside his chest.

Stumped, he watched as Val lifted out a Tupperware tray of deviled eggs and a basket wrapped in a matching napkin.

"Define 'conflict of interest,'" he suggested.

She looked at him directly. "You work for my father."

"That doesn't have to be a conflict."

"Look, I didn't go to business school, but I'm not stupid. If money is missing from my account, then the bank is involved. And if the bank is involved, then my father could be, too."

"Someone at the bank might be, certainly. Money doesn't disappear. If you aren't paying expenses from cash—"

"I write checks for everything," Val insisted.

"Then it could be a teller mis-added the receipts and pocketed the difference. Or someone altered the cash-in ticket and then debited your account. If the problem's significant enough, there'll be a pattern. And I'll find it.''

"If my father wants you to."

He narrowed his eyes. "Why wouldn't he? He told me he wanted you to succeed."

"No, I don't think so. What he'd really like is for me to fail in spite of all he can do for me and move back under his roof and take my rightful place as a Cutler."

It was so ludicrous, Con laughed.

"It's not funny," Val said ruefully. "Do I look like Junior League material to you?"

"Maybe not the earrings. But what about all this?" He waved a hand over her picnic spread.

She surveyed the star-stitched quilt in confusion. "All what?"

"Where I come from, Dixie, a picnic is beer and brats and paper plates. Not little sandwiches with the crusts cut off and cloth napkins and matching salt and pepper shakers.''

She raised her chin. "Cloth napkins are better for the environment."

He raised his eyebrows.

Her eyes danced suddenly. "Well, all right, maybe a little Junior League. But just because I pack a lunch basket like my mother doesn't mean I want her life."

"So, what do you want?"

Val closed her eyes a moment. Out on the river, a mallard squawked, breaking the silence with a splash of water and a flurry of wings.

Opening her eyes, she looked at Con, relaxed and confident, as if all he had to do was stretch back on that blanket and smile that slow, collected smile and women would crawl all over themselves to get to him.

She sighed. Probably most women would.

"I want my independence. I want my restaurant to succeed. And even if I'm not the status symbol they want me to be, I'm trying very hard to reconcile with my parents right now." She shook her head, making her earrings jangle. "Though it's tough building a mature relationship with a man who calls you 'punkin.'"

"I can imagine," Con said dryly.

His blue eyes were bright with humor and dark with understanding. She felt his regard deep in her midsection, sweet as raspberry trifle and comforting as bread. A woman could learn to depend on the sustenance of that warm regard. Briefly, Val hungered for…what? His support? Approval? Love?

No.

"What I don't need," she continued, "is a…a boyfriend looking over my shoulder and telling me what to do."

"Or a lover?"

His deep, rough voice plucked at her nerves, making her insides quiver.

"I tried that. I'm not some little innocent, you know. It didn't work. It wouldn't work."

"Why not?"

"Expectations. You let somebody into your bed, and all of a sudden he wants the keys to your apartment and a chance to run your life."

"Your life? Or your business?"

"Either one." Bravely, she met his eyes. "I won't give up control, MacNeill."

His thumb rubbed his jaw. "You know, it's possible you're letting your prejudices blind you to a good thing. You're stuck with me, anyway. Why not use me? I've got expertise and I've got experience. Hell, I can get you references if you want."

Her cheeks scorched. "Are we still talking about the restaurant here?"

He went very still. His stillness was an active quality, as

unmistakable and expressive as another man's shout. And
then his slow grin sizzled clear down to her toes. "I was.
But feel free to take advantage of any services you want. I
won't be in town forever."

Chapter 7

After the cool and shaded riverbank, the interior of the car
steamed like an oven. Val unrolled the windows, fussed with
her seat belt, snapped on the radio—anything to avoid looking at the man beside her.

Feel free to take advantage of any services you want.

Oh, my.

She started the car. The men she'd known saw sex in
terms of conquest and surrender. In Naomi's words, once a
woman admitted a man into her bed, he expected to be allowed into her decisions as well.

But there was something so seductive about Con's invitation. Take advantage of him? As if she could have all that
intelligence and intensity and confidence at her command.
The prospect made her heart beat faster.

Reversing, she caught a glimpse of her flushed cheeks and
bright eyes in the rearview mirror and pulled a face. Valerian
Darcy Cutler, Rebel Without a Brain.

She'd always been afraid of being taken over. Not just
physically, though she had to accept that Con could over-

power her if he wanted to. She was afraid of losing control. Even worse, of giving it away, of letting the potent combination of liking and desire compromise who she was and what she wanted. Look at her mother, frozen into the model of a perfect wife by status and affection. Or Ann, locked into an abusive marriage by her need to give her son the advantages she'd lacked.

The old car bumped up the graveled drive through the avenue of trees. Val snuck a glance at the man beside her. She couldn't see Con MacNeill using sex as a club to force a woman's compliance. Heck, with his glacial good looks and volcanic sexuality, he probably used a stick to beat women off.

Suppose she took him up on his offer. He wasn't going to be around long enough to try to change her. Would sex complicate their working relationship?

You betcha it would.

The car turned onto the main road. Air flowed through the open windows, flattening her shirt to her body and rushing in her ears. A husky female voice, balanced between pain and melody, streamed from the car's tinny speakers promising an unseen lover that tonight would be enough.

In the passenger seat beside her, Con grimaced and stretched. His feet pressed the floorboard. His shoulders flexed. Her own muscles squeezed in sympathy, as if they inhabited the same body. Shared the same bed.

She cleared her throat. "Crowded?"

He shook his head once, not denying it, just dismissing his discomfort as of no importance. His new position planted his shoulders against the door, so that he angled toward her. His left knee brushed her thigh. Her hands grew clammy on the steering wheel.

"I'm not a big country fan. Mind if I change the station?" he asked.

She shrugged. "Be my guest."

He paused with one hand on the radio dial. "I won't if you don't want me to. MacNeill Road Rules."

She couldn't have heard him correctly. "What?"

His blue eyes gleamed. "Driver chooses the music. MacNeill Road Rules. You sure you don't mind?"

She smiled, stupidly reassured. "Not as long as you ask. Go ahead."

He fiddled with the dial. Bruce Springsteen leapt from the dashboard with gritty vocals and a crash of his guitar.

"Yankee music," she drawled.

He laughed.

She did fifty-five returning on Highway 40, but it felt like speeding with her hair streaming in the wind and the music blaring from the radio. For the first time since her return home, it felt like she was going somewhere new, someplace exciting.

They hit the first stoplight on the three-block stretch that was Cutler's downtown. Val slowed past the bank and the old hardware. An elderly man escorted his wife from Arlene's Café. A trio of bored teens hung on the bicycle rack in front of the new video store.

Con nodded toward them as they passed. "Takes you back, doesn't it?"

She smiled in quick understanding. "Nothing to do, no place to go?"

"I couldn't wait to grow up and get out," he confessed. "Or at least get my driver's license, so I wasn't always begging the back seat in Patrick's car."

She looked down her nose at him sideways, difficult to do without driving up on the curb, but his comment seemed to call for it. "You spend a lot of time in back seats, MacNeill?"

"As much as I could get away with," he admitted coolly. "What about you? You ever take a walk on the wild side back in high school?"

Her smile flattened as she remembered. "There was no wild side in Cutler."

He looked amused. "Dixie, there's always a wild side. Sometimes the nice girls just need a tour guide to find it."

I won't be in town forever.

On impulse, she turned the wheel and coasted to the curb in front of Wild Thymes.

In the passenger seat, Con sat solid and still as the bronze statue of the Confederate soldier on the courthouse lawn. "My motel's at the other end of town."

She turned the key in the ignition. The street was quiet. The silence pounded in her ears.

"I know."

He gave her a level look. "Your restaurant's closed on Sundays."

"Yes. I live upstairs." Thump. Her heart jumped and lodged in her throat. She cleared it. "Would you like to come up?"

His voice roughened, silk pulled over stone. "Dixie, do you know what you're doing?"

She shook her wind-tossed hair away from her face, impelled by bravado and curiosity and instinct. "Well, now, I'm not sure. Maybe if I get it wrong, you could show me?"

Those cool blue eyes kindled at her teasing. She felt a rush of heat to her midsection. "I'll do my best," he promised.

She gave him an uncertain smile and swung out of the car, leaving the doors unlocked.

A small-town gesture, Con thought. A small-town girl, for all her easy warmth and open ways. He sat where he was for a second, feeling lucky. Feeling stunned. What had he said or done to change her mind?

He rolled up his window, and hers. Slowly, he got out of the car. Why question his good fortune? Sean would hoot with laughter at Con's hesitation in going upstairs with a woman he both liked and desired. What was his problem?

His mind engaged, clicking along familiar tracks like a train pulling out of the station.

He did like Val Cutler, he realized, Gypsy hair and mismatched earrings and all.

Maybe he liked her too much?

He respected her loyalty to her friend and her painful attachment to her family. He was impressed by her determination, drawn to her openhearted hopes. That friendly free spirit she presented to the world was deceptive, like the warm shallows of a sandy beach that invited you to play. Beyond and below the sparkling surface, she was deep and private as the sea. The thought of exploring those quiet depths was enough to tempt a man to drowning.

"I thought you didn't want complicated," he said.

She lifted her chin, regarding him over the hood of the car. The swaying silver hoops glittered in the sunlight. "It seems pretty simple to me."

His own words on her pretty lips… He was no saint. He was a man. And he wanted her.

"Fine. I'd like to see where you live. You can offer me a cup of coffee or something."

Her wide gray eyes were serious, but a smile flirted with the corners of her mouth. "I don't drink coffee."

He ached with wanting her. And, as he'd warned her—God, was it only three days ago?—he was used to going after what he wanted. "Then I guess it'll have to be the something."

He followed her under the restaurant's awning and waited while she fumbled with her keys. Under the turquoise tank top, her breasts rose and fell. Her hair, waving close to his chin, smelled of cinnamon and sunlight. He discovered his hands curled into fists and consciously relaxed them.

She led him through the dark green door to another door set in a corner of the tiny white-tiled entry. Unlocked, Con noted with the portion of his brain not fixed on her. They were going to have to have another talk about security soon.

Dingy linoleum covered the steps. Their footsteps tapped against the metal strips tacked to each edge. Their breathing echoed up the narrow staircase. Ahead of him, Val moved with familiarity and unconscious grace. He felt too big, too loud, following her.

And then he heard a barely perceptible sound ahead of them, around the corner. An indrawn breath. A scrape.

Dammit. Living alone, she should lock her doors. All her doors.

He put his hand on her arm. "Wait."

She half-turned on the step. "What?"

A voice quavered from the top of the stairs. "Val? Is that you?"

A woman's voice. Con barely began to relax when Mitchell appeared around the corner, his thin face twisted with concern and red with crying.

"Aunt Val? It's Mom. She's hurt bad."

Val moved. Fast. "Oh, my God. Oh, Annie. Oh, honey."

Ann huddled on Val's doorstep, her arms cradled across her stomach, a broken figurine in an ironed T-shirt and denim jumper. She pressed a tea towel to her face, the sunflower pattern almost obscured by blood.

A mugging? In Cutler?

Val dropped to her knees beside her friend, one arm already reaching protectively over her shoulders. "Annie? Are you all right?"

Con noticed she didn't ask what had happened. Comprehension sliced through him, and cold fury coiled in his gut. Had Ann's husband done this? Had that slick Southern son of a bitch used his fists on this thin, quiet woman?

"I'm sorry," she said thickly. "I didn't know where else to go."

Val touched her, feather-light touches on her back, her hair, her arm, like a mother reassuring herself her child was all right. Like a wisewoman, bestowing healing with her hands. "No, this was right. This was good. What can I do?"

"I'm calling the police," Con said.

"No! No," both women said.

"Give her a minute," Val added.

"Was it Cross?" Con demanded.

"It was an accident," Ann said.

He swore.

Val raised her head from Ann's shoulder. A smear of blood disfigured her pale cheek. "Please."

Despite her firm tone, her eyes appealed for his patience. Con balanced on the balls of his feet while everything inside him screamed for action.

"I'm sorry," Ann said again, tears welling.

The two women were looking at him as if he were the one they had to be afraid of. Hell.

"Don't be," he snapped. "You haven't done anything to apologize for."

"He's right," Val soothed. "It's all right. Can we get you inside?"

Silent in a corner of the hall, Mitchell watched the three adults with guarded eyes.

"Would you help me get her inside?" Val asked Con directly.

A muscle worked in his jaw. Val held her breath. Would he listen to her?

Stiff-necked, he nodded.

Ann's face contorted as she dragged her legs under her. "I don't think I can…"

"I've got you," Con said. His expression could have been carved in granite, but his deep voice was gentle. His big hand cupped Ann's elbow. His muscled arm supported her. "Easy, now. Easy. There we go."

His tenderness made tears burn at the back of Val's eyes. She unlocked the door to her apartment and then stood back as Con escorted Ann inside and helped her to a chair.

Val glanced back over her shoulder. "Mitchell? Come on, honey."

The eight-year-old shuffled forward. "Is she going to be all right?"

She gave his bony shoulders a reassuring squeeze. When he didn't respond, she sighed and dropped her arm. "I think so. I hope so. I'm going to get her some ice, okay? You want a soda?"

He shook his head.

Ann hunched at the kitchen table, her arms protecting her body, one hand pressing the towel to her face. Blood spotted her neat denim jumper. Swallowing fury and frustration, Val stalked to the refrigerator to load a plastic bag with ice.

"Frozen peas," Con said beside her.

She frowned. "What?"

"For her face. A bag of frozen vegetables conforms better to the site of the injury, and it won't leak all over her."

She remembered. "Boxing."

He didn't smile, but the gleam in his blue eyes momentarily lightened the burden in her chest. "Plus I fought with my brothers a lot." Glancing over her shoulder, he lowered his voice. "You want to get her to a doctor."

Val spoke with a bitterness born of experience. "She won't go."

She wrapped up a bag of frozen corn and carried it to the table. Kneeling at Ann's chair, she pried gently at her friend's hands. The short, neat nails bore quarter-moons of blood.

"Here, honey, it's a clean towel. Can I get you something? Aspirin?"

Ann shook her head, which restarted the flow of blood. "Oh! No. I took some before we came. I'm sorry. I'm so sorry. I just wanted...I just had to get out of the house for a while."

Val's gaze flew to Ann's son, watching beneath the guard of his lashes. "He didn't...Mitchell?"

"No," Ann assured her. "No. But Rob's been so keyed up the past two days. I wanted to get away. Just until he settled down. And I couldn't leave Mitchell alone with him.''

Neither one of them bothered to identify *him*. They both knew. There had only ever been one man for Annie Barclay Cross. And Val, God help her, knew him too. She swallowed convulsively at the memories and dabbed gently at Ann's face with a napkin. The kitchen towel wrapping the frozen corn was already bright with new blood.

''She needs to get to the hospital,'' Con said.

Ann made a choked sound. ''No.''

Val glared. Con was going to scare Ann right back to her husband. ''You're upsetting her.''

''*I'm* up—?'' Con bit off whatever he'd been about to say. ''She needs to see a doctor,'' he repeated quietly. ''I think her nose is broken.''

Oh, dear heaven. Oh, poor Annie.

''Mom?'' Mitchell took a hesitant half step out of his corner.

''It's okay,'' Ann said bravely through the blood-soaked towel.

But it wasn't, and Mitchell knew it. His realization showed in his defeated posture and defiant eyes.

Con dropped his big hand on the boy's shoulder. The boy turned to him, green eyes blazing.

''Will you take us?'' he demanded.

''Yeah, sure, kid. We'll go.''

Ann made a broken bird cry of distress. ''No. I can't. The insurance… If he finds out…''

''Ann.'' Val drew a careful breath to still her internal trembling, to steady her voice. She had to be steady, for Ann's sake. Val knew better than anyone but Ann herself the difficulty of standing against Rob. But Con, with his stranger's eyes, saw what Ann did not, what Val herself had avoided seeing. It was time to act.

''Come on, honey. You need help. We're going to the hospital.''

Eventually Ann, who was used to obeying, allowed herself to be persuaded. Val squeezed her hands on the way down to the car, as if she could infuse her friend with her own conviction. Con folded himself into the back seat beside Mitchell.

Glancing in the rearview mirror, Val saw that he kept constant, unobtrusive contact with the boy—his palm curled over his shoulder, his crossed foot nudging his knee—and that Mitchell permitted his touch. At the hospital, he smoothed their way, requesting a wheelchair, parking the car.

He caught up with them as Val steered Ann's wheelchair past the half-empty rows of chairs in the waiting area. A toddler with an ear infection screamed from her mother's lap. A flush-faced boy leaned against his father's arm.

Just another quiet Sunday afternoon in Cutler, Val thought bleakly. Nothing to demand attention but bee stings, boating accidents and battered wives.

As if conjured by Con's arrival, the nurse appeared, a solid woman in white pants and jacket, her dark hair shaved close to her head. Tucking her clipboard up on her hip, she bent close over the wheelchair.

"All right, now, honey, want to tell me what happened to you?"

Ann's gaze slipped past the nurse to Mitchell. Her swollen eyelids squeezed shut. Val's heart constricted at her friend's dilemma. What could she say in front of their son?

"The explanations can wait. She needs attention now," Con said.

The nurse straightened, her round face disapproving. "And who are you?"

Val could imagine what she suspected. A beaten woman accompanied by an overbearing man had to be a typical sight in the ER.

"A friend," she said hastily. "We're her friends."

The nurse's guard relaxed. "Well, you brought her to the

right place." She took the back of Ann's wheelchair. "Okay, honey, let's get you down to X ray. This your boy?"

Ann nodded. "Mitchell."

"We've got a real nice waiting room. How about we get one of the other nurses to show Mitchell where the Nintendo is while we go take some pictures?"

"I don't want to play Nintendo. I want to stay with my mom."

"I'm sorry. No children in the treatment area."

Mitchell's voice shook. "No! I want to stay with my mom."

Ann moaned. Val rubbed a circle on the back of her hand, her insides churning.

Con dropped to his heels so that he was eye to eye with the boy. "Look, I'll stay with you. Val will go with your mom. As soon as she knows anything, or it's all right for you to go back, she can come get us. Okay?"

Mitchell searched Con's face, his own expression troubled. Apparently he trusted whatever he found there, because at last he nodded jerkily.

"Good man," Con said quietly.

The boy's thin shoulders straightened.

Val released her pent-up breath. Thank God for Con. His compassionate firmness was just what Mitchell needed. Not what he was used to, but what he needed. No wonder he watched the man with that hopeful, hungry expression. She wondered uneasily if she looked at Con the same way.

"Thank you," she said.

He shrugged. "No big deal. We'll be here when you're ready for us."

No big deal, Val repeated to herself. But as she followed Ann's wheelchair down the hall, she brooded over Con's quiet assumption of responsibility. He determined what needed to be done and did it. She was grateful and more than a little surprised. No other man she knew would have taken his cues from Ann. No other man would have shouldered the charge of a frightened boy for an indeterminate hospital wait. His calm cooperation bewildered her.

This time, his support hadn't felt like interference. And that was a very big deal for her.

On the animated screen, the monster roared and lunged for the jeep. Mitchell, his pale face set, pressed buttons with rapid-fire accuracy. Tiny sparks flew from the car and ignited. The jeep's attacker disappeared in a red-and-yellow fireball.

Mitchell grunted in satisfaction, and Con gave a silent sigh of relief. Maybe it wasn't politically correct, but he was all in favor of a little therapeutic destruction. Let the kid defeat his demons, even if it was only on TV.

He felt Val enter the room before he saw her, with a new sixth sense that operated only in her presence. She'd been by twice before, once to reassure Mitchell and once to tell them it would be at least another hour before Ann could be discharged.

Somewhere along the way, he saw, she'd wiped Ann's blood from her face, but drying streaks still stained her pretty tank top, brown against blue. She looked tired, and so beautiful she made his heart ache.

She perched beside him on the vinyl couch, backbone straight as a debutante's. "Hey," she said in a Southerner's greeting.

He wanted to pull her onto his lap and kiss the worry from her mouth and rub the tension from her shoulders. Except that she held herself so stiffly he was afraid the wrong touch might shatter her.

He nodded instead. "Hi."

She glanced at Mitchell. "How are we doing?"

He debated telling her about the tears and the five trips they'd made to the vending machines and then decided that some things were best kept between men.

"Okay, all things considered. We seem to be beating the bad guys."

Her smile was wan, and still it stopped his breathing. "That sounds nice."

"Yeah. Score one for our side. How about in there? Is she pressing charges?"

"No. At least she's agreed not to go back to him tonight. And she let them take pictures."

She sounded discouraged. He wondered if she ever let herself lean on anyone. He wondered what it would take to make her lean on him.

"That's good, right?"

"It's evidence," she agreed wearily. "They'll keep it in her record. But it doesn't do any good if she won't file charges."

"You want me to have a talk with the husband?"

Val looked at him as if he'd offered to beat the guy's head in. Which, come to think of it, wasn't a bad solution.

She primmed up her mouth. "No. It would only make things worse if she decides to go back. The nurse told me if Rob suspects Ann's seeking help, there's no telling what he might do."

In one short, graphic phrase, Con suggested what Rob could go do.

"Well, if you think that would help…" Val deadpanned.

Reluctantly, Con grinned. Even drooping with fatigue, she was no fragile Southern flower.

Another monster exploded on the screen. Mitchell watched the television with blank intensity, his thumbs jigging and pressing the controls as if the safety of the world rested on his reactions. Con's jaw tightened. Maybe, in his kid's mind, in his kid's world, it did.

He turned back to Val, still erect on the couch. "So, what's the deal? Are they going to a shelter?"

"No. She's not ready. She's staying with me."

Fear fisted in his gut. "Bad idea," he said instantly.

"Why? I have two bedrooms. It will be better for Mitchell—more like a sleepover."

"It's not safe."

She tilted her chin. "Safer for her than going home."

"And what about you? What if Cross comes after them?"

Her slim throat moved as she swallowed, but she replied resolutely. "I'll call the police. I can take care of them."

He would have admired her bravery if he weren't so worried about her. "You can't even take care of yourself. You forget to lock your damn doors."

She sighed in exasperation. "So, tonight I'll remember."

"I have a better idea," Con proposed.

She arched her brows.

"I'll sleep at your place tonight."

The offer surprised them both.

Con didn't intend to jeopardize his professional plans by thrusting himself into Val's personal life. Besides, after seventeen years of sharing bedrooms, first with Patrick and then with Sean, he guarded his space. But despite his reluctance to get involved, he didn't question his instincts. Staying at Val's apartment was the right thing to do.

He wasn't going to fail her.

Apparently, she didn't see things that way.

"You must be kidding," she said.

Chapter 8

Con raised dark eyebrows. "It's the logical solution."

Val frowned. It was one thing to accept his help parking the car. And maybe a bodyguard wasn't such a bad idea. But just whose body did Con imagine he'd be guarding tonight?

"I have a ten-year-old boy sleeping in my guest bedroom. Or had that little fact escaped your attention?"

His eyes narrowed. "It's because of Mitchell that I'm spending the night. Unless you'd like him to see what his father does to his mother after Cross breaks into your apartment?"

The calculated brutality of his response should have offended her. But he was right.

"All right. But you sleep on the couch."

"Of course."

His matter-of-fact acceptance shamed her. She had no business reacting like an outraged virgin while Ann and Mitchell's safety was on the line.

"Although," Con added smoothly, "I'll be disappointed if you don't at least offer me…a cup of coffee?"

Val bit back her smile and stared down her nose at him in her best Aunt Naomi fashion. "I don't drink coffee," she reminded him again. "And it's just for one night."

"Understood."

"Tomorrow, if I can talk her into it, Ann has an appointment with one of the advocates at the women's shelter."

His expression sharpened. "A lawyer?"

"More like a cheerleader, I think. But it's a start."

"Yeah. How's her face?"

Val glanced at Mitchell, engrossed in his game, and kept her voice low. "You were right. He broke her nose. They packed it and gave her a prescription for pain pills."

Con nodded. "That's about all they can do."

She tried not to stare. "Did you ever…?"

"Once. Regional tournament." He rubbed the slight bump on the bridge of his nose. "Sean's the pretty one now."

His quick grin scrambled her insides. She'd thought Rob Cross had cured whatever susceptibility she'd once had for high school athletes. It was disconcerting to discover her immunity didn't extend to ex-jock Con.

"You'll have to introduce me to your brother," she said lightly.

"No."

She thought he was joking. "Pardon me?"

He didn't smile. "I don't share."

She ignored the primitive feminine thrill created by his possessive tone. She wasn't anyone's possession.

"Nobody's asking you to share. Nobody's asking you to do anything." She pushed her hair back over her shoulders and stood. "Mitchell, honey?"

The boy cocked his head, his eyes still fixed on the TV.

"Let's go check on your mama, all right?"

* * *

Well, he'd blown that one, Con thought.

He stood in the middle of Val's living room, a pillow clutched to his chest, listening to the quiet murmur of women's voices in the other room. At least she hadn't thrown him out on his ear.

She'd told him she didn't want anyone telling her what to do, running her life or her business. He knew she had control issues with her old man. So what had possessed him to fall back on the primate routine at the hospital?

She worried him, Con admitted. Without a thought for her own safety or convenience, she'd opened her home and her heart to Ann and the boy. He could admire her loyalty and compassion. He even respected her decision. But the thought of Val mixed up in the middle of an ugly domestic dispute threw a punch at his cool appreciation of her finer qualities.

And that worried him, too. He didn't know what to make of his instinctive response to protect her no matter what she wanted. Val reached him on an elemental level that had once been closed to everyone but family. He'd certainly never felt the need to drag Lynn by her hair to the nearest safe cave.

Con tossed the pillow down on the couch. Hell, if he was going to react like a gorilla, he might as well make himself useful. He was here. He would keep her safe.

The bedroom door cracked open. Val appeared in the widening rectangle, her face in shadow and her curling hair haloed by the soft yellow lamplight.

Con's heart thumped in quick anticipation. He crossed his arms over his chest. "How's it going?"

"All right. We've almost got Mitchell settled." Her smile flickered. "I had to convince him he'd be okay in one of my T-shirts for the night."

It sounded like a good deal to Con. He wouldn't mind getting into Val's shirt, especially if she were still wearing it. Unfortunately, he figured she wasn't making him the offer. He tried for cool. "And?"

"I found an old Knicks shirt that wasn't too sissified."
She hesitated. "He wants to say good-night to you."

He was surprised and a little embarrassed. From years
ago, the memory surfaced of five-year-old Sean, his dark
hair sticking up from his bath, coming down the hall to the
big boys' room to say good-night. *I love you, Con.* And
himself, touchy with eleven-year-old consequence, not
knowing what to say in reply.

Patrick had known. Even at fourteen, Patrick had known
what to say. *I love you, buddy. Now get to bed, or I'll have
to sit on you.*

Con cleared his throat. "Yeah, sure. He coming out?"

She turned her head, speaking over her shoulder. "Mitchell?"

His skinny body edged past her in the doorway. He
dragged his feet over to the couch and stood an arm's length
away. Close enough to touch, if Con took the initiative; far
enough away to retain his dignity.

"Good night, Mr. MacNeill."

"'Night, kid."

"Will you be here in the morning?"

Beneath the casually voiced question, Con heard the
child's need for reassurance. He felt the grave, sweet weight
of Val's regard. He didn't want to be found lacking in either
one's eyes.

He reached out, pretending not to notice the boy's invol-
untary flinch, and messed up his short, neat hair.

"You bet. Now get to bed, or I'll have to sit on you."

A gleam lit Mitchell's too thin, too solemn face. "Okay.
Good night, Aunt Val."

"Good night, honey. Give your mama a kiss for me."

She waited until the bedroom door had closed behind him
before she turned to Con, a rueful smile on her face. "I wish
I knew how you *do* that."

He lifted one shoulder, uncomfortable with her praise.
"It's a—"

"—guy thing. I know. It was very nice." She didn't fidget—she was too well brought up to fidget—but her gaze slid from his. She toyed with her earring, a sparkle of silver in the dim light. "I don't think I've thanked you for all your help today."

"Yeah, you did. At the hospital."

"Oh. Can I…can I get you something to drink?"

It was just one more example of her thoroughbred manners. He knew better than to ask her again for coffee. He knew better than to imagine she was offering anything more. What he needed was a cold drink. A cold shower would be even better.

"Water would be good."

Nodding, she slipped by him on her way through the narrow living room to the big kitchen. The air moved with her. As she passed, he could almost smell the afternoon sunlight on her hair, almost feel a subtle rise in the room's temperature. Her unconscious sensuality made him sweat.

Easy, genius. You're imagining things.

The refrigerator light blinked on and off. Val returned carrying a tall blue tumbler. Ice tinkled as she set it on the low table in front of him.

"Thanks," he said hoarsely.

"You're welcome."

To his surprise, she sat on one end of the couch designated as his bed and, leaning back her head, put her feet up on the table. In the center, a metal dragonfly hung suspended over a green glass bowl. It shivered at the soft impact of her feet.

"Comfortable?" Con asked dryly.

She closed her eyes. "Tired."

His voice roughened. "You should go to bed."

Her head moved slowly against the cushions, back and forth. No. "I'm too excited to sleep."

He was perilously close to too excited himself. Damn, but she was pretty. Under her turquoise tank top, her breasts rose and fell. Her lashes fanned against her cheeks. The necessity of keeping their voices down and the lights low wrapped them in intimacy.

If she didn't hustle back into her own bedroom where she belonged, he was going to sink down on that soft couch and dive into her like a swimmer into water. Con rocked on his heels, stuffing his hands into his pockets. Right now, he was trying real hard to remember he had scruples about things like that. He wasn't proud of the idea that he would take advantage of his role as Val's protector to jump her bones.

To shock himself back to sanity, to scare her back to her room, he said deliberately, "I could help you to sleep."

She chuckled. "You can cut the Big Bad Wolf routine, MacNeill. It won't work."

He was irritated. Curious. "Why not?"

"Because you're being nice tonight," she explained, still without opening her eyes. "I don't buy it."

Nice. Hell.

He tried to remember the last time a woman had accused him of being nice. Nothing came to mind. Patrick was decent. Sean was charming. Con had been called smooth and, occasionally, generous. Never nice.

"Well, that puts me in my place," he said acerbically.

She chuckled again, almost asleep. Her hair streamed over the overstuffed pillows and rolled arm of the couch. She was spread out like a banquet for his starved senses. He wanted to thread his fingers through that heavy fall of hair, to nuzzle the hollow just below her ear, to glut himself on the scent and the taste and the texture of her.

She sighed, and his breathing jammed, doing funny things to the rhythm of his heart.

If he had half the brains his brothers credited him with, he'd get the hell out of Dodge.

Instead, he eased down beside her, stretching one arm along the back of the couch. The soft cushions gave beneath him. She shifted as the springs adjusted to their relative weights. Her head rolled against his shoulder. She kept it there.

Hunger leaped inside him.

She rubbed her cheek against his shirt. "This is nice."

Con groaned silently. That word again. He ordered his libido back into its cage and slammed the door shut. And it was…well, not satisfying, precisely, but pleasant, he discovered, to sit in the half light with Val's head resting on his shoulder and her hair tickling his jaw.

Even…*nice.*

He brought her carefully closer. She felt small and soft and desirable in his arms. But quick and determined in Ann's defense. Sergeant Major John MacNeill would have approved, he thought.

"You were a good friend to Ann today," he said quietly.

Her muscles tensed under his palm. "If I were a good friend, she wouldn't be in this mess."

He understood her frustration. He wished he could do more himself. But Bridget MacNeill had brought home enough tales from the hospital to convince Con that Val had done everything she could.

"You can't force someone to seek help before she's ready," he offered, borrowing from his mother's store of wisdom.

"I know that," Val said. "But I should have prevented Ann needing help in the first place."

She took too much on herself. He honored her sense of responsibility, but he couldn't let it pass unchallenged. "So, what could you do? It's not your fault the jerk beats his wife."

"No. But it's my fault she married him. I should have told her. I should have warned her."

"You can't blame yourself. You couldn't know."

"I knew."

The words were muffled against his chest. They struck at his heart.

"How?"

Val raised her head. "I used to go with Rob in high school."

He didn't want to hear what she was saying. Didn't want to accept it. "Define 'go with,'" he suggested evenly.

Her chin lifted. "Dated. Went steady. Slept with." She enunciated clearly, leaving him no choice but to hear and understand.

"When?" He bit the word out, fighting the cold realization that trickled down his spine.

She sat back against the cushioned arm, facing him. "He asked me out my freshman year. He was the senior class president, the star of the football team. I was flattered. My parents knew his parents. Everyone thought we were the perfect couple." She shrugged. "For a while, maybe, it was even true."

The thought of Val, young and vulnerable, joined to a man who punched his wife's face, who broke his wife's nose, raked at Con's gut. It was in the past, he reminded himself. It shouldn't matter. But it did. It mattered so much it terrified him.

He sought refuge in facts, as if the dispassionate examination of her history could somehow make him care less. Define the problem.

"Did you love him?"

"I thought I did, at first." Her eyes met his without apology. "Everybody told me I did. What did I know? I was fifteen. And Rob could be—can be—very charming."

The son of a bitch. Con's jaw ached. He realized he was grinding his teeth. "Did he hit you? Hurt you?"

Against the kitchen light, her shoulders squared. "This was a million years ago. What difference does it make?"

"Did he?"

"Why would he? I was such a *nice* girl back then. No trouble to anyone." Her voice was mocking. "Besides, he wanted a job with my father."

Rationally, Con knew better than to fault Val for her fifteen-year-old judgment. A nice girl from a good family... Why wouldn't she do the accepted, the expected thing and date the high school hero? But resentment churned his gut.

Val clenched her hands in her lap. "By my senior year, I'd grown up enough to want out. I was tired of being Rob Cross's girl, and I surely wasn't ready to be his Junior League wife. But to everyone else, we were a couple. *The* couple. All our friends... My mother had practically booked the club for the reception. I felt like I couldn't breathe."

Even with his emotions rioting like the exchange floor at closing, Con could still put two and two together. "And that's when you went to your aunt Naomi."

She hesitated. "Around then. Yes. And Rob married Ann. I felt terrible. I should have kept in touch with her. I knew how persuasive he could be. I knew how lonely she was."

Con inhaled sharply, as if oxygen could clear his brain. Maybe, in some fuddled way, he wanted to blame Val for giving herself to a bastard like Cross. That didn't mean she should accept the blame for her friend's lousy marriage.

"That doesn't make what happened your fault."

"Maybe. But sometimes I wonder if he didn't marry her because..."

"Because...?"

She shook her head. The silver hoops swung back and forth. "It sounds crazy."

"Dixie, he is crazy. Any man who uses his fists on a woman is out of his mind."

Her gaze met his with that directness he admired. "I sometimes wonder if he married her partly to get back at me. Rob doesn't like to give things up. I was gone, but Ann was still here. And she was my best friend."

For a vegetarian given to feathered earrings, she sure took her ties seriously. Tenderness assailed him.

"Look, did Ann deserve for her husband to hit her?"

Val straightened indignantly. "Of course not!"

"Okay. Now, I took the guy on at the bank on Friday. He's probably been stewing all weekend. Is it my fault he hits his wife?"

"Well…no."

He pressed. "Then, if it isn't Ann's fault or my fault, how is it yours?"

Her wide gray eyes considered him a moment. "Are you always this logical?"

"Always," he said firmly. Until he met her.

"It makes it pretty difficult to argue with you," she complained.

But there was a lift in her voice and a curve to her lips that hadn't been there a minute ago. Con felt a profound, unfamiliar satisfaction.

"So, don't argue," he suggested.

She put her head to one side. "What else did you have in mind?"

At her teasing tone, his blood ignited. The woman was a witch. His mind flamed with a thousand images of things he'd like to do with her, to her, on her.

He extended his hand from the back of the couch. "Come here."

Con MacNeill's deep invitation made Val tremble. She regarded the space he'd made for her with longing, the haven bounded by his sleekly muscled arm, his powerful chest, the strong column of his throat. He would be warm and solid and real against her. She swayed closer, mesmerized with wanting him, with the sure knowledge that he wanted her, too.

But wanting wasn't enough anymore.

Maybe it had never been enough. The confidences whispered in the semidarkness had dissolved her concept of casual intimacy. The things she'd confessed and the things she hadn't yet told him formed both a bond and a barrier between them. In the car that afternoon, Val had contented herself with the notion that Con would never want more from her than she was prepared to give. Now she didn't know if she could be content with giving him less than everything.

The prospect made her weak with yearning and sick with anxiety.

She glanced over his arm to the closed bedroom door, seeking an excuse for her uncharacteristic wavering. "I don't know. Ann…"

"Sh. It's okay. Just come here."

She hesitated, torn. She wanted his closeness, his warmth and his strength. She didn't want to send him the wrong signals, or start something she wasn't prepared to finish.

He waited, his expression enigmatic in the darkness. Obeying instinct, she went into his arms.

He wrapped her close. She sighed with relief, burrowing closer. His skin was hot. She shivered in response. Her hands slid over him, seeking, finding, claiming hard muscle under the soft cotton of his T-shirt.

Con drew in his breath, making his chest rise under her head, and then his large hands trapped hers. He raised her fingers to his mouth. He kissed them and folded them and returned them to her lap.

"Easy, Dixie. Don't rush."

Confused, hurt, she pulled back. "More instruction from the expert?"

He didn't release her. "No. I just don't want to do anything you're not ready for."

"And who decides when I'm ready?"

"You do," he said quietly, and deflated her defensive pride.

She sighed and subsided against his chest. "Well, shoot. I think I'd like you better if you didn't know what you were talking about."

His amusement rumbled under her ear. "No, you wouldn't. You'd just find me easier to boss around."

She gave an unladylike snicker.

His jaw rubbed the top of her head. His scent, soap and sweat and cotton, enveloped her. She nuzzled his shirt.

Con cleared his throat. "You've got a pretty name," he said hoarsely. "You know where it's from?"

She pulled her scattered thoughts together. "Valerian? It's a kind of flower. Heliotrope, I think. Mother's choice."

"You don't like it," he guessed.

"Better than 'punkin,'" she offered wryly. "I guess it sounds like the kind of daughter they wanted. You know, all pink and white and fragile?"

His hand stroked her arm. "Valerian was also an emperor. A Roman general, I think."

The image pleased her. "You made that up."

"Nope. I take weird first names very seriously."

She drifted, lapped by the sound of his voice and the warmth of his body, anchored in his arms. "Connor's not so bad."

"My name's not Connor."

She nestled closer. "Conan, then."

"Sweetheart, you don't get it. The folks are Irish. Really Irish. Heck, they named their first-born Padraig."

"Patrick?"

"Close enough. And no one calls him Paddy anymore, unless they want their faces beaten in."

She smiled against his shirt. "Sean sounds pretty normal."

"Yeah. At least he got named after an uncle and not one of the flipping kingdoms of ancient Ireland."

She raised her head, prepared to offer comfort. And saw the flat-cheeked control he exercised to hide his laughter and the devil dancing in his eyes.

The fake, she thought, amused. He was proud of his family. He probably loved his name. She envied him the close family identity he regarded with such humor, that gave him such strength.

"A kingdom?" she drawled. "Really? What did they name you, Camelot?"

He laughed and gathered her back against him. Pleased, she relaxed against his chest, drawing comfort from his nearness and the steady thud of his heart under her ear.

"Connaught," he told her. "My name's Connaught."

"Connet." She tasted the syllables in her mouth, as beautiful and uncompromising as she imagined the stones of Ireland itself. She was a product of North Carolina clay. How could anything grow between them?

And yet, for a tiny space of time, drowsing in Con's arms, Val imagined a whole new world opening before her.

Pounding woke her. She struggled to sit, to drag open her eyes, to find her balance and her shoes in the dark. Something warm and solid heaved under her.

"Ann! I know you're in there. Open the door."

Rob.

Chapter 9

Her tongue was fuzzy. So was her head. Val floundered getting off the couch, and her foot swung out over the coffee table and struck something. She heard the crack of glass as whatever it was rattled to the floor.

Rob battered on the door. "Val? Are you home? Open up."

Lunging, she stepped in a spreading puddle of ice water and yelped.

"Easy."

Con's voice, warm in her ear. Con's arm, hard around her shoulder. Grateful for his support, she leaned on him a moment only, to orient herself.

He steadied her and then, in one smooth move, put her behind him on his way to the door.

Shoot, Val thought. She snapped on the lamp beside the couch and hurried after him in squishy cold socks. This was her home. Ann was her friend. She didn't need Con's intervention, however well-intentioned.

Rob's voice deepened, coaxed. "Come on, Val. I need to talk to my wife."

Ann appeared in the bedroom doorway, her hair sticking up, her face swollen and ugly with bits of packing still under her nose. She'd snatched up Val's robe, an incongruous flow of emerald silk, to cover her borrowed T-shirt.

She reached behind her with one hand to pull the door shut, as if she could physically shield Mitchell from what was about to happen. "I'll get it."

Val stopped. "No. Annie, you don't have to see him."

"Ann? Baby? I can hear you in there."

Con moved smoothly to the door. "We hear you, too. Keep it down."

"Don't open the door," Val ordered.

Con glanced at her, brows drawn level over blazing blue eyes. "You want me to call the police?" he asked quietly.

"No," Ann protested. "No police. You promised."

I won't make you do anything you're not ready for.

Strangled by her own assurances, Val looked to Con. "Rob played football with the police chief's son," she explained. "There's a chance Chief Palmer won't take Ann seriously."

"That's bull. He'll take a broken nose seriously."

The door rattled. "Ann? You don't want to blow things out of proportion here. If you know what's good for you, you'll let me in."

Ann twisted her fingers together. "He means what he says. He won't go away."

"I'll send him away," Con said.

Val could feel the situation spinning from her control. She didn't want a brawl in her apartment. But Ann was right. Rob wasn't just going to leave.

She sucked in her breath. "I'll talk to him."

"The hell you will," growled Con.

She stiffened at his tone. "This is still my apartment,"

she announced in Aunt Naomi's sternest manner. "I won't have fighting in it. I will get the door."

Con narrowed his eyes. But he stepped back, out of her way.

Heart hammering, Val made sure the chain was still secure and slowly slipped the lock.

The door snapped inward and jammed against the chain. Val jumped back. Rob's large, flat hand pressed against the outside edge. His knuckles were red. His face squeezed close to the opening in the door.

"Val, what the hell is this? Open the door. Where's Ann? Is she all right?"

Keep calm, Val ordered herself. Keep control. "She's safe, Rob. Now go home."

"You're kidding, right? I'm not going anywhere without my wife. Let me in, damn it. I've been going out of my mind."

Con advanced, a bulwark behind her, his low, cool voice cutting through the other man's bluster. "You've got a funny way of showing concern, Cross."

"MacNeill." Confusion spiked Rob's voice. And then he rallied, seeking allies, speaking man-to-man. "What's going on?"

"Maybe you should tell me."

Rob sighed theatrically. "Hell, I don't know. I woke up from a nap, and my wife and son are missing. I checked my mother's. I checked her parents'. I even checked the goddamn hospital. I thought she might be with Val."

"Yeah, well, now you don't have to worry. Like Val says, she's okay."

Rob pushed against the door, held at bay by six inches of tarnished chain. "Let me talk to her."

Val felt a shiver run up the backs of her arms. "No."

He swiveled his head against the opening, trying to see in. His face was flushed with alcohol or anger. His trim blond sideburns were dark with sweat. "Ann," he called softly. "Let me in."

Ann took a step toward the door.

"No," Val said.

Rob ignored her. "Ann, can you hear me? I know things got a little out of hand earlier. I'm sorry. Let me in, baby. Just to talk, I swear."

Val wanted to throw up. Baby, he called her. As if he loved her. As if endearments and excuses could wipe away bruises and a broken nose.

Sickly, she realized that they might. Because Ann was wavering in the doorway, knuckles pressed to her swollen mouth to keep herself from answering her husband.

"Have you got our son in there? You don't want to do this to him, Ann. You don't want to get him all confused. What's he going to think of his father if you take him away like this? Let me see him. Let me talk to him. Mitchell!"

Ann jerked as if he'd slapped her. "Let him in," she whispered.

Familiar, helpless anger at Rob's manipulation coiled in Val's gut. "Annie…"

Ann looked at her, her face and her tone flat. "I have to. He'll wake Mitchell."

Rob dragged his "just folks" smile from somewhere and pasted it on. "Come on, Val. It's all right. I'm not going to do anything. Let me in just for a minute. Just to talk to her."

She didn't believe him. But what could she do?

"Don't do it," Con said.

His warning rankled. She knew her anger was misplaced, and yet she resented being dictated to in her own home.

She glanced at Ann, hugging her elbows behind them. A tiny crust of blood had formed under one nostril beneath the packing. Her bruises were slowly turning the color of eggplant.

"Please, Val. Just for a minute, and then he'll go home."

Val tugged hard on her earring, as if the tiny pain could

help her think. She had to consider Ann's safety. But she didn't want to take away Ann's power of decision. She'd had too many of her own choices thwarted or ignored to do that.

"Just to talk," she warned through the crack in the door.

She had to close the door part way to take off the chain. For a moment she was tempted to slam it and bolt it and lock all her troubles outside. But Rob would come back, of course.

He always came back.

She took off the chain and opened the door.

He didn't muscle in, as she'd feared and half expected. He took two quick steps past her, his blond hair tousled and his starched shirt limp, the picture of a distraught husband.

His voice was soft, a masterpiece of reproach. "Ann, you made me very worried. I didn't know where you and the boy had gone. You couldn't even write me a note?"

Ann's gaze fell. "I'm sorry, Rob, I—"

"Maybe she didn't want to drip blood on the paper," Val drawled.

Rob's mask slipped a moment as he glared at her. Good. He'd always hated it when she'd talked back.

And then he took another step toward his wife. "You should have let me drive you to the hospital, baby."

Slowly, he reached out his hand. Val sensed more than saw Con tense beside her. Ann flinched and then went still under Rob's soft, exploring touch. His fingers trailed along her jaw.

"You look pretty bad."

Ann pressed broken lips together. "I'm—I'm all right."

Another lie. Val pushed her hair back over her shoulder. "Except for bruises, black eyes and a busted nose, she's fine."

"Your nose is broken?" His concern sounded almost genuine. "Aw, baby, that's too bad. Let me take you home."

"I don't think that's a good idea," Con said evenly.

''Butt out,'' Rob said. His hand drifted down Ann's arm to curl around her wrist. ''Come on, Mrs. Cross.''

Ann slumped. ''No, Rob, I—''

Rob's grip tightened. Even from several feet away, Val could see the muscles in his arms flex and tense. ''You're coming home now. You belong at home.'' He turned to Val, his voice still smooth, his eyes bright with triumph. ''Get my son. We're leaving. Ann needs to rest at home.''

Dread uncurled in Val's stomach and forced its way up her throat. The situation was spiraling beyond her control. Once Rob got Ann home, who knew what he might do?

''Rob, it's late.'' She had no idea what time it was, but *late* seemed safe. ''We're all tired. Ann's not dressed, and Mitchell's asleep.''

Val didn't believe for a second that Mitchell had slept through Rob's arrival, but she was miserably certain the child had practice ignoring things that went bump in the night. Inside her wet socks, her feet were clammy cold.

''Why don't we call it a night?'' she suggested, blinking away the sight of his knuckles bunching on Ann's thin arm. ''In the morning you can come back, and we'll talk this—''

A stifled sound of pain escaped Ann, and Con moved. Close enough that Val felt the rush of his passing, fast enough that she barely saw him grab Rob's other arm and twist it up and out behind his back. Rob grunted. Ann screamed and then covered her mouth with her free hand.

''I have a better idea,'' Con said. ''Let's take this out into the hall.''

Rob swore. Con jerked on his arm, putting pressure on his elbow and shoulder, forcing him to release Ann's wrist. His feet scuffled on the bare wood floor as he launched a punch behind him. Con slid to one side, jerking upward. Rob groaned and doubled over. They were both big men, former athletes, evenly matched. Rob was heavier, but Con's grip was implacable. His face was set in stone.

''Outside,'' he repeated.

"What in hell do you think you're doing? She's my wife, you jackass."

"That's right. Your wife. Not your punching bag. Out."

Val watched, shocked, as Con grappled Rob over to the door and kicked it open. Of course she wanted Ann to be safe. She wanted Rob to leave. But she would have preferred to persuade him to go. Con's violence dizzied and dismayed her. She had no control over it. She had no control over *him*.

In the doorway, Rob lunged and lashed out with his feet. "Let me go, damn you. I'll have you up on assault."

"And Ms. Cutler could have you arrested for trespassing."

"No, she couldn't. She wouldn't. You don't know who I am."

"You're a sorry son of a bitch," Con rasped, and bumped into the hall.

Val ran to close the door behind them. Should she call the police? She had bitter experiences of Rob's ability to sway the town's opinion. Would Chief Palmer allow the arrest of Cutler's one-time champion quarterback?

Behind her, Ann sobbed quietly, gulping because of the packing in her nose. The two men scraped and thudded on the landing.

"You're crazy," Rob gasped. "I'll see you fired. Old man Cutler listens to me. I'll ruin you."

Something hit the wall so hard a picture jumped inside the apartment. Val flinched.

"Tell Cutler what you want. And while you're at it, explain what you were doing at his daughter's apartment."

"Collecting my wife. A man has a right to his wife."

"Not if he beats her," Con said, and threw him down the stairs. Val heard the heavy thumping and the crash.

"Oh, Lord. Oh, dear Lord," Ann moaned.

A painful silence penetrated from the hall.

"I'll be back," Rob called thickly. "This is my town, and

that's my wife, and the law around here doesn't look kindly on keeping a man from his wife.''

''Just keep away from here,'' Con said coldly. ''Or the law will be the least of your worries.''

The downstairs door slammed. Val drew a deep breath and swung open the apartment door, prepared to offer bandages, aspirin and a piece of her mind.

Con's head jerked around. She stopped in her tracks. His face was taut. His eyes were hard. The dim light overhead revealed a sheen on his forehead and high, carved cheekbones. He radiated heat. Energy. Tension.

Her heart rate bumped up. Adrenaline, she told herself firmly. There was simply no way she was getting weak-kneed and short of breath because of some uncivilized female response to the all-conquering male. She hated violence.

She inhaled sharply and shook back her hair. ''Finished?''

Con grinned, making his warrior mask even more attractive. ''For now. Were you waiting to thank me?''

''Not particularly. You didn't even give me a chance to talk him into leaving.''

He raised his eyebrows. She wished she didn't find his unconscious arrogance so appealing. ''You're assuming you could have. My way, we didn't need to wait to find out.''

''Your way, Rob is angry and vindictive.''

''Aw, hell, Dixie, that guy was born angry. And beating me in a fight wasn't going to make him less vindictive. What did you want me to do, lose?''

No, of course not. If she were honest, she wanted Rob hurt. She wanted him punished, both for hurting Ann and for…other reasons. Reasons she had long ago schooled herself to forget. Her stomach contracted.

She lifted her chin. ''Not lose, no. But was it really necessary to throw him down the stairs?''

Con shrugged. ''If it's worth fighting, it's worth fighting dirty.''

She didn't understand him. Where was the cool, dispassionate businessman now?

"More MacNeill Road Rules?" she asked.

"Not really. Patrick fought because it was his duty. Sean will fight for fun. I fight to win."

She understood that. Edward Cutler liked to win. So did Rob. Under the circumstances, Val supposed, she should be glad tonight's champion had been in her corner. She shivered, both attracted and repelled by his victory.

"And what if Mitchell got up? Don't you think he's seen enough violence in his short life?"

Con narrowed his eyes. "As a matter of fact, I do."

His words lay like a challenge between them. Con had taken action to prevent Rob from hurting Ann, from dragging Mitchell from his bed. Val flushed. The uneven light of the overhead bulb picked out the grim set of Con's mouth, the swelling rising along one cheekbone. Somewhere along the way, he'd taken a punch that could have been directed at her or Ann or Mitchell. Her annoyance thawed, an unfamiliar warmth spreading to take its place.

"Well, you were certainly…effective. At least in the short term." She reached tentative fingers to the angry reddening under his eye. "Let me get you some ice."

"I don't need—"

Her touch drifted to his mouth, stopping his protest. She smiled wryly. "It's got to be ice. We're all out of frozen vegetables."

The blaze in his eyes banked to a slow burn. Capturing her hand, he pressed warm lips to the center of her palm. Her heart pounded. The man was dangerous, all right. Dark and dangerous and desirable.

"I can think of something else that would make me feel better," he said huskily.

Heat collected inside her. She felt like a teakettle threatening to explode. She didn't want this attraction to a confident, combative Yankee. She didn't trust it. She didn't trust

herself. She blew out a quick breath, as if she could somehow let off steam, and tossed her head.

"In your dreams, MacNeill."

She retreated to the apartment, leaving the door standing
open.

Con stayed where he was, on the landing. He figured Ann
Cross could use some time to recover from the latest ruckus
in her life without him looming over her. He needed time
to come down from the fight himself. He flexed his hands
and heard his knuckles crack. They hurt.

That was okay. As long as Cross hurt worse.

He listened to Val as she urged her friend back to bed,
snagged by the contrast between that soothing silver voice
and her iron backbone.

The woman was a messy bundle of contradictions, a rebel
with too many causes. Con steered clear of messes. And yet,
he admitted, something drew him. He didn't know if it was
her sudden blush or sexy drawl, her determined independence or fierce loyalty, her open ways or guarded heart.
Maybe it was the whole unlikely package.

She hadn't conformed to the neat little box her parents
had wrapped her in. She fit even worse into Con's blue-
collar background. Val Cutler, with her wild hair and mismatched earrings, calmly eating Sunday dinner in his parents' white frame house? He shook his head. It would never
work. They were meat and potatoes, and she was sprouts
and tofu.

He heard the click of the bedroom door and the soft pad
of Val's footsteps as she crossed the apartment to her
kitchen. Thoughtfully, he rubbed his face, assessing the
damage to his jaw.

Boston might appeal to her. After all, she'd lived in New
York. But even if he could coax her to the city, to his de-
signer-perfect condo, Val had no place in his plans for his
future. Her roots were here. Her restaurant was here.

Con grimaced, pulling a cut inside his mouth where a

lucky punch had slammed his teeth into his cheek. The fight with Cross had obviously addled his brain. What made him think that after bucking her wealthy family Val would embrace the restrictions and pretensions of Boston's moneyed circle? She wouldn't, of course. He wouldn't want her to.

So, if they had no common past and no shared future, what could he do but convince Val to make the most of the present?

He pushed away the fleeting wrongness of the thought. Val herself had made it plain she wasn't looking for a permanent relationship. That didn't mean she was uninterested in exploring other options. She'd kissed him, hadn't she? Invited him up to her apartment? She was free and over twenty-one. Available.

She called him from the kitchen, impatience edging her smooth drawl. "I'd like to patch you up before I go to bed. Or were you planning on staying out there until the ice melts?"

He grinned at the fantasy he'd concocted from inflated ego and overactive hormones. Valerian Darcy Cutler available? Sure. *In your dreams MacNeill.*

At eight o'clock on Monday morning, Ann's face was a Technicolor map of Rob's brutality. The harsh bathroom light and cold white tile leached her complexion of natural color and highlighted her bruises.

Val rinsed out the washcloth and silently handed it back.

Ann tried to smile. "I can wash my own face, you know."

"I know. But it makes me feel better to do *something.*"

Ann dabbed carefully under her nose with the warm washcloth, avoiding her own eyes in the mirror. "I have to leave."

Disquiet stirred inside Val at her flat voice. "Leave Rob?"

Ann set down the washcloth. "Leave here. He knows where I am now. He'll come back."

"If he does, I will call the police. He can't touch you here, Annie."

"You don't know that. You don't know what he's like."

But Val did. Nine years buried, the memories squirmed, feeding in the dark on fatigue and fear and the smell of blood. She shifted on the cold, closed toilet seat. She remembered.

"It doesn't matter," she said firmly. "You're still safer here than you are with him."

"And what about you? I've done enough to you already. I can't put you in more danger."

"Don't be silly. I'm a big girl. I can take care of myself, and I can handle Rob." She hoped.

Her teeth worried the inside of her lip. She didn't want to offer her next argument. She didn't want to suggest that she was dependent on Con MacNeill for safety or protection or anything. But she couldn't place her pride before Ann's need.

"Besides," she said, "Con's here."

"Mmm. But he won't stay." A ghost of a smile flitted across Ann's swollen face. "I mean, what would your mother say?"

"I'm a little old to worry about what my mother says. Ann, you have to leave him."

Ann's smile faded. "I can't. He'll take Mitchell."

"No, he won't."

"He will. You don't know. I've done things…"

"Nothing to deserve being beaten. Annie…" Val flung out her hands in frustration. "Can't you see what he's doing to you? Can't you see what he is?"

"I know what he is." Ann's thin hands clenched the rolled edge of the white pedestal sink. "I know he hits me. I know he cheats on me."

The last was news to Val. Her jaw sagged. "He cheats on you?"

Ann nodded. "With Donna at the bank. Your mother told

me. But I knew who he was when I married him. The Great Rob Cross, who could have any woman he wanted. And he wanted me, Annie Barclay. I thought I must be someone special, for Rob to want me. I thought...well, it doesn't matter anymore what I thought. But he's been a good provider. And I made promises, Val, to him and to myself, that I can't break.''

''What about Mitchell?''

''Rob's never hit Mitchell.''

''Maybe not. But what is he teaching him? What kind of example is he setting?''

''I know. Oh, God, I know. But what can I do?''

''You can get a restraining order. You can press charges. You have to stop him.''

Wearily, Ann said, ''No one can stop Rob.''

Memory writhed again. Val set her jaw. ''Then you need to get away from him.''

''To New York?'' Ann asked softly.

Their eyes met in the mirror. There were things Val had never told anyone, not even her best friend. She wondered what Ann knew and how much she had guessed.

''If that's what it takes,'' Val said. ''You do what you have to do.'' She laid her hand over Ann's on the edge of the sink. ''But maybe you don't need to go that far. You're a grown woman with friends and a child. You could get legal help. You could keep your appointment this morning with the court advocate—''

''At that shelter?''

Ann couldn't keep the dismay from her voice. Val knew the joy with which Ann had left her parents' loveless, profitless farm, the hope she'd invested in the four-bedrooms-three-baths on Stonewall Drive. Domesticated Ann had taken such pride in her spotless kitchen with its matching canisters, her custom-made drapes and coordinating wallpapers. More than leaving her husband, leaving her house would be the desertion of her vows, the abandonment of her dreams.

"Ann," she repeated softly, urgently. "You do what you have to do."

Ann's throat moved as she swallowed. "What time?"

Relief made Val almost giddy. "Nine-thirty. I'll drive."

Chapter 10

Val blew into the office like a miniature force of nature, wearing a loose blue dress that should have looked like a sack and instead flowed over her curves like water. Her hair curled wildly in the suffocating Southern humidity.

Her oversize canvas bag hit the floor with a thump. "I need you to find me enough money to offer Ann a job."

Con looked up slowly from his laptop, fighting the swift, helpless rise of lust. It was eleven o'clock on a Monday. The restaurant was closed, the bank was open, and he was frustrated by his failure to find a paper trail. He didn't need Val Cutler trashing his concentration.

"Good morning to you, too," he said.

She smiled then, making his insides knot, and ran slim fingers through her hair. "Good morning."

Her eyes were gray as rain and smudged with fatigue. She looked tired, he thought, and felt a quick squeeze of concern.

"How'd things go at the women's shelter?" he asked.

She shrugged. Under the fluid front of her dress, her breasts moved. He was pretty sure she wasn't wearing a bra.

His jaw set with annoyance. He felt like a pervert, drooling over her while they discussed her friend's predicament.

"All right, I think. Ann's agreed to counseling. If she and Mitchell decide to stay at the shelter, I'll take her back to the house this afternoon to pack a bag."

The risks she was willing to assume scared him. His own protective reaction scared him even more. "We'll take her," he corrected her evenly.

She rolled her eyes. "You can come along if you insist."

Meaning, she didn't want him. She didn't *need* him. Hell, he knew that. "I insist."

"Okay." She came forward into the office, her full skirt flirting with her calves. "Ann said she'd call me when she decided what to do. In the meantime, can you find me the money?"

"How much do you need?"

"Enough to hire Ann full-time. Enough for her and Mitchell to live on."

Con raised his brows and picked up a pencil. "What can she do? What skills does she have?"

Val perched on the corner of the desk, propping one foot on the arm of his chair. Her ankles were slim and tanned and sexy. He was in sorry shape when even looking at an ankle turned him on.

"Well, she can operate the cash register. She greets and seats customers for me sometimes. Types menus. Runs errands. I was thinking something at the front end of the house?"

"You do all that stuff already," he felt compelled to point out. "You can't afford to pay someone else to do it."

"That's why I came to you."

So she needed him, after all. Too bad it was only his business skills she wanted.

Feel free to take advantage of any services you want.

Never mind that. Define the problem, he told himself.

"Well, if you're hiring new staff, you either need to increase your income or decrease your expenses. This could be a good time to open the restaurant for dinner. Maybe just on weekends for a start,'' he added in response to her quick frown. ''You could still handle lunch, and evenings Ann could take over.''

''I'd have to do dinner,'' Val objected. ''Ann needs to be home for Mitchell at night.''

''Whatever. However you want to do it.''

She regarded him for a long moment, her eyes amused and aware. ''I'm not sure I want to do it at all. But you knew that.'' She blew out her breath. ''All right. What else?''

''As for reducing expenses,'' he said carefully, ''I've put together a list of cost-cutting measures that—''

''I'm not sacrificing quality,'' she interrupted.

His lick of temper surprised him. It was perfectly rational of her to question his recommendations. But he found himself wanting her trust. ''I'm not suggesting you should. Why don't you at least review the damn list before you reject my ideas?''

''Well, excuse me.'' But she took the list. Scanned it. ''I think you're right about standardizing portion sizes,'' she said at last, looking up. ''I'll talk to Steven. But these two menu substitutions won't work.''

''Look, I'm no cook, but I checked with several area restaurants. The most popular lunch items for your target market are—''

''Fried chicken salad and french fries. So what?''

''So, you should offer the same as your competitors. I know marketing.''

''And I know my clientele. I offer a Greek salad and a roasted potato medley.''

''That's not the same.''

''That's the whole point. My customers can go to any one of half a dozen places for the same-old same-old. When they come here, they want something different.''

''Will you at least try it?''

''Maybe.'' She grinned. ''If I can send the complaints to you.''

''There won't be any complaints.''

''Then you don't have anything to worry about, do you?''

She was quick. It was one more thing to like about her, however difficult it made his job. ''Sure of yourself, aren't you?''

''Aren't you? Mr. Business Solutions.''

He wouldn't apologize. ''It's what I get paid for.''

''It's not just your job. You like being in charge. Look at the way you jumped on Rob last night.''

Her quick change of subject drove him on the defensive. ''I was protecting you.''

''Thank you. But I don't like feeling that I need protection. As long as Rob was talking, I had the chance to change his mind. Once the confrontation got physical, I lost all control over the situation.''

''Not quite,'' he said dryly. ''You did have me.''

''But I didn't. I can't control you. I have no control over your actions.''

''Look, Dixie, you don't need to control my actions. You just need to believe that I can.'' It all boiled down to trust, he figured. She still didn't trust him. ''So what if I can beat on Rob Cross and you can't? You think that makes us less than equal?''

She put up her chin. ''More to the point, is that what you think?''

''This isn't an arm-wrestling contest. I think you can hold your own.''

''My father wouldn't agree with you.''

Damn. Was that what this was about? Growing up under her father's rule, was it herself—her strength, her spirit, her own resolve—that Val didn't trust?

''Yeah, well, I had different examples growing up. They

don't come any tougher than my dad, but my mom matched him and kept us all in line."

"That's because your father was overseas all the time."

Con grinned suddenly. "You wouldn't say that if you'd met my mother."

Her answering smile was wistful. "I'd like to."

"Tell you what, why don't you come to my brother's for dinner sometime?"

The invitation surprised them both. He saw her eyes widen. He wasn't sure he wanted her that close himself. He had plans, and she wasn't part of them. Not to mention that the last time he'd brought a girl to "meet the family" could hardly be called a resounding success.

"I don't know…"

Oddly enough, her uncertainty convinced Con it wasn't such a bad idea. At least she wouldn't look down her nose at Patrick's family, or worse, try too hard to please and impress.

"Maybe Wednesday, before I go. Or we could do it when I get back," he said.

Her brow creased. "Where are you going?"

"Boston. I've got a trip at the end of the week."

It was none of her business where Con MacNeill went or when, Val reminded herself. It would be a relief to get him out of her hair and off her mind.

"What kind of trip?" she asked, and bit her lip. She sounded like her mother.

He leaned back in his chair, looking faintly amused. "Job interview. Going to miss me?"

"I haven't thought about it." But she was afraid she might. She twitched her braid over her shoulder. "I just thought you might stick around to deal with things here."

"It's important, or I wouldn't go. Vice president of Northern Ventucom," he explained, as if that would have some significance for her.

The only significance Val could find was that she'd let herself rely on him and he was leaving.

Something of what she felt must have shown in her face, because he added, "I'm not leaving your restaurant in the lurch, Dixie."

"I'm not worried about the restaurant. I'm worried about Rob Cross. You questioned his handling of my account. You humiliated him in front of his wife. He's not going to just go away while you fly off somewhere."

Con straightened, all amusement gone. "I'll deal with Cross."

"From Boston?"

A muscle jumped in Con's jaw. "Are you asking me to stay?" he asked quietly.

Oh, dear Lord, she wanted to. The thought appalled her. Was she already so dependent on him that his very presence comforted her?

"Of course not." She'd told him she could take care of the situation herself. She preferred taking care of things herself. Nothing had changed. His leaving proved that. "I'm simply suggesting that the next time you're tempted to get involved you consider the consequences."

"I don't need you to lecture me on responsibility."

"No?" she asked crossly. She was tired. Her head pounded, and the odd hollow feeling inside her had spread. She wrapped her arms around her stomach. Maybe it had been a mistake to skip breakfast this morning. "What about Mitchell? At the moment he imagines you're some kind of cross between Daddy Warbucks and Sir Lancelot. What am I supposed to tell him about you leaving?"

"You could try telling him I'm coming back. It's an overnight, Dixie, that's all."

"And if you get offered the job?"

He hesitated.

She tossed back her hair. "Yeah, that's what I thought."

His eyes narrowed with temper. "Any commitments I

make will naturally be contingent on my fulfilling my obligations here.''

"Big words," she scoffed. "Try asking an eight-year-old sometime how he likes being considered an *obligation*. I know I sure as heck don't." She hopped off the desk, disappointed in him and furious with herself for letting it matter. For letting it show. "I've got to run."

His voice stopped her at the door. "What time are we picking up Ann?"

She jerked one shoulder irritably. "I don't know."

"What time?"

"You don't need to come."

He met her glare with a long, level look of his own. "Maybe I do."

Her thighs went as soft as butterscotch left in the sun. Darn him. Did he have any idea what it did to a woman when he looked at her with promise in his eyes?

Of course he did, she scolded herself. The man had a mind like a calculator, adding, ticking.

"Ann's supposed to call me," she said coolly. "I'll let you know."

Con watched her sweep from the room in her rainy day dress, frustration twisting inside him. What did she want from him, anyway? He drummed his fingers on the desk. The ceramic pig that held her pencils smirked.

Hell. For a moment there, he'd actually considered calling Josh Wainbridge to put off the interview until next week some time, when the situation here was more settled.

Which was ridiculous.

Opportunities like Ventucom didn't wait. The vice president position represented his best chance for a corporate comeback, to recoup his place in Boston's moneyed set and recover his self-respect. It was everything he'd worked for, everything he'd wanted.

Damn Val Cutler's stubborn priorities for blunting his enthusiasm for the trip.

His hand closed around the pencil. *Con is very motivated,* his fifth-grade teacher had written on his report card. Driven, his Harvard classmates had acknowledged. Ambitious as hell, his co-workers had muttered.

He wasn't used to being hedged by another person's hopes, fettered by someone else's trust. It was a kind of connection, an accountability, he hadn't felt since leaving home. A sense of belonging. Of limits.

He had every intention of fulfilling his contract with Cutler. But what was he supposed to do with this nagging sense of obligation to Cutler's daughter?

The furious echo of her words challenged him. *Try asking an eight-year-old sometime how he likes being an obligation. I sure as heck don't.*

Val rested her forehead on the steering wheel as if she could drive her headache away. The last place on earth she wanted to be was the bank. The last man on earth she wanted to see was Con MacNeill. The shark. The rat. He was probably in there right now reporting to her father on his clever cost-cutting measures before he flew away to Boston.

But Ann had been so relieved by Con's offer to go with them that Val had promised to fetch him. So, here she was, baking in the bank parking lot in her little tin can of a car, waiting for Con to finish his business inside and come out.

"I won't take long," Ann had said, her face swollen and her eyes pleading. "We just need a few things. But it would be so nice to have him there. Just in case…"

In case Rob came.

Shoot. Val raised her head and glanced at her watch. Two forty-nine. If Ann was going to get packed and be gone before Rob returned home from work, Val needed to collect Con now. She pulled her keys from the ignition, hitched her canvas tote over her shoulder and crawled out of the car.

Cool air rushed to envelop her as she tugged on the bank's thick glass door. The bank lobby was nearly empty. A farmer in clay-coated work boots and a NASCAR cap waited by the velvet rope. A harried mother held her squirming toddler on the counter while a glossy-lipped young woman with styled dark hair counted out bills. Val squinted at her brass nameplate. Donna Winston.

Donna? As in, he-cheats-on-me-with-Donna-at-the-bank Donna? What could that polished, pretty woman possibly see in Rob?

But Val already knew. A blond bank vice president with a thirty-four-inch waist, an eight handicap and a six-figure salary probably looked pretty good to a bright young thing tired of shooting pool with the good old boys down at Tim's Tavern. Pickings were slim in Cutler.

Con's words came back to taunt her. *I won't be in town forever.*

She bit her lip. Nodding to the security guard—Alex? Eric? His brother had been a year behind her in high school—she pushed through the gate that separated the lobby from the private offices.

Back here, the walls were a deep rich gray and the floor marble. Very tasteful. Very cold. Shivering in her sleeveless blue dress, Val passed the open cubicles that served the loan and proof departments. Rob's office door was open, but his lights were off. She hadn't seen him after his fight with Con. Had he stayed home rather than explain his bruises?

Or was he out looking for Ann?

The marble hallway ended in a pool of carpet. A big empty desk floated in the center, banked by a couple of red leather chairs and some waxy-looking palms. Her father's efficient secretary must have stepped away, leaving the citadel unguarded. The inner office door was ajar.

Val hesitated. Edward Cutler had never been an advocate of Take Our Daughters to Work Day. Sylvia Cutler had raised their daughter not to bother Daddy at the bank. On the other hand, Con was probably in there discussing the financial future of her restaurant. A discussion about her business *was* her business.

She skirted the desk, the sound of her chunky-heeled sandals absorbed by the deep-pile carpet. Her soft tap on the door was overpowered by the raised voices within.

"That's nonsense," her father was insisting. "Rob's department exists to prevent exactly the kind of mistake you're talking about."

Con's deep, cool voice answered. Good, Val thought. At least she'd tracked him down.

"I'm not saying there's a mistake. From where I stand it looks like a deliberate manipulation of deposits."

What deposits? Her deposits? She stopped with her hand on the door.

"Do you have any proof of that?" Edward Cutler asked sharply.

"There won't be proof if the original receipts have been destroyed."

"But what you're suggesting is impossible without the collaboration of someone in the bank."

"Precisely."

Edward laughed shortly. "God, you've got some nerve. It's not me, if that's what you're driving at."

"Then let me find out who it is."

"Let you go snooping around, casting aspersions against members of my staff... Certainly not. I won't have you interfering in my business."

"You didn't have any trouble with me interfering in your daughter's business."

"I hired you to advise her. Not cook up some cockamamy excuse for her mismanagement. What's she giving you to come in here and make unjustified allegations against my bank? It sure as hell isn't money, because she hasn't got any."

The insult hit like a slap in the face. Val sucked in her breath.

"If you weren't her father I'd deck you for that," Con said quietly.

She pressed her hands to her stinging face. She didn't need Con's backing. She'd trained herself—she thought she'd trained herself—not to care what Edward Cutler thought of her. It surprised her how much his words still had the power to hurt and how comforting she found Con's support.

"Don't threaten me, MacNeill. I'll see you pay."

"You're the one who will pay if something's going on and you don't get to the bottom of it."

"You don't know what you're talking about. It doesn't cost you anything to waltz in here and throw around accusations."

"You think it should cost me something? Fine. Name it."

Oh, no. Squaring her shoulders, Val pushed open the door. "I wouldn't recommend it," she drawled.

Edward stiffened, but for once her father's disapproval carried little weight. Her gaze automatically sought Con.

He turned. His eyes narrowed. "How long have you been out there?"

She smiled, not the least bit intimidated by his I-eat-nice-girls-like-you-for-breakfast tone. He was being honest and decent and brave. And if he didn't like her knowing about it, that was just too darn bad.

"Long enough to know you're making a mistake. Both of you. Con's trying to help, Daddy. And, Con—" she faced him squarely, realizing her heart probably showed in her eyes and not caring "—never offer my daddy a bargain. There're men walking around all over town without their shirts who could tell you that."

His gleam of appreciation sent warmth curling through her stomach. "Thanks, but I'll stand by my report. And my offer."

Edward Cutler pursed his lips. Here it comes, Val thought. "Let me make you a deal, MacNeill. If you can prove that someone at my bank is somehow at fault, you get my handsome apology and a nice bonus for the job. But—'' Edward raised a manicured finger ''—if there's no evidence of wrongdoing, I fire you from this job. And I'll do my damnedest to see you don't get another one.''

Val shook her head. ''No.''

''Fine,'' Con said at the same time.

She glared at him. Couldn't he see he was playing into her father's hands?

''Two conditions,'' Con added. ''I want access to your records and cooperation from your staff.''

''I'll see you get access. For the other, well, you can talk to whomever you want. Whether or not they cooperate is up to them. And you.''

''We've got a deal, then,'' Con said. He turned to Val, one eyebrow lifting. ''You ready to go?''

She was ready to spit. Con had his career to consider. And she had her pride. What if he got sacked? What would he do then? And what would she do without him? She let him take her arm and escort her from the office, her brain whirring like a high-speed mixer.

She waited until they'd passed the potted plants outside before demanding crossly, ''What's the matter with you? Do you want to get fired?''

His lips tightened. He held open the gate to the lobby. ''I told you I'd take care of Cross.''

He had. She just hadn't believed him.

''My father means what he says, you know. How badly do you want that Ventucom thing?''

He looked down at her as she passed under his arm on the way out of the building, his blue eyes cool and enigmatic. ''The vice president position? I want it.''

''Why?''

''Aside from the big bucks and the office on Federal Street?''

She wanted to tell him he was worth more than that. But

maybe that perspective was a luxury that came from having every advantage purchased for her by status-conscious parents. Con's background was very different.

"I suppose the money would be important to you."

His mouth crooked up. "Let's say it's the most convenient way I've found of keeping score."

They exited the bank. Heat slammed down on the concrete steps and shimmered up from the parking lot. Val squinted against the haze, fighting guilt. She'd never intended her challenge to provoke Con into jeopardizing his goals and career. She didn't want that responsibility.

"This isn't a game. It was a stupid risk to take."

He raised both eyebrows. "Only if I'm wrong."

She snorted. "Oh, and you're never wrong."

"Very rarely."

"What if my father's involved?"

"Your father just agreed to let me investigate." They crossed the asphalt. "Besides, someone would have noticed the bank president pocketing bills from the teller's desk, don't you think?"

"And if he knows and is covering up for someone else?"

Con stopped by the driver's side, waiting for her to pull out her keys so he could open her door. "Is this the conspiracy theory? You think I could be in on it, too?"

She felt the betraying blood spread in her cheeks. "Don't joke. This isn't funny."

His gaze was sharp as a blade, his voice cool as steel. "No, it's not. The only remotely amusing part is that I hoped you might have started to trust me."

She turned to face him and found herself trapped in the triangle formed by his arm and the door of the car, between the heat of the car behind her and the heat of his body in front. He smelled like clean cotton and expensive aftershave and Con. He watched her, his face expressionless. A welt rode one cheekbone, where Rob's fist had connected.

He'd been hurt, fighting for her.

Beneath his clipped speech, smooth manner and superior education was a deeply feeling man capable of great pride and loyalty and hurt.

Had she, unthinkingly, hurt him?

Standing on tiptoe, she pressed her lips to the swelling under his eye. She felt him shiver.

"Not that funny," she whispered. "Maybe I do."

Chapter 11

Ann moved silently from drawer to drawer collecting socks and lingerie, her image flitting dimly across the mirror of the heavy Chippendale dresser. Like a ghost in her own home, Val thought, and her heart wrenched with pity.

They were the same age, was all she could think. One choice, one chance, was all that separated Val from drifting through these rooms picking salvage from the wreck of a marriage: this slip, that purse, this pair of stockings. And all the while Ann was packing away the bits and pieces of her life, Val felt Con's waiting presence in the other room. An ending and a beginning, crowded together in a house of secrets.

Val shivered. Con's steady, quiet presence threatened her more than his corporate raider pose ever could. He hadn't once looked at his watch to suggest he had anything better to do with his time than to sit, an intruder in Rob's home, on Rob's BarcaLounger, while Rob's wife packed and prepared to leave him. If Val were some poor, dependent female whose life could only be validated by association with a handsome, strapping male, she could do a lot worse than Connaught MacNeill.

And just look at where that line of thinking had led poor Ann.

She tugged on the closet door. "What about shoes?" she asked practically.

Ann picked up and put down a folded knit top. "What?"

Val gestured to the tidy rack where Ann's shoes lined up like matrons at a wedding. She couldn't begin to choose among them. Her own sneakers and sandals were so tumbled together on the floor of her closet, it was a wonder she found a match each morning. "Which shoes?"

"Oh." Ann drifted over to stare, her arms protecting her stomach. "I don't know. You pick something. I need to pack for Mitchell."

"Sure." Val turned from the closet, a pair of flats in each hand, and wrapped her friend in an awkward hug. "You go on. I'll close up the suitcase."

Ann nodded and faded down the hall. Val tucked the shoes into pockets and dragged the suitcase over the rose-and-cream comforter to wrestle with the zipper.

"Give you a hand?"

She whirled. Con loomed in the bedroom door, big and dark against the ivory walls, out of place among the carved furniture and eighteenth-century botanical prints that hung in the hall. He didn't belong here. And yet there he stood, framed in Ann's doorway, smack in the middle of issues and memories Val was trying hard to ignore.

"I've got it, thanks." She yanked and coaxed the zipper closed.

He strolled forward. "Let me take the suitcase to the car."

He hefted it easily. She fought a buzz of irritation. Surely she wasn't so petty that she had to insist on carrying the bag herself? But the homey intimacy of the scene chafed her. They could have been lovers or husband and wife packing to go on vacation, instead of two people caught up in the sad end of someone else's domestic drama.

Outside the bedroom, Con paused, nodding down the passage toward Mitchell's room. "Is she ready?"

"I'll go check."

She hurried down the hall, her focus on Ann blurred by Con's distracting presence. Her awareness of him permeated everything, investing mundane actions—locking the house, loading the car, trailing down the walk—with heightened significance. He did the things men do without thinking about it, moving with grace inside his powerful, long-boned body. He jingled his keys. He slammed the trunk.

When he hooked an arm up over the seat to say something to Annie in the back, Val noticed he'd rolled his sleeves, exposing muscled forearms. She caught herself studying the pattern of dark hair and flushed with annoyance.

At the shelter, Con got out and opened Ann's door.

"What about dinner?" he asked her. Asked both of them? "Are you hungry?"

Ann shook her head. Her smooth brown hair brushed her battered jaw. "No. That is, yes, but…I have to get used to doing things on my own. For myself and Mitchell."

Val wanted to cheer her friend's difficult bid for independence. But it was pretty early for Ann to be dismissing support. "Are you sure?" she asked quietly.

Ann attempted a smile. "Sure."

Con inspected her face and then nodded. "Okay. Let me get your bags, then."

"If you need anything…" Val said.

"Call," Con finished for her.

Val sat in the car as he unloaded Ann's suitcases, trying not to feel as if her helpfulness had been usurped.

Even with the windows rolled down, the interior of the car was stifling. She got out for some air. When Con came back to the car, she was leaning against the driver's side door.

On edge and uncertain, she smiled, trying to diffuse the heavy atmosphere between them with humor. "Need a lift?"

He rocked back on his heels, assessing her mood. "How about a tip?"

"Wash your hands before you eat?" she offered straight-faced.

"Not exactly what I had in mind." Quietly, he studied her. "How are you?"

"I'm fine. It's Ann I'm worried about. She's not used to being alone."

"In her case I'd say it beats the alternative."

"In most cases, I'd say."

His eyes narrowed. "What about us?"

Her breath quickened. "What about us?" she asked lightly. "I mean, don't get me wrong, I like you. I like being with you. But essentially, haven't we both chosen to be alone? Two separate individuals."

"Maybe that's because we haven't explored all the alternatives yet."

He stepped close to the car, blocking her escape. Her heart tripped into overtime. His thighs crowded hers. His body pressed hers. His long, clever fingers stroked a frame around her face.

She half resented his effect on her. She didn't like being at his mercy, at the mercy of her hormones. Silly, she chided herself. What could he possibly do to her out here on the street, in full view of the windows of the women's shelter?

His mouth swooped down on hers, and she had her answer. *Plenty.*

The kiss was hot, hard and possessive. He knew exactly what he was doing, and did it so well she couldn't bring herself to object. He thrust one hand into her hair, angling her mouth to receive his kiss. His lips parted hers. His tongue probed and sought. In spite of the warning tick in her brain, she welcomed it, welcomed him, felt the surge of need roll inside her and crash the careful structure of her casual pose.

When he finally lifted his head, her hands had fisted in the fabric of his shirt.

"Well." Satisfaction gleamed in those blue, blue eyes. "What next?"

If he hadn't said anything, she might have dragged him into the car and home. But he asked deliberately, forcing the choice upon her.

And she wasn't ready for it.

She drew a deep breath, instinctively pushing for distance, reaching for control. "I haven't made up my mind."

Some of the light went out of his eyes. He released her, jamming his hands into his pockets. "That's honest, anyway."

"You asked," she said defensively.

"Yeah, I asked for it, all right." He took three short, impatient strides down the crumbling walk and back again. With an uncomfortable combination of relief and regret, she saw he once again had himself under perfect control. "Okay. You want to drop me back at the bank? My car is there."

His backing off surprised her. Another man would have pressed his advantage—either her undeniable physical response or her uncomfortable sense of obligation.

"You could come back to my place. I could make us something to eat...." It was easier to offer food than sex.

"No." He caught himself. "No, thanks. It's been a long day. I'll follow you back, though. See you get in safely."

"Ann's not staying with me. I don't need—"

His mouth compressed. "You may not need me, Dixie, but you've got me. Deal with it."

Indignation burned up her brief regret. She closed her mouth and set her jaw and got into the car.

Shutting off the shower, Val reached for a towel. The pounding spray hadn't soothed her headache or cleared her brain. Without the sound of running water, the apartment was quiet. She told herself she liked it that way.

Maybe that's because we haven't explored all the alternatives yet.

Nonsense, she thought bracingly, in Aunt Naomi's best style. Living alone suited her. An only child, she'd been relieved to escape her parents' home, ruled by her father's strictures and decorated to her mother's exacting tastes. As a teenager, she'd hated her own bedroom, which Sylvia Cutler insisted she keep in a state of glossy perfection, as if the photographers from *Southern Living* might walk in at any moment.

New York had been a breath of freedom, a blast of fresh air. Okay, smelly, noisy, exciting air. But at seventeen, Val had been thrilled at the chance to make her own way, to create her own space, to define her own style. Oh, a succession of friends had camped on the floor of her tiny studio. One lover had even spent a night in her bed. But overall Val discovered she preferred the freedom of solitude. Outside of Wild Thymes, she protected her privacy.

So why did this apartment suddenly feel so empty?

The curtain hooks clattered as she shoved back the shower curtain. Maybe she missed Ann. Maybe she was worried about Mitchell. Patting water from her breasts and thighs, Val stepped from the shower. Maybe she should look into getting a cat?

She swiped at the mirror and pulled a face at the misty glass. It wasn't a cat she was missing, or Ann or Mitchell. If she was honest with herself, it was Con.

Deal with it.

She squeezed her hair over the drain. She'd always resisted her father's manipulation. She wasn't in the market now for some take-charge kind of guy to run her restaurant and her life.

She knew he wanted her. Other men had wanted her without tempting her from her safe isolation. But Con's apparent willingness to treat her as an equal drew her. Swayed her. He might disagree with her, but he never ignored her opinions or belittled her ideas.

This isn't an arm-wrestling contest, he'd told her. I think you can hold your own.

She tugged absently on her empty earlobe. Could she believe him? Did she really believe she was a match for Con MacNeill?

Wrapping her hair in a towel, she padded naked into her bedroom. It didn't help that the man had a mind like a computer and a body like a decathlete. But she could have admired him without loving him. It was the deep heart and decency beneath that cool, logical facade that seduced her: the loyalty he showed his family, the gentleness he revealed with Ann, the risk he took for what he believed was right.

I'll take care of Cross, he'd told her.

And this afternoon in her father's office, he'd put his career on the line for Ann's sake.

For Val's sake. Because she'd taunted him with not facing the consequences of his involvement.

The thought made her squirm. She thrust her arms into the green silk robe. She owed him now, and she didn't like it. In her experience, emotional debts were always collected.

What would Con expect in payment? And what did she want to give?

The doorbell chimed. Fear jammed her lungs. Had Rob come back looking for Ann? Or seeking another victim?

Val clenched her hands on the belt of her robe, infuriated by her own vulnerability. Like Rob would walk up and ring the doorbell. With Ann taken from him, he was more likely to try to kick down the door.

She forced a deep breath, tied the robe tight and went to answer the bell.

"Who is it?"

She was learning, Con thought. She hadn't just opened the door. "Con MacNeill."

The chain rattled, and she let him in. Con sucked in his breath. Holy saints, she was beautiful. Her hair streamed dark and damp behind her shoulders, and her narrow feet were bare. She was wrapped in something shiny that made his palms feel empty.

"You should've looked," he said.

She stepped back to admit him. "I recognized your voice. What do you want?"

He wanted her, but he figured now was not the time to mention it. His brothers hadn't nicknamed him Genius for nothing. Her sleepless night was in her face for any moron to read, along with a vulnerability he thought damn few people had seen.

"You look done in," he said roughly. "You eat yet?"

Her eyebrows rose. The Belle was back, he thought admiringly. "Thank you for the charming compliment, and no."

"It wasn't a compliment." He held up a white paper bag. "I brought dinner."

She blinked. "Dinner?"

"Yeah."

"I…" She took a step forward. The green thing she was wearing shimmered and clung. He remembered seeing Ann Cross in the same robe last night, but it hadn't had this effect on him. "Not many people bring food to a chef."

No, they probably all expected her to feed them. He felt a spurt of irritation at her distant family, her user friends. He'd taken note of the number of free meals she served to hangers on and genuine charity cases.

He shrugged. "I figured you shouldn't have to cook on your day off."

The warmth in those wide gray eyes embarrassed him. He barely stopped himself from shuffling his feet.

"That was so—"

"You call me nice again, so help me, I won't answer for the consequences," he warned.

She laughed. "Thoughtful. It was very thoughtful. What did you get?"

He hefted the sack for her inspection. "Arlene's barbecue. I could have gone for Chinese, but I didn't trust Szechwan shrimp cooked by somebody named Debra Sue."

"Snob."

He grinned, not denying it. "I didn't know if you'd eat the fried chicken, so I got macaroni and slaw and stuff."

Her hands played with the tie of her robe. "It sounds wonderful. Let me just get dressed. There's beer in the refrigerator if you want one."

She'd bought beer? That was progress. He found he liked thinking of his beer in her fridge, his shaving things above her sink. His body in her bed. He almost groaned. It was the robe, he decided. He'd be okay once she took it off. And found that train of thought didn't help at all.

"I'll only be a minute," she added.

A minute. Sixty seconds. He could probably control himself that long. As long as he didn't think about the slide of silk on skin....

She didn't go. She stood there, her gray eyes steady on him and her hands still twisting the ends of her belt.

"Thank you for the food." She made the simple thanks sound like a challenge.

"You're welcome."

She still didn't move. His control was wearing dangerously thin. Con cleared his throat. "Hurry up, or it will get cold."

She regarded him a moment longer, and then one corner of her mouth dented in and her smile slowly spread. "I guess it's up to me to warm things up, then," she said, and closed the distance between them.

She smelled of soap and woman. The placket of her robe brushed his jeans. He could glance down the V in front and see where her smooth, golden chest rose to plump, pale breasts. His jaw tightened, his whole body tightened, in a downward spiral of need.

"Dinner," he reminded her. His voice was hoarse.

Val drew back and studied his face a moment, his glacial eyes half-hidden beneath heavy lids, his stubborn jaw, his compressed mouth. A band of intransigence loosened around her heart. You decide, he'd told her last night, and this afternoon she hadn't made up her mind. But his determination now to restrain his own needs, to consider hers, gave her the courage to take the next step.

"Dinner," she agreed. "Do you want it before or after?"

He went very still. The room was perfectly quiet. Over the whoosh of a passing car on the street outside and the hum of the refrigerator, she could hear the rasp of his breathing and the thunder of her own heart.

"Are you asking me to go to bed with you?"

She gave up fussing with the belt of her robe and stuffed her hands in its pockets. "Why is it I'm so good at communicating what I don't want and so lousy at saying what I do?" She sighed. "And I never asked what you wanted at all."

He stroked her cheek with his thumb, pressed it gently against her bottom lip. She felt the unfamiliar thump of desire deep in her stomach. "No mystery there. I told you, up front and early. I want you."

She wanted him, too. She wanted to ignite those cool blue eyes and soften the laughter of that clever mouth. She wanted to burrow beneath his formidable defenses and find the passionate Irishman she was pretty sure lived inside. She wanted to wrap his strength around her like a blanket to ward off the chilly residue of fear.

She wanted Con MacNeill. For a brief while, she'd even imagined she could enjoy him without penalty, without forever altering the landscape of her heart. She hadn't known that she could need him, that need could pulse in her bloodstream and melt the marrow of her bones. The feeling ex-hilarated her. Terrified her.

"Yes," she said baldly.

If possible, he grew even more rigid. "No games, Dixie. Yes, what?"

He was going to make her spell it out. There would be no pretending for either one of them that this wasn't her decision. "Yes, I'm asking you to go to bed with me."

"Thank God."

His fervent response startled a laugh from her that his descending mouth sweetly, firmly silenced. He wasn't cold. His lips were warm, his hands were warm, his back under the wilted cotton shirt was warm. She held on tight. His chest felt solid and hot against her breasts. His hips radiated enough heat to toast her down to her toes.

She lost herself in the textures of his kiss as his tongue drew the outline of her mouth. She welcomed it with her own, coaxed to trace the slick inner surface of his lower lip, to explore the recesses beyond. She tasted his hunger and his challenge, and her own hunger spread in response. A slow, melting heat uncurled inside her, diffusing through her veins.

He lifted his head, inhaling through his teeth. "Dixie, let me put down the bag. You don't know what you do to me."

Actually, Val was getting a very good idea. She could feel his response, hot and snug against her belly. She trembled, but not with fear. How could she fear anything this man could do when the evidence of her own power was so unmistakable?

She pulled away. The white bag from Arlene's Café was crushed in Con's right hand. Twisting it from his grip, she paced to the kitchen and ditched it in the refrigerator.

She crossed her arms over her chest to contain her skipping heart, to hold close her slippery robe, and turned to him with a smile. "Satisfied?"

"Not by a long shot."

Her breath escaped in a soft whoosh of surprise as Con swept her up into his arms. "What are you doing?"

"I've been waiting for this. I want to do it right. Where's your bed?"

Off balance, she put an arm around his shoulders, amused by his immediate response to her challenge and secretly delighted by his care. "I usually keep it in the bedroom."

He carried her through the apartment. She was very conscious of his size, his easy strength, but her awareness came without anxiety. She was grateful for that. Grateful for him.

"Show off." Her fingers combed the silky hair that curled against the back of his neck.

He grinned. "Yeah. Through here?"

At her nod, he turned, elbowed open the door and carried her over the threshold. Twilight seeped through the slatted blinds, spilling across the tumbled laundry and bright toss pillows. It glowed from the big square mirror, glinted off the cheap glass bottles and silver-backed brushes that littered her dresser.

From her perch in Con arm's, Val surveyed the usual comfortable disorder, and the ghost of her mother rose to chide her.

"I did pull up the quilt," she offered self-consciously.

Tenderness curved his mouth. "Very nice." He was looking at her, not at the room.

"You don't mind?"

"Dixie, you could have an elephant in here right now and I wouldn't mind as long as it stayed off the bed." He bent his head to kiss her again.

His mouth was sure and sweet. Val sipped and sucked from it. A Baptist-born girl could get giddy on such sweetness, dizzying as stolen sherry on a Sunday afternoon. Her head fell back, and his lips took shameless advantage, moving, sliding to explore her face and throat, pressing tiny, teasing pecks along the tender line of her jaw to her ear, inciting fires in their wake.

She trembled, or maybe it was his arms that shook. Her robe gaped as she turned into his chest, her hands stretching, reaching for taut muscle and solid bone. How could such pleasurable contact create such an ache inside her?

Val was a sensual creature, comfortable and accustomed to satisfying her taste and touch with the flavors and textures of her kitchen. But she was overwhelmed by the hungers Con stirred, by the banquet he promised. She wanted to pull him to her, wanted full, close contact with his weight and his strength. Frustrated by the way he cradled her, she slipped her hand into the neckline of his shirt to feel warm flesh and coarse hair.

"The bed?" she reminded him.

He rumbled an affirmative, but his lips had reached her ear now. The wonderful things his lips knew how to do there distracted her. She gasped and clung. He shifted her in his arms, testing her desire and his restraint. She heated like a pastry in the oven, melting, swelling, bursting with sweetness. And impatience.

"MacNeill," she warned.

He lifted his head from her throat. "What?"

"Put me down."

He turned her so that she had the contact she craved. His eyes were dark, the black nearly swallowing the blue. He slid her slowly down his long, muscled, fully aroused body until her robe rode up around her hips and her naked feet skimmed his shoes and touched the floor. With his gaze intent on her face, he cupped her buttocks over the slippery silk and pulled her close, closer, into intimate friction with every inviting inch of him. She sucked in her breath.

"Like that?"

"I was thinking—" she cleared her throat; it was hard, so hard, to insert that little note of amusement when everything inside her wept for his attention "—of the bed."

"Good thinking. So was I."

And then he lunged with her across the room and she had

the mattress at her back and the full, welcome weight of him along her front. Sighing with satisfaction, she opened to his kiss. Warm and urgent, his tongue sought hers. His hand spanned her rib cage, gliding up to part the silk, to capture one breast. Excitement tightened the peak between his long fingers. She moaned as he deftly worked the tender nipple. He swallowed the sound.

Sensation bombarded her overworked senses like an explosion of spices. Feet flat against the rumpled quilt, she slid her bare legs up along the outside of his powerful thighs, the khaki fabric at once abrasively exciting and horribly in the way. She gasped an inarticulate demand, her hips rising off the mattress. He rocked her with his body. She wrapped her arms around his strong back and clung. An answering rhythm woke deep inside her, and suddenly she could not bear to have anything between them.

She tugged at his shirt, frustrated by buttons and then by the long tails tucked into his narrow-waisted pants. He lifted away enough to help her, pitching his balled-up shirt into a corner of the room before he lowered to her again. The heat of his skin scalded hers to tenderness. His body hair licked like flame against her breasts. She was melting, her heart and her womb melting within her.

Her hand groped blindly between them. Again, he helped her, yanking at his belt, stripping the pants from his body. He stroked the silk back from her breasts, worked the tie. He told her something as he uncovered her nakedness for the first time. Lost in lust and wonder, she heard the awe and exultation but not the words. She reached for him. He rose against her, hot and potent, and a purely feminine doubt tensed her stomach. He was so large. He would have her, and she would never possess herself again.

But his kiss on her mouth was tender, and his hand, smoothing her abdomen, trembled slightly. And she knew that as surely as she gave herself to him, he was giving up himself to her. She opened herself to receive his gift.

He reached over the side of the bed for his discarded khakis. She waited while he ripped open a foil packet, her legs apart, her palm pressed to the powerful planes of his chest. She could feel his heart beat under her hand. There was something solemn and significant in this moment of preparation, an intimacy more deliberate than sex itself. Unease lapped at her. She had made herself into who and what she was. Would this act of loving somehow remake her?

Her choice, she reminded herself. She would not regret this. She would only regret it if, through fear, she denied herself loving Con MacNeill.

And yet she tensed as she felt him rigid above her. He came into her a little way, bracing himself on his elbows, giving her time to adjust to his invasion. Her body resisted and then tightened in need. He groaned, and rested his forehead for a moment against hers. She felt his exertion and his heat, wet against her face and against her palms on his back. Her nails curved into him.

"You're making this—" he inhaled sharply "—hard."

She loved him for his control, for his consideration. It was wickedly tempting to test how far it extended. She stroked him. "I thought that was the point."

Laughter ruptured his restraint. He pressed into her, his body surging at the break in his command. She drew him down, drew him in. He thrust. Her breath caught.

Each thrust, each slow withdrawal and urgent reentry, built the heat between them like the inexorable climb of temperature inside an oven. His breathing grew ragged. Her arousal grew sharp and raw, a silver knife twisting inside her. Faster, harder, he moved in her and on her, his intent face too beautiful to bear. She closed her eyes. Brilliant colors melted in the velvet darkness behind her shut lids. She was molten, too, and changed. Needy, she clung to him, murmuring. He plunged into her. Until the last, white hot explosion transformed and fused them together.

Chapter 12

He was drowned. When he could breathe again, when control crept back to his muscles and blood pumped sluggishly to his brain, Con found himself someplace he'd never been. Cautiously, he levered himself slightly away from the soft, receptive body under his and tried to get his bearings.

A streetlamp outside Val's window glinted off her mismatched possessions like the moon shining off the river at night. Easing over onto his back, he picked out a Lenox vase and a Plexiglas earring tree, the outlines of an elegant dresser and a pillow shaped like a giant tomato. He grinned into the darkness. Who'd have figured he'd find himself cast ashore in a room that looked like a cross between an antiques showroom and a garage sale?

His hairy calf rubbed Val's sleek one. The satisfaction that sapped his muscles was more than the physical release of good sex. Great sex, he corrected himself. Okay, the best sex of his life. But sex alone didn't explain this floating sense of well-being. He felt connected, committed, tied to a woman and a place that were all wrong for him.

He was in major trouble here. So why didn't he feel more alarmed?

Con turned his head. Val's hair rioted across her face, his arm and the pillow. She was so beautiful his heart ached. He didn't know what to do with the feelings that crowded his chest, impossible to define or solve. They were too new, too big, too disturbing for a Boston boy on the corporate comeback. No way in hell could he squeeze what he felt into words small enough to make it past his throat.

Instead, he propped himself on one elbow and threaded his fingers possessively through her hair, combing it back from her face.

"About the bed?" he said.

Her eyes slitted open, gleaming in the twilight room.

"Good idea," he told her.

Her sultry mouth curved in a private Mona Lisa smile. "I do get them occasionally."

He glided his hand along her shoulder, liking the way she lifted involuntarily to his touch. He let his gaze drift to her breasts and lower. Incredibly, his body stirred. He wanted… Hell, for the first time since seventh grade, he wasn't sure what he wanted. But short-term, at least, he wanted her.

She was probably sore, he cautioned himself. So beautifully tight, and he'd held nothing back at the last.

He forced himself to speak casually, trying to ease the acute need twisting his gut into knots. "Yeah? Well, let me know when you get another one."

Her lashes dropped, shutting him out. "I'll do that."

He touched her cheek with his fingertips. "Of course, if we don't eat pretty soon, I could pass out on you."

Not tender words, Val thought. The lack of them hurt.

She told herself she was being inconsistent…and unreasonable to boot. No regrets, she reminded herself. What did she want, a proposal? A declaration of undying love? Now, wouldn't *that* be inconvenient?

She pushed away the memory of Con's deep voice. *Sex is inconvenient, Dixie girl.*

Surely she wasn't so old-fashioned, so needy, as to believe that the pleasure Con brought her was more than a mutually satisfying interlude. Liberated Aunt Naomi could have lectured for a week on a woman's judgment being compromised just because she'd fallen into bed. Tumbled into love.

Val's eyes opened wide. Oh, Lord. Oh, no. Was that what she'd done?

She needed to get out of bed. She needed to buy space to herself and time to think. She wanted to be in her kitchen. "Let me get dinner."

"I'll help you."

He rolled from the bed, unselfconsciously naked, and reached for his pants. Val switched on the bedside lamp. The Tiffany shade cast a multicolored glow around the room. A bar of gold light slid across Con's back and buttocks. Struggling to push her arms through the tangled sleeves of the creased silk robe, Val stopped, transfixed by the shift of light and shadow over the hard planes of his back, the glide of muscles under his skin, the dark tuft under his arm. By the body of her lover.

Con tugged on the buckle of his belt and glanced over his shoulder to catch her staring.

Her cheeks scalded. She lifted her chin.

"Ah, Dixie girl."

The mattress depressed as he knelt beside her. He drew her up beside him, so that the sensitive crests of her breasts pressed the hard planes of his chest. His breath was warm against her hair.

"I really am starving," he said.

His mouth brushed the top of her head, his kiss as soft as his words were harsh. Desire pulled in the pit of Val's stomach. She resisted it, resisted the slight tug of his arms as he brought her more firmly against him. She didn't need to be soothed with kisses or placated with promises. Just because his expert lovemaking was beyond all her experience and expectations didn't mean she'd let herself be reduced to a quivering lump. She'd gone into this relationship deliberately, understanding its risks and restrictions. She wasn't going to complicate her life by changing the rules of the game now.

If Con could be casual, she could be cool. Mustering her self-possession, she climbed off the bed.

"Then I guess we'd better eat," she said brightly.

Forty minutes later, Val pushed away her plate and sighed. A sweating cup, a wrinkled bag and crumpled paper napkins littered the table. Nothing was left on the chunky blue china but hush-puppy crumbs and a smear of cheese.

"I didn't realize I was so hungry. That coleslaw was good."

Con tipped his long-necked bottle to his lips. "Bet it was better on my barbecue than on your macaroni and cheese. You ever consider adding pork to your menu?"

She narrowed her eyes in warning. Taking her to bed didn't give him license to meddle in her kitchen. "Not since I read *Charlotte's Web*."

He flashed his wolf grin, and she realized he'd been joking.

Resolutely, she ignored his teasing. "It was nice eating someone else's cooking for a change."

He shrugged. "It was okay. Nothing to come home to. Not like, say, summer squash bisque and vegetable stir-fry."

Laughter fermented inside her. But even as a smile rose to her lips, a hard, indigestible lump remained. Maybe Con MacNeill wasn't out to change her vegetarian ways. But how long before he started to change her?

She shook the thought away, piling napkins and silverware. "I do appreciate your bringing dinner."

"No big deal. I needed to eat. You needed to eat. I wanted to eat with you."

She pushed away from the table to carry their plates to the sink. "Oh, and you always get what you want."

He strolled over, tossing her empty cup in the trash. "Usually."

Blocking the drain, Val squirted soap into the metal basin and turned on the tap.

"This Boston job..." She wasn't sure how to proceed or why she was asking. She plunged in anyway, immersing her hands in hot soapy water. "Do you think you're going to get it?"

He parked against the counter next to her, warm and close, his hips by her elbows, his gaze on her face. "I think I've got a shot at it, yeah."

And then he'd be gone.

She picked at the subject like a hangnail, knowing it could hurt but unable to resist.

"How important is my father's recommendation to you?"

"It would help."

She swished around in the bubbles. "But you have other references, right?"

"Why?"

"Well..." She floundered. "I'd feel bad if I thought because of Ann or—or me—you might not get the job, that's all."

His expression shuttered. "You don't think your old boyfriend is dipping into your account?"

Val stared down at the scummy dishes in her sink. Admitting Con to her bed was one thing. Letting him into her past was something else entirely.

She temporized. "You said it would be hard to prove."

"And you don't trust me to prove it," he said flatly.

It was her own heart she didn't trust, and her growing obligation to this man. If he was willing to put his future on the line for her, what exactly would he expect in return?

"I'm just not sure what you're hoping to accomplish."

He set his beer bottle down precisely on the counter. "Did your father tell you I was fired, is that it?"

She gaped at him. "What?"

"The sudden lack of confidence. Is it because I screwed up my last job?"

She was appalled that by protecting her own feelings she'd led him to think that way. Wiping her hands, she turned to examine the hard, handsome face staring back at her: the intelligent forehead, the stubborn jaw, the bump in the bridge of his nose.

"I don't think you're the kind of man who makes mistakes." Or forgives yourself for them, she thought. "What did you do? Punch out the boss?"

He hesitated. When she only waited, he shrugged and said, "I made one bad call. Millennium was approached for a loan by a startup software company—a couple of kids working out of their dorm room with an idea for a new video game."

He reached again for his beer, turning the bottle around in his hands. "I liked the idea, liked the guys, liked the game. But before the board voted on approval, they asked me if the probable return outweighed the risk of investing in an unproven business. I had to tell them no."

Val pulled the plug from the sink, letting the dirty water escape. "And?"

"And the kids made a fortune selling the idea to someone else, Millennium lost the chance to make a bundle, and I got canned."

Indignation swirled inside her. "But it wasn't your fault."

"It was my account. My mistake." He took a swallow from the bottle and set it back on the counter. "So, now you know why I'm down here working for your father."

"And why you want to go back. To prove yourself."

"A comeback. Yeah."

"Well, you don't have anything to prove to me." She

smiled, hoping to melt the frightening frost from his eyes.
"For a bean counter from Boston, you've done a wonderful
job balancing my books."

"Any halfway decent accountant could have done the
same."

"You don't think I'd let just any accountant into my business."

He raised his eyebrows. "Not anyone, no. Just someone
forced on you by your father."

"That has nothing to do with it. Well, all right, it did, but
it doesn't anymore. I trust your judgment." Even as she said
the words, she acknowledged they were true. She did trust
him, his integrity, his fundamental decency, his honor. "I
trust you, Con."

He pushed away from the counter with both hands. One
finger tipped up her chin. "Maybe you shouldn't."

His cool blue eyes were molten now. Sensual awareness
flooded her, and with it the recognition of her own emotional
danger. Standing barefoot in her kitchen in her thin green
robe, she felt naked. Vulnerable. This man, his moods and
his motives and his approval, were rapidly becoming too
important to her.

Blindly, she reached behind her for the drainboard, for
support, and missed. Her hand landed on the pile of cutlery
stacked to dry by the side of the sink, and pain lanced her
finger.

She jerked it back. "Ouch."

"What is it?"

"Nothing. I pricked myself."

"Let me see."

"No, I—"

Disregarding her denial, he took her hand, twisting it for
his inspection. Blood welled up, a small, dark jewel on the
pad of her thumb.

She tugged against his grasp, embarrassed by her outcry,
discomfited by his possession. "It's nothing."

"You're right," he said, but he didn't let her go.

Instead, he held her hand tenderly, so tenderly her breathing got confused.

His dark head bent over their clasped hands. His warm mouth closed over her thumb. Gently, he sucked at the tiny wound. She felt the pull in her breasts and the hollow of her stomach. Need uncurled, warm and urgent, inside her, escaping her throat in a muffled cry. Val pressed her lips together, disconcerted and yet excited by the sound.

Con straightened and looked her in the eye. "Dixie, you can make all the noise you want."

She put up her chin. "I do not make—"

His mouth took hers. She tasted beer and the dark, sweet flavors of her blood and his hunger blended on his tongue. Desire shuddered through her. She'd told herself she could handle this, could handle him. She'd never expected the craving Connaught MacNeill evoked from her blood and her bone. She wasn't prepared for the crash of her defenses.

Breathless, she wrenched her mouth from his. The wall clock swung wildly in her line of sight.

"Con…it's getting late."

He lifted his head from her throat. "I want to spend the night," he said bluntly. "I want to sleep with you."

She tried to distance him with humor, to cool the fire that sparked through her at his possessive tone. "You just did."

"Not have sex. Sleep here, in your apartment, in your bed."

She wet her lips. "I don't think that's necessary. Rob's not coming back."

The polite, precise way she spoke alerted Con to trouble. She'd tried on that tone at their first bank meeting, like a lady of the Ascendancy explaining English rule to some thickheaded, thick-handed Irish peasant. No way. After mind-numbing, body-flooding, heart-stopping sex, after baring all his professional dreams and failures, he'd be damned if he'd let her exclude him now.

Her unexpected encouragement after his confession had been like getting a gold star on his math homework or a promotion, validation on a level he hadn't sought or known he'd needed. He wanted more of it. More of her. Wanted to possess, to claim.

"Cross has got nothing to do with it," he growled, and purged his frustration in another kiss.

Her mouth was hot and slick. Sweeter than the tea she drank, with a kick like eighteen-year-old whiskey. He flexed his hands in the glorious coils of her hair, holding her still while he devoured her.

This wasn't her idea, Val thought dizzily. Maybe it wasn't a good idea. Did she trust him enough to let him seduce her? Did she trust herself enough to be seduced?

His hands unfisted in her hair. His long fingers skimmed the curve of her jaw, the line of her throat. She could feel her blood beat beneath his touch. She swallowed.

His eyes were dark with desire and almost bewildered. "You are so beautiful," he said hoarsely. "I don't think I've ever seen anything so beautiful."

Against the nakedness of his voice, it didn't matter anymore whose idea this was. Nothing mattered but Con and the way he felt against her, solid and strong, and the way he made her feel.

Beautiful.

She wrapped her arms around him and kissed him back. It wasn't enough. Her bare toes climbed the tops of his feet, and she felt him swell against her. She nipped his earlobe.

He jolted. She wrapped one leg around him, moving, sliding, reveling in the friction. His neck was corded, his shoulders rigid, his desire hard against her belly. He reached down and around with both hands and cupped her bottom. Bracing, he lifted her. That was good. She wiggled, trying to find a fit between her heat and his hardness.

"Not here." He bit out the words. "I'm not making love to you on the kitchen table."

"I don't mind," she answered honestly.

She felt his chest expand with his breath. "The bed," he said tightly. "I can make it to the bed."

She clung to him as he strode with her down the hall. Her heel grazed a wall. Bumped off balance, he laid her against the cool plaster and ravished her mouth. She cooperated, grabbing at his shoulders, tugging at his hair. Need spiraled inside her. Heat climbed between them. He hauled her up, staggered to her room and fell with her onto the mattress.

Beautiful. Con's heart stopped at the look in those candid gray eyes. Her lips were swollen from his. Intimacy quivered between them as she lay all open beneath him, pink and beautiful, warm and vulnerable. His.

He framed the perfect oval of her face with his hands, drawn to seek an affirmation it seemed only she could provide.

"Now can I spend the night?" he asked, deliberately provocative.

He felt her infinitesimal resistance to his challenge. She closed her eyes, closed him out. "I'll have to think about it."

"Fine," he said silkily. "Don't mind me. I'll just… occupy myself while you're thinking."

Her brows twitched together, but she didn't open her eyes. She would, he promised himself.

The rich dark robe, spilling to both sides, framed her rose-and-cream torso like a work of art. Bending his head, he kissed the soft underside of her breast and the pretty pouting nipple.

She shifted, shrugged. Undiscouraged and intent, he opened his mouth wider, feasting on the feel and the scent and the taste of her. She wanted him earlier, he would swear. She'd practically begged.

He pushed the uncomfortable thought away. Valerian Darcy Cutler wasn't a woman used to begging.

''Like honey,'' he muttered against her flesh. ''You are so sweet.''

Her nipple was hard under his tongue. When he felt the rhythm of her breathing change, he raised himself on one elbow and softly, warmly kissed her mouth. Her lips were hesitant answering his. He nipped slightly on the lower one and followed her indrawn breath with his tongue.

''Sweet,'' he whispered.

He probed the corners of her mouth like a kid searching for the last taste of candy. He rubbed his mouth over hers, tasting her response, tangling with her velvet tongue. She smelled like nutmeg, like cotton sheets and sex. Her breathing was erratic now. He shaped her breasts with his hand, making a sound of rough pleasure at the tight little points pressing his palm.

''Yeah,'' he whispered. ''I like that.''

He took another kiss, warm and full-bodied, while his hands rubbed slow circles on her breasts. ''Do you like that?''

He plucked at the sensitive tip. She made a choked sound in the back of her throat, and her hands came up off the mattress to curl into his shoulders.

''Yeah, you like it, too.'' His hand slid down her belly, flirting with her navel, before it found its way between her thighs. ''How about this? You like it here?''

She arched. She liked it, all right. He stroked her, his touch firm, satisfaction burning up in his own building desire. And all the while his fingers worked her body, his tongue plied her mouth. Her legs moved restlessly to capture his. Her head tossed from side to side against the pillows. He shifted her against the crumpled covers, positioning himself between her thighs.

For an endless moment, he hovered over her, snared by the sight of her taut, flushed body, enmeshed by her scent, trapped by that exquisite little catch in her breath. So beautiful she could lure a sailor from his ship or the sun from the sky or a man from his purpose. So beautiful, and his.

Her eyes were still closed.

He shifted again, sliding down her silky slick body to the sweet heat between her thighs.

''I love this,'' he rasped, and put his mouth on her.

She almost came off the mattress.

She struggled, not against but toward him, close, closer, moaning now, moving. It wasn't enough. He wanted more of her. He wanted everything she had to give, every nuance of response, every hidden corner of her heart. He felt her muscles clench beneath him and around him, her hands fist in his hair. He drove her up, up, until he felt her topple, and caught her shuddering descent.

He was almost crazy for her, desperate, and hotly, heavily aroused. Dragging himself over her body, he laced his shaking fingers with hers.

''Open your eyes,'' he commanded. ''Damn you, look at me.''

Her eyes opened. Wide. Dark. Stunned.

He joined with her in one possessive stroke, staking his claim with his body. He took her. And she took him just as fiercely, as deeply and completely, seducing his senses, stealing a part of his soul. He was greedy. She was insatiable. When her inner shock waves began again, they carried him away like burning branches swept up in a flood.

Chapter 13

"**G**ood morning."

Con MacNeill padded in from the bathroom, a fluffy pink towel hitched around his waist and another draping his shoulders. He should have looked silly. He didn't. He looked good. He looked great, in fact, lean and dark and male, confident as a runway model with his broad hairy chest and her pink towels.

Val's insides pinched with wanting him and with doubt. What had she gotten herself into here?

"Sleepy?" His voice was deep with satisfaction.

She stretched between the wrinkled sheets, taking cautious inventory. Just looking at him made her blood flow thick and slow as molasses. And yet...and yet he'd certainly made himself at home in her apartment. Had he left her any hot water?

She rubbed her face with one hand. "What time is it?"

"Eight o'clock. I called your dad already. I'm going in to the bank today."

"You called him at home? From here?"

His eyes narrowed. "Why not? Does he trace his calls or something?"

"No. No, of course not." Feeling foolish, she started to fold back onto the pillows and then sat up again. "Do you want me to go with you?"

"Why?"

"Well, I...it is my business."

"It started as your business. If someone at the bank is falsifying bank records, it's gone beyond that now."

"But—"

He raised an eyebrow. "Need to keep an eye on me, Dixie?"

"Maybe I'm just trying to watch your back."

He smiled appreciatively, and some of the coolness left his eyes. "I'll handle it. I've got some paper to chase and some people to talk to. I'll give you a report at lunchtime."

Prowling to the bed, he sat on the edge of the mattress. The towel parted high on one side, exposing the pale skin of his upper leg, solid with muscle and dusted with rough hair. She yanked her gaze back to his face. Even relaxed from sex and sleep and steam, it was an intimidatingly intelligent face. Focused. Hard. The face of a man who would demand as much from any woman who loved him as he did of himself.

Recalling the way he'd evoked her response in bed last night, she shivered.

"Cold?" he asked silkily. "We could do something about that...."

He leaned in to kiss her, a long, sweet kiss. She could smell her shampoo on him and wanted him hot. She wanted him sweaty. She wanted to know she could get to him the way he got to her. Maybe the earth *had* moved for her last night. That didn't mean the ground rules had changed. She didn't want her objections brushed off with a kiss.

"I'm fine, thank you," she said politely.

"Can I get you something? Coffee?"

She tried to appreciate his consideration, tried not to feel like a guest in her own home. "I don't think I have any. Would you like a soda?"

She felt his faint, unmistakable recoil. "In the morning?"

Sylvia Cutler had always disdained her daughter's soda habit as lower-class. Val shrugged and anchored the sheet under her armpits. "It's caffeinated."

Con's look said clearly that there were more important considerations than caffeine.

She lifted her chin. "I could make tea."

He stood, adjusting the towel at his waist. "I'll put the kettle on for you. I don't do tea."

"Or there's beer," she drawled.

That earned her a sharp look. And then the mattress sank beneath his weight again as he sat beside her.

"D'you mind letting me in on our problem this morning?"

She pleated the top sheet. "Sorry. I just... All this just takes some getting used to."

He swore softly, tipping her chin up. "I knew I should go easier. Are you okay? Sore?"

His instant concern eased her chagrin. What *was* the problem, anyway? A lover most women would die for was sitting half-naked on her bed, and she was obsessing over beverage selections. It was possible her past experiences with men had made her a little too sensitive. Not to mention unfair.

"No. Maybe. It was— You were wonderful." She gave up fussing with the sheet to meet his gaze directly. "It's not having a man in my, my bed. Though you're right, I'm not used to that, either. It's having you in my apartment. My space." She disliked the sound of her own voice, prim and breathless, and forced a smile. "I'm not fit for company in the morning, I guess."

Con thought of the way Val had opened her home to Ann and Mitchell, the way her restaurant welcomed all comers, and struggled not to feel offended. "Well. I'll be out of your hair in a minute."

"No." She laid her fingers on his arm, detaining him with a touch. "It's not having you here. It's having you—" she pressed lightly "—*here*."

Con absorbed that.

Hell. She'd told him she wasn't in the market for a boyfriend. If she wanted to keep this thing between them on a purely physical level, he could do that. He could... His gut constricted. No, he couldn't. Whatever last night had meant to her, it had mattered too damn much to him to write it off as terrific sex.

"You're sorry I spent the night," he said at last, flatly.

"It's just going to take some getting used to, that's all," she repeated.

She made being with him sound like adjusting to braces or living with a debilitating disease.

"Thanks a lot."

"I'll buy coffee," she offered.

He stood and paced across the room. "I can buy my own damn coffee."

"I know."

The elegant dresser brought him up short. In the beveled glass he could see Val's reflection watching him doubtfully from her bed. The bed he'd carried her to. The bed he'd made love to her in.

His competitive streak and his pride demanded that he have this out with her now. Remembering the way her barriers had shattered at his touch, he was tempted to force the issue. Two falls out of three. Winner take all.

But her eyes were wide and wary, her face as beautiful and remote as the moon. He wanted to throw back his head and howl.

Yeah. Like *that* would reassure her.

"No flavours," he said.

"What?"

He turned around. "No mocha-Swiss-almond-decaffeinated stuff, okay? Just regular coffee."

She smiled faintly, and something eased between them, so that he caught himself smiling reluctantly back.

"I'll see what I can do," she promised.

Ruth Ann Minniton nudged the edge of her plate and frowned apologetically. "I'm sure it's very nice, dear. It's just not what I was expecting."

Val knew that. In fact, she was counting on it. Removing the offending plate, she offered a smile in return.

"Of course, Miss Ruth Ann. Why don't we let Doralee take this back to the kitchen for you, and I'll ask Steven to make you something else."

"Anything wrong?" a cool, deep voice inquired behind her.

Con.

She turned slowly. Just for an instant, at the sight of him, how big he was, how dark he was, there in her restaurant, her heart thumped in her chest. And then she got a grip. The last thing she wanted—this morning of all mornings, with their relationship on shaky new footing—was to lose it the minute the man walked into the room.

"Oh, nothing," she said breezily. "Just a little problem with today's side dishes."

He prowled forward, confident as a lion presented with a nice hunk of antelope. "What kind of problem?"

Doralee, sliding by to refill table five's iced tea, paused to top off Miss Minniton's glass. "Somebody decided to replace all our sides with french fries today," the waitress said. She arched her eyebrows. "You wouldn't know anything about that, would you?"

Con eyed Val warily. "French fries?"

She squelched a bubble of guilt. Mr. Business Solutions needed to learn he didn't have all the answers. "You told me to try it."

Doralee picked up her pitcher. "And the customers are not happy."

"Don't you worry, Doralee," Val said. "Mr. MacNeill told me to send any complaints to him."

Con narrowed his eyes at her. So he remembered. Good.

"It's not that I don't *like* french fries," Ruth Ann contributed in her soft, plaintive voice. "I'm just not in the mood for them today."

"Did you order fries?" Con asked.

"She didn't need to. Wild Thymes provides a side with all its lunch entrées," Val said.

Ruth Ann fluttered her fingers in appeal. "It's just not what I was expecting."

Con moved smoothly to take her plate from Val, his eyes meeting hers in brief acknowledgement. "I think I understand." He flashed his Big Bad Wolf smile at Ruth Ann, making half the women in the dining room sigh with envy. "When you come here, you expect something different."

Flattered by his attention, Ruth Ann confided, "That's it. I like that pasta salad. I didn't think I would, but I do. And that thing she does with the basil and potatoes? That's good."

"I like that myself," Con said. He slid the plate onto an empty table. "Let me see what's in the kitchen. And the next time you're in—" he pulled an order pad from the front pocket of Val's apron, scribbled something and presented it with a flourish "—lunch is on us."

The elderly woman beamed and clutched the slip of paper. "Ooh, well, really... How lovely."

Val stood by while Con shed his cool Yankee charm over the dining room and Ruth Ann preened and cooed. Finally, she picked up the rejected plate and carried it off to the kitchen.

Con followed her.

She ducked under his arm, extended to hold the door. "Free lunches?" she murmured, looking at him sideways.

"It's good public relations."

"It's expensive public relations."

"You can't put a price on client goodwill."

Val set the plate down on the long prep counter and pulled open the door to the walk-in refrigerator. "We may have to. I've got four tables with complaints, two that sent their meals back and one that up and left because fatty foods offend her. Who's going to pay for all this goodwill?"

"I am."

She dumped a tray of gingered carrots—prepared ahead of time for last-minute substitutions—on the counter and turned to face him. "Is that in your job description?"

He regarded her cooly down his not-quite-straight nose. "I like to provide full service."

Yes, he did. Memories of the night before assailed her: his devastating thoroughness, her needy response.

Swallowing, she replied, "Well, you may have to. Goodness knows I can't afford to."

"I'm aware of that," Con said stiffly.

She frowned. She'd intended to tease him, to remind them both that she was still in control of her restaurant and herself. But there was a set to his mouth and shoulders that worried her. "What's wrong?"

He glanced around the kitchen, at Ronnie shaking flour into the chugging mixer, at Steven turning vegetables on the grill.

"We can go into it later."

"Go into it now," she said. "They can't hear us."

"Don't you want to wait until you're less…distracted?"

"For your information, it's only men who can't work and listen at the same time. Women are used to doing more than two things at once. We're genetically programmed for it or something."

A corner of his mouth quirked, but the smile didn't touch his eyes. "Pretty sexist."

"Coming from you, I'll take that as a compliment." She dished up. "So, what happened at the bank?"

"Nothing."

"I don't appreciate being kept in the dark, MacNeill."

"I'm not keeping you in the dark." Frustration edged his voice. "I'm reporting what I found. Nothing. Nada. Zip."

Unease prickled her skin like a chill. She put Ruth Ann's plate up on the counter for Doralee to collect and re-covered the carrots with plastic wrap. "What sort of thing were you looking for?"

"Evidence. Some kind of proof that someone diddled your accounts. There isn't any. Only the one unjustified debit, which Cross corrected."

"Rob corrected it?"

"After I called him on it. Remember? The teller mis-added your receipts, and his department didn't catch it. Hey, mistakes happen."

She pulled a bowl of peppers toward her and began to gut them to go on the grill. "That's what you said when you took over adding the daily deposits."

"And that's why. But when I went back to the bank to-day, a lot of the original receipts from your restaurant that should have been with the cash-in tickets were gone. Missing. That tipped me off. And I got even more suspicious when I saw that for more than half the days they're missing, you had lower-than-average deposits." Con leaned against the counter, crossing his arms against his chest. "What I can't figure is whether Cross is covering up bad bookkeeping or outright theft."

She was confused. "You mean someone withdrew money from my account?"

"No. That would leave a trail. This is even simpler. Like taking money from the till. What I'm thinking is someone kept out cash when you made your deposits."

"Could Rob do that?"

"Sure. He had the means. But then, so did anyone at the

bank with access to your deposit bag.'' Con's eyes were bleak. ''What I can't nail down is when he had the opportunity. No one remembers the vice president of the proof department playing teller in the lobby.''

Tension rolled from him like steam off ice. He'd staked his bonus, his job and his future on proving that her money problems were not her fault, and he had no hard evidence.

Val set down her knife. ''Donna,'' she said suddenly.

''What?''

''Maybe Rob had help. Ann told me her husband was cheating on her with Donna from the bank.''

Con lifted an eyebrow. ''One of the tellers? That would certainly provide him with the means. I'll talk with her tomorrow.''

He didn't sound hopeful. She didn't blame him.

''Of course, we've still got the problem of motive,'' he added. ''Cross is a bully and a jackass, but it's hard to see what he hoped to gain by screwing you.''

Val concentrated on making perfect strips of peppers, like slashes of colored confetti. ''Money?''

''Could be. He got any expensive habits you know about? Gambling? Drugs?''

''No. Nothing like that.'' She squelched her distaste. ''He *is* having an affair.''

''Yeah, well, unless his girlfriend charges for the kinky stuff, I don't see him needing an extra twenty thou a year for that.''

Val bit her lip and was silent.

''If there were something else…'' Con's fingers drummed an impatient tattoo on the counter. ''Does Cross have a problem with his wife working at your place?''

Val bent her head over the cutting board. ''I don't know. He wouldn't let her accept a salary, but he never objected to her coming to the restaurant. He encouraged her, actually.''

''Why, do you think?''

She shrugged. She'd been too grateful for Ann's liberty to question it. "It was a...connection."

Con's eyes narrowed. "Are you telling me that after all these years Cross is still carrying a torch for you?"

The notion made her queasy. "No. Oh, no. The opposite, in fact. He dislikes me. But he doesn't like letting go. And we were nearly engaged once."

"Yeah, well, I *was* engaged, and I can't imagine a less fascinating project than keeping up with my ex-fiancée." He looked briefly surprised by the discovery before he refocused on her. "Come on, Dixie. Help me out here. Why would Cross want to put the squeeze on you?"

Across the kitchen, the mixer thumped. The range fan clicked and buzzed. Val's pulse thundered in her ears. She felt boxed in between the refrigerator and the worktable, trapped between reluctance to resurrect her teenage ghost and the knowledge that Con wasn't going to stop. A rational man, he would seek the reassurance of facts, looking for answers, picking her responses apart.

She positioned the knife over the cutting board. Her knuckles on the handle were nearly white.

"Because I got away," she said.

From the corner of her eye, she could see Con watching her, his casual pose at odds with his almost unnatural stillness. Beneath her knife, the peppers glistened, red and yellow and green. Her stomach almost heaved in protest.

"Explain." The single word rang between them like a pot dropped on a hard tile floor.

She drew a deep breath, steadying her voice and the blade. "Because before I left for New York, Rob tried really hard to make me stay, all right? He was my boyfriend, remember. Three years older than me. He figured he had the right to stop me. He figured he had the right to do anything he wanted."

Con never moved. But the very quality of his stillness changed. He froze as cold and solid as a glacier, and anger emanated from him in waves as chill as the air that rolled from the refrigerator. Standing in the warm, close kitchen, Val felt goose bumps prickle along her arms.

"You said he never hit you," Con said.

"He didn't."

She hadn't made it necessary. She'd only said "No" and "Stop," and once, she was pretty sure, "Please don't."

That was one of the hardest things she'd had to face and overcome since, that "please." Because "stop" and "no" hadn't been enough, and she hadn't fought Rob hard enough to make it necessary for him to hit her to get his way.

"I was stupid," she said. "We'd been arguing. He'd been drinking. I should have known better than to get in his car."

Con expressed his opinion of that in one tight word. "Maybe trusting yourself alone with a jerk is bad judgment. But forcing a woman against her will is a felony."

She was stunned by his swift understanding, by his immediate support. Tears pricked her eyes. And then he ruined it.

"I'll kill him," he said, very quietly.

She shivered. "No. I've dealt with it. I'll deal with him."

"You haven't dealt with it. The bastard is still alive."

She put up her chin. "And so am I. I'm not claiming victim status. I won't be defined by something that happened to me nine years ago."

"Nine?"

"Years ago. It wasn't even really…" But she'd spent too many years working through the trauma to lie. "It's ancient history," she finished firmly.

"So, you were, what? Eighteen?"

"Seventeen."

He pushed away from the side of the refrigerator, radiating suppressed violence. "I'll kill him."

"You will *not*." She slammed the knife down into the board.

The sound made Steven turn around. Con scowled at him, and the cook turned hastily away.

Val lowered her voice. "I'm not letting you turn this into some macho demonstration of don't-mess-with-my-woman. If Rob is abusing his position at the bank, we need a long-term solution."

"I'll bury him," he said through white, even teeth. "That's a permanent solution."

"It's not a solution at all." She struggled to take charge. Healing was learning to be in charge again. "We need something we can take to my father and the police. What happened to me is only relevant to the extent that it sheds some light on motive."

"It's damn relevant to me."

Val didn't like his assumption that she was still somehow a victim. She felt him snatching control of what had happened to her, relegating her to the needy, brutalized girl who'd fled home nine years ago. She was beyond that.

"Well, that's too bad. This isn't about you. This is about me, and I've put it behind me."

He froze. There was a savage look in his eyes that was almost like hurt. But his voice when he spoke was soft and sneering.

"Fine. That makes things real clear. I'm not supposed to get involved in something that's 'about you.' But what about your friend Ann? What about the next woman Cross decides to abuse? Am I allowed to get involved then?"

Her hands were shaking. She hid them in her apron. "You're misunderstanding me. I appreciate what you've done for Ann. What you're trying to do for me. But does it really make a difference to us, to you, something that was over nine years ago?"

"Hell, yes, it makes a difference."

He might as well have socked her in the jaw. Her head snapped back. Her eyes burned with tears. She'd wanted to think—she'd fooled herself into thinking—that because Con had met her as the woman she'd become, he wouldn't be concerned with who she'd been: a frightened teen running from what her parents would think, running from what the town would say, running from what Rob insisted were her only options....

Because Con had given her choices, because he'd respected her decisions, Val had imagined one episode of coerced sex with an angry high school boyfriend wouldn't make a difference to him when he looked at her now.

Who was she kidding?

Of course it made a difference.

"Val, I..." Ann Cross rounded the bank of shelves and stopped dead in the aisle. "I'm sorry. Am I interrupting?"

"No," Val said.

"Yes," Con snapped at the same time. Ann flinched, and he visibly clamped a lid on his temper.

"No," he corrected himself. He treated her to a dose of the patented MacNeill smile, half-strength but still remarkably potent. "First day on the new job, right? You go on ahead. I've got work to do." He leveled a look at Val, the smile fading.

"We'll talk," he warned her. "Later."

She fought the sick lurch of her stomach. She could hardly wait.

Chapter 14

"Come on," Con ordered. "We're getting out of here."

Val straightened stiffly from wiping down a lunch table, one hand to her aching back. The dining room was empty. Steven had already clocked out, and Ann had gone home—back to the shelter, Val corrected herself. Con braced open the swinging kitchen door, alert and impeccable in pressed khaki pants and a crisp blue shirt that matched his eyes. Val almost cried with frustration. She was dog-tired and dirty, in no shape to go a couple of rounds with the Yankee contender and in no mood to be pushed around.

She brushed her hair from her face. "And going where?"

Threading his way through the tables, he took the rag from her hand and tossed it on a nearby serving cart. "My brother's for dinner. They're expecting us around five."

She didn't need his pity invitation. She could feed herself. She could take care of herself. "I didn't agree to dinner at your brother's."

"Sure you did. Yesterday, in your office." He got behind

her and tugged at her apron strings, putting her braid over her shoulder.

He was being nice again, she thought crossly. It made him harder to resist. "When you got back from Boston, you said."

He turned her around and lifted the apron over her head. "Yeah, well, I called my sister-in-law, and they're free tonight."

She pulled down the apron to get a better look at his face, sure she'd been set up. Con's expression was just a little too straight to be innocent. And then his mouth crooked. Not innocent at all. But she felt herself softening, anyway.

"Please?" he coaxed. "You're going to love them."

She frowned, annoyed at the way her heart responded to his persuasion after his caveman act that afternoon, irritated by her worry that she would somehow fall short in his eyes, in the eyes of his family. She couldn't even impress her own mother.

"But are they going to love *me?*" she muttered, wadding up the apron between them.

"Relax." His thumbs rubbed over her shoulders before he released her. "It'll be fun. You need the night off."

She needed something. And what did it matter, what the MacNeills thought of her? Once Con went back to Boston she would never see these people again. Funny how that thought failed to soothe her.

At least if they were at his brother's, Con wouldn't be prowling the streets hunting for Rob and looking for a fight or quizzing her on her past relationships.

"I have to go change," she announced.

"Are you asking for my help?"

She ignored the lick of excitement she felt at his suggestion and tipped her head to one side. "When did you say we were expected?"

He laughed. "Five o'clock. No time, then. Go on. I'll wait."

She hurried upstairs to dress and then wasted precious minutes scowling at the contents of her closet. So what did you wear to meet the family of a man who dressed like he'd stepped out of a glossy ad page in *GQ?* She finally settled on a long full flowered skirt, a skinny white ribbed top with narrow straps, silver hoops and silver bracelets and a peacock feather earring.

His eyes kindled, tiny pilot lights deep within the blue, as she approached him down the stairs. "Very nice."

Val lifted her chin. "Thank you," she said, and followed him out to his car.

She wasn't a car person, but the Jaguar impressed her, with its sleek lines and contained energy. High maintenance, she reminded herself. Like its owner. She didn't have room in her life to tend either one.

Still, there was something seductive about all that understated drive. The car wrapped her in comfort, deep seats, smooth leather, soft music playing from the radio. The road was a hum, the landscape a blur. Con's long, lean hands clasped the wheel with easy control. His profile as he scanned the road was hard and a little intent. She remembered his absorbed expression as he moved strongly on her and in her, and pressed her knees together.

The car crested a hill and swooped down a hollow. Val gazed out her window at a spreading ancient oak and the tangled glory of summer roses. Through the windshield up ahead she could see a white farmhouse on a hill and a pale-coated dog and a child playing in the sunshine.

It was a dream of all a home should be, a vision of domestic perfection, warmer and more welcoming than her parents' showcase house.

And the man coming down the porch steps as the car pulled up the graveled drive completed the fantasy.

Con glanced over at her. She didn't think the drool showed on her chin, but his eyes narrowed. "Forget it, Dixie. He's married."

Secretly amused, she glanced from one dark-haired, blue-eyed, beautifully built male to the other. ''Your brother?''

''One of them.''

Con got out of the car. Val had both feet flat on the gravel before she realized he'd come around to open her door. With a little shrug, she accepted his guiding touch on her elbow and preceded him up the walk.

''You must be Val.'' Patrick MacNeill offered her his hand and a smile. ''Kate'll be right down. She just got off rounds.''

''It's very nice of you to invite me. I—''

A small, sturdy boy in jean shorts and a Michael Jordan jersey came running up from the yard, the dog bounding at his heels. Close up, Val could see that beneath the brim of his baseball cap the whole left side of his face was puckered and scarred. The result of a long-ago car accident, Con had explained on the drive over.

''Uncle Con!''

''Yo, buddy.''

The two embraced before Patrick drew the child to him with an arm around his shoulders. ''This is my son, Jack.''

Val smiled into the MacNeill blue eyes that watched her intelligently from the boy's scarred face. ''I could have guessed. He looks like you. Like both of you.''

The child's watchfulness dissolved into the MacNeill grin. ''That's what Mom says.''

Con's look of quiet approval brushed her like a kiss.

The screen door opened behind them and another early-model MacNeill stepped out on the porch. Val looked up. And up. This version was even taller than Con, younger, leaner and less finished than Patrick. He wore his dark hair longer than his brothers', and a small gold hoop in his ear like a pirate.

''Well, hi there, pretty lady. I thought I heard the muscle mobile.''

''Hell,'' Con said. ''Who invited him?''

Patrick shrugged. "Kate let it slip you two were coming. He invited himself."

The pirate possessed himself of Val's hand and assessed her with impudent brown eyes. "So, you're the woman the Boy Genius is so eager to keep to himself."

Val bit down on a smile. "I take it this one's not married?" she murmured to Con.

Patrick overheard. "No one can catch him," he explained.

Con snorted. "No woman in her right mind would *want* him."

"Don't listen to them," the pirate urged. "They're just jealous."

"I can see how that must be a constant problem for you," Val drawled.

The younger man laughed. "You'll do," he said. "I'm Sean."

"Val Cutler."

"Nice to meet you." He sounded like he meant it.

"You can let go of her hand now," Con said.

"Are they here?" a woman's voice called from inside the house, and the screen door opened again.

Val drew in her breath. The MacNeill men had not intimidated her. This MacNeill woman did.

Dr. Kate MacNeill was small and neat and proudly pregnant in a pale blue tailored jumper that managed to look both comfortable and expensive. She had masses of curling light brown hair, astute brown eyes, and a diamond on her left hand that flashed like the Cape Hatteras lighthouse. In her flowing skirt and bangles Val felt like a thirteen-year-old pressed into passing canapes at one of her parents' parties: conspicuous and young and underdressed.

"Welcome," her hostess said warmly. "I'm so glad Con brought you. Has anyone offered you a drink yet?"

There was a general shuffle on the porch.

"Let me—"

"Would you like—"

"I'll get it."

"Sean," Kate said firmly. "Would you get Val something to drink? And bring me a lemonade, please, while you're in there."

"Sure thing, gorgeous." The pirate stooped to kiss his sister-in-law's cheek and then looked at Val. "What'll you have?"

"Lemonade sounds wonderful."

Val wasn't sure just what she'd expected from the gathered MacNeills, but what struck her was their clannish unity. It was evident in the way Patrick cradled his pregnant wife, the confiding way she leaned into his arm, the breezy insults and casual gossip exchanged between brothers. The conversation was noisy and general. Upright on the swing, Val sat a little apart as they laughed and joked and drank beer.

Crayons were scattered across the planked porch floor. Jack drew, sprawled on his stomach by the steps, getting up every now and then to chart his picture's progress with his mother. Stepmother, Val reminded herself. Con had shared a little of his brother's family history in the car. But the obvious, poignant bond between Jack and Kate MacNeill constricted Val's throat.

Observing them, she realized that here was the other reason behind that I-can-eat-the-world assurance of Con's that had set up her back at their first meeting. Love. His confidence sprang from this family foundation of casual love and support. She had nothing to compare it to but silent breakfasts and angry afternoons and evenings she'd been banished to her room for unacceptable dress or behavior.

She was, she realized, jealous.

Patrick hooked another bottle from the ice-filled cooler and handed it off to Con, lazing on the swing beside her. "So, how's the Comeback Kid?"

Con shrugged and twisted off the cap. "I'm doing all right. Wainbridge called on Sunday. I'm still in the running for the Ventucom job.'' That was news to Val. She listened intently.

''You don't sound so enthusiastic, bro,'' Patrick observed.

''They want me, that's the important thing.''

''Yeah, yeah, everybody wants you,'' Sean teased. ''Harvard man.''

''Your mother would be glad to have you back in Boston,'' Kate said.

''Yeah.''

''You could stay down here,'' Patrick observed. ''Keep at the consultant shtick.''

''Play in the minors?'' Con smiled but shook his head. ''That's not for me.''

''I thought you liked being your own boss,'' Sean said.

''I do, actually. More than I thought I would. I like the whole business of working with a client to solve a specific problem. It's just…'' Con shrugged.

Val couldn't sit silent any longer. '' 'He who dies with the most toys wins'?'' she quoted back at him dryly.

Everyone turned to look at her. She felt the quick wash of heat sweep from her collarbone to the roots of her hair. But surrounded by Con's laughing, quarreling, normal family, she could not contain her indignation. They were the real prize, the true measure of his success. How could he not see that? How could he not want that?

''You have so much more to offer than that,'' she said.

Con's eyes glinted beneath lowered lids. ''As I recall, you weren't all that thrilled with my interfering in *your* business.''

She raised her chin at his challenge. The glass sweating in her lap helped her ignore her clammy palms. ''That was before I knew what you could do. Maybe we both need to adjust our expectations.''

Patrick saluted her with his bottle. ''I like the way this one thinks.''

''I like the way this one looks,'' Sean said.

Con turned his head, allowing Val to catch her breath. "You like her too much and I'll break both your arms."

"I'm shaking. You hear anything from Lynn?" Sean asked.

"Sean…" Kate protested.

"Last I heard, she was getting married." Con raised his bottle. "To her happiness."

"I'll drink to the poor bastard she's marrying," Sean said.

"Cut it out, Sean," Patrick ordered. "Though I'll agree. You're well out of that one."

Val sat back shakily. It was none of her business, she reminded herself. None of her business who Con saw or where he went or whether he placed a proper value on himself. She'd known all along he wouldn't stay.

And then his hand, strong and sure, closed over her thigh. Surprised, she glanced over to find him watching her with a look in his eyes that stopped her breathing again. It was more than simple physical need this time. Question, demand, acknowledgment—all lapped at her defenses, undermined her assumptions.

"You could be right," he said.

To her? Or to Patrick?

His brother cleared his throat. "I need to get dinner pulled together. You two can give me a hand."

Val surfaced and started to stand.

Kate shook her head. "He means the guys," Patrick's wife told her. "I don't cook very often, and Con says you cook too much. Besides, Patrick keeps telling me I need to take it easy."

Well. That was different. Val subsided on the swing as Con got up and followed his brothers into the house.

Kate turned her head to watch her husband disappear through the doorway. The naked intimacy in her eyes touched a chord that shook Val's heart. What would it be like, she wondered wistfully, to love and be loved like that?

The woman turned around awkwardly in her rocking chair

and then flushed. ''I suppose you think we're pretty odd. Or that I'm pretty lazy.''

''No,'' Val said honestly. ''It's nice. It's just that my parents... It's just not what I'm used to.''

''Mmm. I'll let you in on a secret. Me, neither.'' Val's confusion must have shown, because Kate smiled and explained.

''Patrick and I haven't been married that long. Eighteen months ago, all I had in my life was my work. I certainly never dreamed I'd find myself—'' her hand encompassed it all, the porch, the scribbling child and the man who'd just left them, before coming to rest on her burgeoning belly ''—here.''

''Well, it's obvious you belong now.''

Kate laughed. ''What do they say? Love changes everything?''

Val turned the silver bracelets on her arm. ''I don't think that's really true. I think it must take a very strong woman to hold her own against one of the MacNeill men.''

''It's not a tug-of-war. The MacNeills pull together.''

''That's true for you and Patrick, maybe.''

Kate's brown eyes were shrewd and amused. ''Don't underestimate yourself. And don't underestimate our Con, either.''

As if summoned by her words, Con appeared in the darkness behind the screen. ''Dinner's ready, Kate.''

She started to lumber to her feet. With quick grace, he was through the door and beside her to help her up. She thanked him and then smiled at Val.

''See? He's good at support.''

Watching Con's tender care of his pregnant sister-in-law, Val acknowledged Kate was right. He was good at giving support. But he was good at lots of things. That didn't mean he would put his ambition aside to offer her his unconditional and permanent support.

She tugged thoughtfully on her feathered earring. And

even if he did, was she, with her fear of coercion, her untidy bundle of independence and insecurities, any good at accepting it?

She looked good at his brother's table, Con thought. She fit in. It wasn't her perfect manners, and it sure as hell wasn't her earring. She passed potato salad and teased with Sean and mopped Jack's spilled milk all without missing a beat. He watched her gradually relax and expand, and pride in her filled his chest so bad the pressure hurt his heart.

Eight hours ago, he'd wanted to slake his rage and frustration with Rob Cross's blood. He'd been primed to find solutions and spoiling for a fight. But Val hadn't asked him for answers. She sure as hell hadn't requested his Neanderthal routine. For the first time in his life, what he wanted had to take the back seat to what another person needed.

She'd needed something else.

He'd needed to give her something else.

Watching Val unwind, watching the brittle belle and flamboyant flower child slowly soften into her natural, genuine warmth, he thought maybe he had. But whatever he'd managed to give her, it couldn't equal the soul-deep satisfaction he felt seeing her in the midst of his family.

The realization should have worried him. He had a job waiting for him in Boston. He wasn't looking for a nice Southern girl to bring home to mother. And the nice girl in the peacock feather who'd just charmed the pants off his brothers had told him in no uncertain terms she wasn't looking for a permanent relationship.

But later, driving her home, he asked anyway, prompted by a little demon of possessiveness he would have denied a year ago. A month ago. Hell, two weeks ago. He hadn't met her two weeks ago. "Have a good time?"

"I did." He would not, he promised himself, be offended by her note of surprise. "I liked them."

"They liked you."

She turned her head on the leather headrest. Even in the dark, he could see her smile. "Sean would like anything that wore a skirt and was under eighty-five."

"No. Sean likes them over eighty-five, too."

Her sultry chuckle raised the hair on his nape and his body lower down. The tires rumbled as the white lines in the road flashed by. Night rushed through the lowered windows. He could smell rain approaching and nearer, wilder, Val's perfume.

"I got along with your sister-in-law," she volunteered.

The slight rise in her voice betrayed her unspoken need for reassurance. It cracked him wide open. She created depths inside him he'd never known existed, caverns of hunger, chasms of yearning. One little push was all it would take to tumble him.

"Yeah," he answered absently. "Patrick did all right there."

"'All right'? Is that supposed to be a compliment?"

"Better be. He said I did all right, too."

The scent of her reached him through the darkness, making his nostrils flare. He didn't want to talk about his family any longer. He wanted to immerse himself in her. He wanted to focus her attention on him, and only him.

Con prided himself on taking the quickest, surest road to success. He never figured on following an irresistible detour through Dixieland. But he switched lanes, anyway, signaled and took the next turnoff.

Val sat up. "Where are we going?"

He glanced over at her, her face pale in the reflected glow of the dashboard. Tonight, he wanted off the fast track. He wanted to pull over with Val in the front seat and explore every curve, every dip, every scenic view North Carolina had to offer. He wanted…

"I figured I'd take you to my motel."

She relaxed at his casual tone, her lips curving. "I've never been to a motel with a man before."

His heart was hammering so loud he was surprised she couldn't hear it. "Yeah, well, I wanted to be your first."

She didn't answer him right away, her silver bracelets chiming faintly as she clasped and unclasped her hands in her lap. "It's a little late for that," she said finally, tightly.

"We can pretend."

"We're already lovers, MacNeill. You don't need to do the big seduction scene with me."

It was starting to rain. The fine mist on the windshield sparkled as he drove under the lit motel sign. He flicked on the wipers, and the moisture collected in streaks and ran down like tears.

"Maybe I want to."

Beyer's Motel straddled the asphalt beside I-40, a low brick relic of the fifties with noisy air conditioners in all the windows. But it was cheap, and it was clean. Tall pines sheltered it from the worst rumble of trucks, and Con's back window looked out on a wooded lot that sloped down to a creek.

He pulled into a parking spot, the tires sighing on the wet blacktop.

"This is silly," Val said.

She looked so young. She sounded so uncertain. He pulled the keys from the ignition, hunger and tenderness twisting inside him.

"Am I going too fast for you? You want to make out in the car first?"

She snorted with laughter. "Oh, that's smooth, MacNeill. Very smooth."

Relieved, he grinned. "Or I could take you down to the gazebo, show you the river by night."

"There's a gazebo?"

"Down by the creek, yeah. If you don't mind spiders."

She arched her eyebrows. "Am I supposed to shriek 'eek' and rush into your motel room now?"

He walked around the hood of the car, then opened her

door. "Only if you feel like it. You could just bat your eyelashes and admit my general usefulness for creepy crawly removal."

"I think I've fed your ego enough for one day."

There it was again, the wry note, the distance, the toughness she inserted between them like a knife. It irritated him. What was she protecting herself from?

I'm not claiming victim status. I won't be defined by something that happened to me nine years ago.

She stood under the glow of the motel lights, her chin raised and that cool and secret smile curving her mouth, waiting for him to lock his car and make love to her in a rented room.

And it wasn't enough.

He'd been too greedy, that was the problem. Too attracted by her beauty and independence, her humor and warmth, to pay attention to her essential loneliness. He'd been too blinded by his fascination to notice her need. She'd had too little cherishing in her life and damn little tenderness from him.

He would make up for it, he vowed. Tonight, he would give her both.

He held out his hand. "Let's walk, then."

She looked surprised, but she let him take her hand. He hoped he could find his way in the dark.

The path picked up just beyond the end unit, zigged beside a rusting playground and zagged into the trees. Some manager with dreams of family vacations and summer picnics must have constructed it in the hotel's heyday. It was crumbling underfoot now, unlit and deserted. But it was private and peaceful and all Con had to offer.

Like a fairy fashioned of fog and night, Val glided along the overgrown path beside him. Only her hand curled in his was warm and real and trembled slightly.

He'd insisted on giving her his protection. He'd pushed her into sharing his family. It wasn't enough. Tonight, he wanted to give her himself, to fill up all the lonely places and heal the hurting ones.

At the bottom of the path, the stream rent the canopy of trees. High above them, the moon floated on a bank of cloud, hazy in the humid air, sparkling on black water. The old gazebo was a deeper shadow in the dark night. Con felt the moisture on his skin. He half-expected it to steam, he was getting so hot. But he pushed the thought away, concentrating on control, struggling for tenderness.

Tonight was for her.

She wore the mist in her hair like diamonds. He stopped and cupped her delicate jaw and kissed the dampness from her cheek.

She stepped closer, lifting on tiptoe, so that her peaked breasts pressed his chest and her thighs pressed his legs. He shivered with temptation. He forced himself not to take, did his damnedest not to rush.

I wanted to be your first.

To be the first. To be the one and only.

And so he gently kissed her mouth and then trailed his lips up smooth, moist skin to kiss her eyelids closed. Murmuring appreciation, she shifted to give him access to her breasts. With an effort, he disregarded her invitation, continuing to kiss her as if he had all the time and patience in the world.

He traced the seam of her lips with his tongue before dipping inside, exploring the sweet, slick inner surface and the sharp, smooth edges of her teeth. She opened, urging him in, urging him on, her arms wrapping around his neck, her fingers threading through his hair. The sensual tug against his scalp dragged at his control. His body hardened.

He grabbed at his fading resolve, bypassing the seduction of her lush mouth to string a line of tiny kisses down her neck to the place where her pulse beat hard and fast. He laved it and then blew on the spot. She whimpered. Even in the shadows, he could see the raised outline of her nipples under the clinging white top.

He returned his attention to her mouth, brushing her lips with kisses, soft kisses, sweet kisses, tender kisses. Her hands reached back into his hair and tugged hard, in earnest.

"Ouch." He lifted his head and glared at her. "What are you doing?"

"What are *you* doing?"

"Kissing you."

She tossed her head. "So, kiss me. Don't treat me like a fourteen-year-old out on her first date."

He stiffened. "Don't treat you with respect? Don't treat you with tenderness?"

"*Don't* treat me like a victim."

Even in the darkness, he could see tears standing in her eyes. They quenched his anger as effectively as flood. His arms fell away from her.

"Is that so bad?" he asked her quietly. "What the hell did someone ever do or say to you, that you want me to pretend what happened to you never happened?"

Chapter 15

Val moved away to look over the ribbon of water, her profile pale in reflected moonlight, her skirt a whisper in the darkness.

"You don't get it, do you? Because that's why Rob did it. To change me, inside."

Con's jaw ached. He realized he was grinding his back molars and exhaled slowly through his teeth. He wanted to shout, wanted to explode, and all he could do was stand there and wait for her to deliver the rest of her story, like a punch to his gut.

"Rob wanted things to stay the way they were," she explained. "He was finishing at State, he had the job lined up with my father. He wanted us to get married. My parents wanted us to get married. And I was threatening all that."

She crossed her arms over her stomach, as if she were cold. She wasn't cold. The night air was warm and soft. Three feet and a hundred miles away from her, Con was sweating.

She licked her lips and continued. "He told me I didn't

know what I wanted. He told me I didn't have a choice, that he'd make sure I didn't have a choice. He wanted me to get pregnant, he said.''

Con moved toward her instinctively. ''Oh, God, sweetheart—''

She shook her head, and he froze.

''I cried. I said I'd tell my parents, and he said they wouldn't believe me. I was so confused. So ashamed. I mean, I'd gone with him, and it wasn't as if we hadn't done it before.'' Her voice was higher and bewildered, a young girl's voice. ''I didn't know what to do. And Rob said it didn't matter. I'd come to my senses, he said.'' Even with her face turned away from him, Con saw her throat move convulsively. ''Whatever had happened, it didn't make a difference.''

''So what did you...'' He broke off, swallowing futile rage and an aching desire to help. But he was years too late. She'd already cut loose from her boyfriend's coercion and her parents' expectations, made a life and a career for herself and come back when she was old enough and strong enough to tackle the bunch. Admiration for her filled him.

''Do?'' Val shrugged, pale shoulders gleaming in the near dark. ''I decided he was right. I decided what happened wasn't going to make a difference to who I was or what I wanted.''

She drew a ragged breath and turned back toward him. ''Only it does, to you. When you look at me now, when you kiss me now that you know, I'm different in your eyes.'' The bleakness in her voice tore at his heart. ''Now I'm a victim.''

So, she'd left him something to do after all. Now that she was open and hurting and vulnerable, he could tell her she was wrong.

''Not a victim.'' He took a cautious step across the splintery plank floor, feeling his way. ''You're a survivor.''

She sniffed, but she didn't back away. "Then what was the kid-glove treatment about?"

Logic wouldn't help him here. He was going with his gut, leading with his heart, and it terrified him. He risked a touch on her shoulder, running a finger along one of those skinny spaghetti straps. "Foreplay?"

She regarded him a moment, eyes luminous in the dark, and then her smile wobbled to life. Relief squeezed his chest.

"As long as it wasn't therapy," she said.

"Nope."

He gathered her to him by slow degrees, his hand on her shoulder, his arm at her back, his kiss in her hair. With a sigh, she relaxed her neck and let her head rest against his chest. They stood like that a long, long time, and it was good. It was nearly enough.

But she was in his arms, warm and close against the front of him, and rising in his blood. He could feel the pressure building and the longing in his unruly body. And he made his hands be still and his arms be loose, but he could do nothing about the pounding of his heart beneath her ear or the slow, helpless rise of his desire.

She murmured and moved against him and pressed a kiss to the center of his chest.

Last night he'd been in control of himself and her response. Tonight, in her need, she destroyed his restraint.

He sucked in his breath. "Dixie…" he warned.

She stood on tiptoe and bit the point of his chin. He laughed shakily while his blood pressure threatened to blow off the top of his head. "Sweetheart…"

Her hands moved sneakily around and over him. She was quick and hungry and irresistible. He tried to be careful of her and tender, stripping his shirt to lay on the damp plank bench, trying to take the time to arouse her with his kisses, to ready her with his touch. But she was urgent, almost fretful in her impatience to get closer.

She pushed him back on the bench and straddled him, her

rapid hands dispensing with his belt and zipper. Feeling her warm and naked and curved against him—when the hell had she ditched her panties?—he almost lost his mind.

"Protection," he groaned.

She wiggled against him. "Do you have any?"

"Pocket."

She dug for it. He grit his teeth, mentally calculating this year's taxes, last year's taxes…

She sat back, flushed and triumphant, waving his wallet. She flipped it open. "That's what I love about you business types. Always prepared."

Thinking she'd find it funny, hoping to buy time to regain his breath and control, he told her, "Actually, Sean offered me some."

"Oh." Her head lifted. Her teeth worried her bottom lip. "Is that… Did you take them?"

He lifted his billfold from her, finding the foil packet inside. "No."

Ever so slightly, she relaxed above him. "Why not?"

Because, he almost said, a man doesn't do that to the woman in his life. He doesn't expose the woman he loves to another man, even a brother.

"They were blue," he explained instead.

He felt the vibration of her laughter and then she fastened her mouth to his. Her kiss was hot. Her skin was damp with perspiration. Her hands trailed fire down his chest to where his pants gaped open. He was burning for her, desperate.

He fumbled with the condom while she hovered above him, tempting, close. And then he was covered. He reached under her skirt. Grabbing her soft, smooth, luscious rear with both hands, he thrust up and into her, groaning at the perfect fit, the snug, wet clasp of her perfect body.

She rode him with sharp, sweet little cries, her knees on either side of his thighs and her skirt spread out around them. The wind picked up, sliding over naked skin, stirring the curtain of her hair. A cloud scudded over the moon, deepening the darkness. Her breasts rose and fell. Her hips moved busily up and down, and her breath rushed in soft, hot pants against his face. He couldn't breathe. He couldn't think. He couldn't stop.

He was wrapped in her so tightly it was no longer possible to tell where he left off and she began, no giving and taking, only joining and need. She gasped and arched. He groaned and thrust, again and again, deep and deeper, losing himself inside her. Somewhere outside, the rain began, sighing on the trees, tapping on the roof, but it was nothing compared to this storm inside. It gathered and broke. She clutched at him, her shudders shaking him at the root and to the heart.

With a force that jerked them both, he poured himself into her.

Smiling, Val rolled over, radiating well-being from her toes to her fingertips, stretching between the motel sheets. Con's unfeigned and uncontrolled response last night had tumbled the last barriers of her mistrust. He'd done more than let her claim him; he'd restored to her her own feminine power. Straddling him in the damp night, in the dark gazebo between the summer bank and the silent moon, she'd felt like a goddess. Inside she was molten, liquid and changed.

But the unreserved sharing, the mingling of their breaths and bodies and souls, had left her in some ways more vulnerable than ever.

Con had restored her confidence and stolen her heart.

He was already up, bending beside the bed to set a plastic tray on the laminate table. The scent of coffee—full and strong and not at all what she was used to in the mornings—teased her. His blue gaze met and held hers. A sizzle of memory, a shiver of greed, quivered through her.

Oh, my.

She glanced at the tray. Two lidded cups steamed side by side. A bottle of orange juice chilled in the motel ice bucket. The devised domesticity of the setup should have disturbed her. She'd never planned on playing house with Mr. Business Solutions. But the makeshift breakfast tray looked charming and felt oddly right.

She moistened her lips. "This is nice."

"This is nothing." He sat on the edge of the mattress, pulling the covers tight across her stomach. "I took a run to the convenience store."

Literally took a run, she saw. His gray T-shirt molded his chest. His short styled hair curled into the back of his neck. He smelled of sun and sweat, and looked good enough to have come from her dreams.

"I'm not used to—people—doing things for me."

"Unless they want something, right?"

"I didn't say that."

"You didn't have to."

"Con…thank you."

"It's no biggie, Dixie. It's just breakfast."

He didn't understand what it meant to her, to have him constantly considering her needs without thought to his personal convenience. Maybe he would never understand. But his care of her pierced her heart.

Helpless to resist, she raised her hand to touch his cheek, testing the heat and dampness of his skin, the texture of his morning beard. He turned his face to kiss her palm, lips warm against the tender center, and her insides liquefied.

Uncertain in the face of her own feelings, unsure of his response, she sought refuge in humor. "Must be that hunter-gatherer instinct."

His mouth, with its disciplined upper lip and its temptingly full lower one, quirked. "Must be. Only, knowing you, I switched the actual woolly mammoth for powdered doughnuts."

"I like doughnuts." She struggled to sit up under the taut covers, hitching the sheet up under her armpits.

"Here." He offered her a cup.

"Oh, um…"

He watched her steadily. "It's tea."

"Oh."

She reached for it, wrapping her hands around the hot cup. And then realized that his gaze had dipped. A muscle tightened in his cheek. His pulse beat in his throat.

Deliberately, she let the sheet drop to her waist.

His blue eyes went black. His chest rose and fell as if he were still running. She was all bare to him, and warm and flushed and more than ready to give what he had not asked for. Wanting to give him all the love stored in her cautious heart.

He leaned forward to kiss her, his mouth closing sweetly and surely over hers. She closed her eyes. He tasted like coffee.

The phone on the bedside table jangled.

"Hold that thought," he whispered against her lips. He lifted the receiver. "MacNeill."

She watched him go away from her, watched the ardent, urgent lover fade and the businessman take his place. His eyes sharpened. His voice cooled. His replies became clipped.

"...gets in tomorrow afternoon," he was saying into the phone. "Yeah, dinner would be good. All right. Grandison, too? Fine. Well, that was nice of him to say. Thanks. I appreciate the call, Josh."

He hung up and sat a moment with his hand on the receiver. She could feel the excitement rising in him, see the tension in his neck.

"Who was that?" she asked quietly.

"Hmm? Josh Wainbridge. He's picking me up at the airport tomorrow. Grandison on the board wants to meet me."

She remembered. Con had a job interview in Boston on Friday. Her heart sank down somewhere near her stomach. The day after tomorrow. "You must be pleased."

"Yeah. Oh, definitely." His quick smile showed the

edges of his teeth. "This could be my ticket out of the mi-nors."

He wouldn't stay.

The certainty of his departure had freed her to be his lover. Now the knowledge of his leaving stretched between them like barbed wire.

"Baseball analogies are wasted on me, MacNeill," she said, more sharply than she intended. "But if that's what you want..."

"Sure, it's what I want."

"What about being your own boss? Solving clients' problems?"

"It has its advantages," he admitted. The amused complicity in his eyes invited her to smile. "And I will work with you on any problem any time."

"As long as it's my problem and not yours."

His eyes narrowed. "I don't have a problem here. I have an opportunity."

"An opportunity for what? To do work you don't care about among people you dislike?"

"Look, I'm not saying that if things were different... But I'm not going to let my family down."

"Let them down?" she repeated, disbelieving. "Do you really think that because you get a job back on Wall Street—"

"Federal Street."

"—whatever. Do you really think some *job* makes you a better man than Patrick or a happier man than Sean? I don't know your parents, but I've met their sons. Do you really think they care how much money you make?"

"Hold on. What the hell is this?"

Fear. She could admit it to herself. Fear that he would leave her, worry that his fast-track, high-profile career would carry him away from her and mold him into someone she didn't want to love.

But she couldn't admit that to Con. She wouldn't bind

him with her expectations the way her parents had tried to bind her, or use sex to coerce his agreement.

"Maybe I just don't want to see you wind up like my father."

"Rich? Successful? A pillar of the community?"

"With a wife who is subordinate to him and a daughter who can't get close to him for fear he'll try to overhaul her life."

He went from steamy to glacial in less time than it took her to remove a simmering pot from the stove. "Is that what you think will happen if you get close to me?"

"I was talking about my father."

"According to you, there's not a hell of a lot of difference, now, is there?"

Somehow, she realized, she'd hurt him, when she'd only meant to set him free.

"You're taking this the wrong way," she said as calmly as she could. "I only meant that you can get caught up in thinking the wrong things are important."

"And what do you think is important, Dixie?"

Panic rolled over queasily in her stomach. He was important. Far too important. But telling him so would tip the balance of power too heavily on his side. So she gave him the old answers, the answers that would leave her pride intact and let him go to Boston with an unchained heart.

"Your personal choice is important. Your independence."

"Big ideas," he observed. "Maybe too big for a simple guy like me."

She tossed back her hair. "Oh, please. You're the Harvard business grad."

"Humor me, anyway. Let's keep it specific. What's important to you?"

Val bit the inside of her cheek. What did he want, a plane ticket and her blessing?

"I don't think you should be bound by someone else's expectations," she said.

He stood up. "Well, that says it all, doesn't it?"

"Con, I—"

"You better get dressed," he said over his shoulder. "You've got to be at the restaurant in half an hour."

Con swore as his computer screen froze and then went blank. He was plugged in at an empty desk in the loan department, out of sight of the bank's customers, waiting for the teller—Donna Winston—to take her break at three-fifteen so he could ask her about her relationship with Rob Cross. He scowled at the blue screen. Bullying an attractive twenty-something bank clerk into revealing the sordid details of her personal life was not his idea of a fun time.

Was that how Val thought of what he'd done to her last night?

He'd stayed away from the restaurant all day. Working, he told himself. And heard his mother's amused judgment in his head: *Sulking, boyo. You're too used to getting what you want.*

Give me a break, Ma.

He hit Control and stabbed at a few keys. Define the problem. Solve the problem.

The problem was Val, with her feathered earring and her stubborn independence and her quick claim not to need him.

The problem was the way he felt about her. Hungry and hurting and raw. He was in love for what was probably the first time in his life, and his nice, logical thought processes were jumbled and his direct, deliberate career route suddenly felt like a dead end.

The real problem was the way she *didn't* feel about him.

In bed, at least, her body answered his. Her quick humor responded to his teasing, her warm heart surfaced when she was with his family. Last night, he thought he'd breached the wall of her reserve, seduced her outside her circle of privacy.

Con ran a check on his hard drive and inadvertently deleted a file. Hell. Maybe he could make her respond to him. But he couldn't make her like it. She was too wounded by her ongoing battle with Papa Cutler to accept another take-charge kind of guy in her life. If he did take the job in Boston, Con suspected he'd have to drive the devil's own bargain even to see her again. She wasn't about to leave her life, her friends and her restaurant to follow him anywhere.

Val didn't need him.

Correction, didn't want him.

And there wasn't a single damn thing he could do about that.

He scowled and snapped his laptop closed. No, she wanted her independence. Her precious personal choice.

Well, damn it, before Con hopped his flight to Boston, he'd prove to her that there were some differences between him and Edward Cutler.

Val sat at her desk, once more in possession of herself and her office, painstakingly adding up the day's deposit. It was Con's job, but she could do it. You didn't need a Harvard degree to operate a calculator.

The second total agreed with the first. So she was handling things fine.

Just like she handled things this morning. She put down her pencil and rubbed her eyes like a tired child.

She heard the kitchen door thump into the shelves and footsteps in the hall. Con, she thought, with a lift to her heart like hope.

She squared her shoulders and summoned a smile to her face. "Come to escort me to the bank?" she called cheerfully.

Rob Cross filled the narrow office doorway, exuding Polo cologne and menace. "No. I'm not going to the bank today. And neither are you."

Chapter 16

Donna Winston had expertly outlined lips and an eager smile. She crossed her legs as she sat down, so that her tailored skirt slid up her stockinged thigh, and used the smile on Con.

Rob Cross was pond scum, but he had a pretty girlfriend.

Con blanked the memory of poor Ann Cross's purpled face and swallowed rage. He was going on gossip and with his gut here, and if he scared this bright young thing all he'd have to take to Cutler was a hunch.

"Miss Winston. I appreciate your coming to see me on your break."

"Mr. Cutler said I should stop by."

She didn't ask him why, didn't give him any kind of opening at all.

"Yes. Thank you." He picked up a pencil, feeling like a rookie cop or a prying reporter. "Mr. Cutler has asked me to look into some recent allegations of misconduct at the bank."

She ran her tongue over the dark pink outline of her lower lip. ''Misconduct?''

''That's right. Concerning Mr. Cross.'' Con balanced a pencil between his fingers. ''Now, of course, if you're not involved, I apologize for taking your time. But if you are, I think the best and safest course is for us to get to the bottom of this as quickly and easily as possible.''

''Does Mr. Cutler *know?*''

Con narrowed his eyes. This was almost too easy. Was she going to confess to the theft just like that? ''We have an appointment later this afternoon to discuss the matter, yes.''

''Oh, God.'' She pressed her clasped hands to her mouth. ''He said no one would find out.''

''Rob Cross said that?''

She nodded.

''But you knew eventually someone always finds out about things like this.'' Con did his best to squeeze some sympathy into his voice. No need to tell her he still didn't have any proof.

''Eventually, I guess. But I was sort of hoping it wouldn't come up until Rob left his wife.''

''That the two of you were involved,'' Con clarified.

Her eyes widened. ''Well, yes, we... Oh, God, were you talking about something else?''

Cursing his quick assumptions, Con shot her a reassuring smile. ''I could be. Your personal life doesn't have to come into this at all. If you wouldn't mind answering a couple of other questions...''

Wary, she sat back in her chair, tugging at her skirt. ''I guess not.''

''You've processed the daily deposits for Wild Thymes restaurant, haven't you?''

''A couple of times, yes.''

''Do you always total the receipts?''

"If the customer asks me to. For Wild Thymes, I think we do."

"Did you ever take cash out?"

She blinked rapidly several times. "To give to the customer, do you mean?"

"Let's say, for any reason," Con said calmly.

"No. No, I don't think so."

"Did Mr. Cross ever ask you to take any cash out?"

"Why would he do that?"

"Did he?"

"No. Look, I don't know what you're getting at, but I take my break every day sometime between three and four. I'm not even at the counter most days when she comes in with the deposit."

"Who is?"

Her manicured nails tapped her knee. "Peggy, I guess, or Cheryl. You want the truth, I don't even like seeing her face, all right?"

"You two have a problem?" Con asked carefully. Was there a history here? A grudge? But why wouldn't Val have mentioned it?

Donna Winston laughed shortly. "A pretty obvious one, I'd think. I mean, she had him, and I want him."

"Then when the deposit bag comes in…"

"I don't have anything to do with it. You'd really have to ask Cheryl. Or Peggy." She stood, tugging the hem of her short, tight jacket. "In the meantime, if you've got a problem with me or my performance, try taking it up with the vice president of the proofs department."

Not a bad exit at all, Con thought dryly. Too bad it left him stuck down another blind alley.

He tossed the pencil down on the desk. But he couldn't rid himself of the frustrating sense that Donna Winston had given him something he could use, if he could only see it.

* * *

Fear danced along Val's nerves. She could taste it in her mouth. Or maybe that was adrenaline, flat and sweet as day-old Coke.

She moistened her lips. "You don't have the right to tell me where I'm going anymore, Rob. What do you want?"

He took a step forward, his eyes hot and his "just folks" smile hard around the edges. "I want my wife back."

"She's gone home."

"No. She's not there. I checked."

"I meant, she's not here."

He shook his head like a disappointed father. "Val, she works here," he said in a reasonable voice. "I want you to talk to her. Tell her to get her skinny butt back where it belongs."

Welcome anger ignited in her gut. She warmed herself at it, let its heat infuse her voice. "She won't be back. She doesn't belong with you."

"She belongs to me, and she knows it. Where else is she going to go?" He chuckled. "New York?"

"Go to hell, Rob."

He took a step closer. "Tell her. Tell her she'll be sorry if she puts me to the trouble of finding her and hauling her back home."

"The way you tried to haul her home from my apartment?" Val edged back from her desk and stood, careful to keep the chair between them. "I don't think so. Even Chief Palmer might have questions about you dragging a screaming woman out of a public place."

Rob smiled at her, and a finger of sweat traced a slow, crawling line down her spine. "Ann won't scream."

"I will."

Another step, closer. His head bent confidingly low. His shoulders bunched forward. She could smell the sweat of his excitement and a remembered blend of bourbon and mint mouthwash that nearly gagged her.

"You didn't before," he said.

"I was seventeen. I'm not that girl anymore."

His lips curled in a knowing smile. "So, what are you going to do now, Val? Call the cops?"

She raised her chin. "If I have to."

He laid his big-knuckled hand on the chair between them. "You're nine years too late to press charges."

"For what you did to me then, perhaps. Not for stealing from me now."

His breath hissed. "No one will believe you."

Certainty steadied her heart and stiffened her knees. "Con believes me."

But the moment she said the words she knew they were a mistake. She should never have allowed Rob to goad her into provoking him.

"Then you'll have to tell him different," Rob said, almost pleasantly. "I'm not letting you ruin me, you little bitch."

Val swallowed. "I let you bully me into keeping quiet once before. I won't do it again." She nudged the seat of the chair. It stopped against his legs. "Let me by, Rob."

"I can't do that. Not until I've given you a reason not to talk."

He shoved the chair into the desk, the sound shocking and loud in the deserted restaurant. Her stomach churned.

"Just like old times," Rob said, and reached for her.

Edward Cutler's desk was as long and shiny as an eight-thousand-dollar coffin. Behind it, Edward was as chilly as a corpse.

"Tell me what you've got," he said to Con, "and I'll deal with Rob."

"I'd like us to tackle him together," Con said carefully. "All I've got at this point is a suspicious pattern of low deposits at irregular intervals for no reason I can find."

"In other words, you have nothing."

Con rocked on his heels, stuffing his hands in his back pockets to avoid taking a swing at something. "I have a discrepancy that your proof department should have caught.''

"If there's a problem in the proof department, I'm sure Rob will look into it.''

"Cross *is* the problem in the proof department.''

"Rob Cross is a trusted member of my management team and a respected member of the community.''

"Yeah, well, personally he's pond scum. The man beats his wife.''

"Whatever his marital difficulties—which I'm sure you're exaggerating—they have no bearing on his performance at the bank.''

"How about the fact that he's sticking it to a teller? Does that have any bearing on his job performance?''

Edward flushed. "You can't know that. Besides, office romances happen all the time. Rob is a very attractive man.''

Con studied the man barricaded behind his desk with an unsettling mixture of pity and contempt. There was no way he would betray Val's confidence by telling Cutler what his golden-haired bank vice president had done to her. Yet there had to be some way to make Cutler see that Rob Cross was not one of the good guys.

"At the very least, Cross is preying on a junior member of your staff. And who's to say she's the first woman he's victimized?''

Edward's face was pale and as hard as the profile on a coin. "If this attack on Rob is some ill-judged attempt to pry remuneration out of me…''

"Hold on. You think this is about the *bonus?*''

"I think it's in your interest to convince me Rob is at fault, yes. It's not hard to understand why. After all, my recommendation is riding on your findings as well.''

And this, Con realized, was what Val had contended with all her life. This was what she feared from him. Somehow, in Edward Cutler's eyes, it all came down to what he was owed and what he might have to pay.

Con stood on the kilim carpet, staring across four feet of polished mahogany at the determined bank president. He didn't kid himself. Val's father was as earnest in his defense of his business, his employee and his judgment as Con would have been.

Con's own future as well as his bonus hung in the balance.

"Go to hell," he said, and walked out.

Val ducked and lunged, trying to get past Rob to the door. He was too big. Too big and too strong and too intent on his revenge.

He grabbed her, his hand fast and brutal on her shoulder, and threw her against the filing cabinet. Pain shot up her back as metal banged and echoed and papers toppled to the floor. The drawer pull dug between her shoulder blades. Her hands splayed, to hold herself up, to hold him off, and Rob laughed, moving in.

"I should have done this the day you came back to town."

She screamed then, startling them both. She used her hands and her knees and her feet and, when he crowded still closer, her teeth. He swore and jerked back. She tried to dive under his left arm, but he raised his right one and backhanded her. Her head snapped back. Pain exploded in her jaw and in her neck and circled her head like a galaxy of sparks.

He let her fall, the cool linoleum flat against her palms, and then hauled her up and shoved her across the room, against the desk. She heard herself whimper as he grunted and pressed against her. Blood, salty and insinuating, pooled in her mouth.

"You should have married me. You needed this all along."

She spat at him, splattering blood in his face and on the collar of the starched white shirt that Annie had pressed.

Rob swore, wiping his face with one big hand, holding her with the other, off balance against the desk. Her back hurt. Her head still spun. He rubbed against her, using his groin like a weapon to insult, to threaten, to punish. Wrapping his hand in her braid, he yanked back her head, forcing her to look at him.

"You can't stop me," he gloated.

Nausea rose in her throat, cutting off her air. Nausea and rage. And Con's voice echoed quietly in her head, inside her. *Not a victim. You're a survivor.*

She swallowed. Her hands groped blindly over the surface of the desk behind her, seeking support, seeking…

"Maybe not," she said thickly. "But I can mark you. I can make you mark me. This time I'll bring charges."

And her left hand closed over something smooth and cool and curved, and her arm came up, and she smashed the smiling ceramic pig against the side of his head.

Pencils and sharp splinters showered them both.

"Stupid bitch!" Rob bellowed, and his fist came up, a blur in the corner of her eye.

In her head, tiny points of dancing color exploded against the dark.

Con paused at the top of the bank steps, surveying the parking lot, considering his options. He could go back inside and type out a letter of resignation. He shook his head. Redundant. He could drive to the motel and pack for his flight to Boston. Premature. Or he could stroll the three blocks to the restaurant and inform Val Cutler of his conversation with Donna Winston and his own most recent personal choices.

He was halfway down the steps when he heard a siren in the distance. Police car? Ambulance? In tiny Cutler, was it more likely to be someone suffering from heat prostration or a cat stuck in a tree?

A shiny red pickup slid through the corner stop sign and gunned down the road. Con stared after it, frowning. And saw, like a pall over Main Street, black smoke rising above the trees.

Fire.

He almost got the Jag. But farmers' trucks and SUVs were speeding down the main drag, converging on the small downtown area. A second siren picked up the wail of the first like a hound joining the hunt. Adrenaline pumped through him. Con started down the sidewalk. His leather-soled shoes were too stiff for running.

It could be anything. It could be anywhere. The hardware store or the laundromat or the county courthouse.

He breathed in evenly, and out, as if governing his breathing could control his rising sense of wrong, his grow-ing fear. He passed another pickup truck, double-parked. A police car hurtled by, blue lights flashing, and pulled up half a block away. An officer in an orange vest jumped out and signaled traffic to stop.

Cars jammed the street. People hurried out of stores and drifted out on porches to watch and exclaim.

Not the hardware store, Con thought, and picked up his pace. His heart crowded his chest. The haze of smoke in-creased, making it difficult to draw breath. Not the laundro-mat.

A block and a half away from Val's restaurant, he dropped his briefcase and began to run.

Hot. She was uncomfortable and hot. Val stirred, rest-lessly seeking a cooler spot between the sheets. Her throat hurt. Her chest felt weighted, as if she'd pulled up too many covers. Her arm moved to shove them off, and her hand brushed a hard, gritty surface. Something rolled away from her fingers.

Frowning, she shifted, but she couldn't get comfortable. The grit pressed her cheek, another irritant to add to her scratchy throat and pounding head. Really, her head was the worst. Her jaw throbbed. Her lips were cracked and dry. A starburst of pain radiated from the side of her head. She reached up, her fingers finding the lump under her hair, and heard a groan. Her own? The sound startled her into full consciousness.

She opened her eyes to haze and heat and terror.

She wasn't in bed. She was lying on her office floor in the shards of the ceramic pig, and smoke was pouring in the top of the open doorway.

Kitchen fire? She forced herself to think, to move, to take shallow breaths. She had to get out.

She began to crawl, ignoring the pricks against her palms, the scrape against her legs. Over the metal lintel, she lifted her head to peer down the darkening hall. No fire. No flames. She caught her breath in relief and then coughed. Keep low to the exit, she thought dazedly, reaching back in memory to fifth-grade fire drills. She had to find the exit. Back door. Down the hall. To the right.

Ahead of her, around her, the fire hissed and roared like a living thing. It sounded as if it were coming from the front of the building, from the dining room. She crawled. Which made no sense. Restaurant fires started in the kitchen.

Unless someone started them.

Rob. Where was Rob?

I can mark you. I can make you mark me. This time I'll bring charges.

Unless she wasn't there to tell. Unless he destroyed the evidence.

She cried out in horror as smoke rolled down the walls like an evil genie and engulfed her. Her eyes stung. Her nose ran. She couldn't see or breathe, and it was hot, so hot. Dragging herself on hands and knees, her cheek almost pressed to the floor, she blundered into one barrier after another.

Where was the exit? Where was the door?

She cut her hand on the sharp foot of a metal shelf. Without the tears or breath to cry, she gasped and gulped.

"Con?"

Oh, God. Oh, Con. She scrabbled forward blindly on he stomach, her seeking hands slapping the floor. Stretchin out, she touched hot metal and shrieked.

Not a victim, he told her calmly and with conviction. *survivor.*

The stove. She'd touched the front of the stove. Orientin herself by the grating at the bottom, she rolled and reverse and crawled for the door of the big walk-in refrigerator.

Con shoved through the gaping onlookers, feet and hea pounding. Wild Thymes was burning. Smoke drifted fror the sealed windows and poured from the roof. Pickups an cars were abandoned all over the street as volunteer firefight ers leapt from their cabs and raced to the scene. Blue lights red lights, orange lights blinked under a canopy of blac smoke.

God, he prayed. Let her be safe.

Men were in his way, in yellow slickers and black hats He pushed and thrust them aside, trying to get to the restau rant door. To Val, inside.

"Hey! Keep back!"

"Is everyone out?" he demanded.

"We don't know. Report of a possible casualty—"

"I've got to get inside!"

"Stop!" a yellow slicker shouted.

"Get him!"

He scattered the first four men who tried, only to b dragged to a halt fifteen yards from the smoking door. A second-floor window—Val's apartment window—explode outward. He heard warning yells and screams as glass show ered the sidewalk. His captors cursed and dragged him bac behind the line cleared by the firefighters.

"Go in, damn you! She's inside. Val Cutler."

"Easy, buddy. We've got to wait for the water. If w break in without it, we're just feeding oxygen to the fire."

Python-size hoses snaked the street. Men ran, shouting instructions. The guy holding Con's left arm dropped it to take up a hose. The young one on his right hesitated, gave him a shake.

"You okay? We're going in after her."

Tight-lipped, Con assented. But his blood surged with adrenaline: fight or flight, the primitive response to terror. His muscles strained, his heart screamed, and all he could do was stand there like a chump and watch as a stream of silver water hit the roof.

Firefighters in heavy brown coats smashed the stenciled glass. It shattered under their axes. Flame roared out, and another burst of water shot inside, throwing back the leaping flame, diverting the rolling smoke. The open window gaped like the black maw of a dragon.

Con clenched his fists, fear and hope twisting inside him in a knot that defied definition or solution. Oh, God. He felt six years old again, standing unobserved and alone in the hall listening as the report of heavy marine casualties overseas came on TV and his mother cried. He remembered the phone call in the night notifying him of the accident that destroyed his brother Patrick's family, and the heart attack that had threatened their father just over a year ago.

Each time, his heart had framed the same desperate prayer, ignoring the probability forecast of his logical mind. *Let them be all right. Oh, God. Please, God. Let everything be all right.*

And he knew from miserable experience that the most heartfelt prayers sometimes went unanswered.

He scanned the crowd behind the fire barriers, as if searching could summon Val into the safe circle of onlookers. And saw, on the outskirts, Rob Cross's avid face.

The big blond man stood at the back of the press. Logical, Con acknowledged, if he'd just arrived at the scene. Casual

posture, perfect hair. Blood on his shirt. Con's eyes na
rowed, suspicion coiling in his gut.

Cross looked directly at him and smiled.

With a snarl, Con lunged across wet pavement and orang
tape to throw himself at Cross.

Chapter 17

Con hit Rob hard and low.

Patrick fought with trained efficiency and Sean with glee. The middle MacNeill brother sparred to win.

He bulldogged Rob down onto the wet pavement, ignoring his high school rules. His slacks ripped, and the skin of his knees tore. He welcomed the haze of rage, the sharp relief of pain. Taking advantage of surprise, he seized Rob's hair and slammed the side of the big man's head into the curb. Rob bellowed. Someone screamed. Con swung his free hand and smashed the heel of his palm up Rob's nose. It crunched. Blood sprayed them both.

"Stop it, stop it!"

"Hell."

"Pull him off."

Rob's eyes glazed from contact with the curb, but he was fighting mad. He twisted away, catching Con's arm and taking him with him. They rolled, scuffling, legs tangling, arms grappling, bumping over a hose and scraping along the wet street.

Beneath his soft padding of fat, Rob was muscled and mean. He scrambled on top like a football player fighting for an extra yard. His fist clobbered Con's throat. Close quarters cramped the blow, but enough hatred powered it to close Con's windpipe. He struggled for leverage, for freedom, for air, as Rob's blood dripped onto his face. He couldn't breathe.

Oh, God, could Val breathe?

Rob's fingers gouged his throat. Con slammed both forearms down to break his hold. When Rob's head dropped, Con curled from the pavement and rammed him with his head.

Rob yowled.

And then rough hands reached in to wrench them apart and haul them to their feet: more firefighters, smelling of smoke, with dirty faces and disgusted looks. Con submitted, ignoring the pain as his arms were yanked behind him. At least Cross wouldn't get away now. And Val...he pulled a breath in through his teeth, refusing to give in to the panic clawing his gut. He struggled to speak, but his throat was still too tight.

"He broke my nose," Rob complained thickly. "Did you see? He broke my damn nose."

The policeman in the orange vest shoved between them. "What the hell's the matter with...Rob?"

Cross nodded, wiping blood from his face. "Did you see? This son of a bitch attacked me. You all saw."

While Con tried to force out words to defend himself, Rob leaned on the cop for support. His hand fumbled. And then he whirled and, with the policeman's nightstick, jammed Con's ribs, hard.

Con heard the crack, felt pain rocket to his head and nausea to his throat.

"Hey!" The officer grabbed back his stick. "You shouldn't have done that. Now I'm gonna have to take you both in."

Con coughed and sucked in air. His throat protested. Pain lanced his side.

"You okay?" the cop asked reluctantly.

Con nodded, fighting through the pain. "Make him...tell you...what he's doing here."

Rob, with his handkerchief balled up under his nose, rolled his eyes in disgust. "I was just standing here when this lunatic attacked me. It was self-defense, Tom. You all saw."

The cop looked from Rob's bloody nose to Con, hanging winded between two firefighters.

Con raised his head. "Standing...how long?"

"I just got here."

"Who saw you arrive?"

Rob shrugged. "I don't rightly know. I mean, every rubbernecker in town is glued to the fire."

The fire. Oh, God. Please, God.

Con stared over his shoulder at the wet and smoking ruin of Val's restaurant. Charred wood steamed around the broken front window. Great black fans of smut reached above the upper ones. Smoke drifted sullenly over the wet street. Where in that mess was Val? His mind refused to picture her flowing skirts and streaming hair and feathered earring consumed by fire.

Standing in his torn shirt, with the wreckage radiating heat not twenty yards away, he shivered. His throat ached. His ribs throbbed. His face was wet, from blood or water runoff or tears. With his arms secured behind his back, he couldn't reach to wipe it. He blinked.

"Did you find her?"

"Miz Cutler?" He recognized the young firefighter who'd held him back earlier, his grip easy on his shoulder. Brown eyes met his, regretful and aware. "Not yet."

"How..." He felt the tightness in his chest, heard it in his voice. "How long?"

"We knocked the fire down. They're going in. They'll pull the walls apart, make sure we've got it all."

Con fumbled for more questions, but answers wouldn't help. Nothing would help. Fear sliced him open and left him dangling like a butchered steer. "How bad?"

"Dining room's gone. Looks like the fire started there. Fire marshall called the police department."

"Why?" Rob Cross demanded.

"What about upstairs?" Con asked.

The fireman's attention slid over Rob and returned to him. "Looks like the fire caught in the exhaust system. The upstairs—with the smoke and all—well, it's pretty bad. I'm sorry, sir."

Oh, God. He struggled to grasp it. The rooms filled with whimsy, the antique bureau and silly pillows, the shivering dragonfly and sturdy table, gone. Val would be devastated. He refused to accept the loss could gouge so much deeper, that she could be gone, too. But the possibility crowded his lungs, making it difficult to breathe. Oh, God. Could she breathe?

His attention jerked back to the building as three firefighters in heavy brown coats and orange helmets appeared in the gaping doorway. Two wore oxygen masks. A third, barefaced and blackened with soot, held his mask over the face of the woman he supported. Her blond braid, dimmed with smoke, swung from his arm.

"Val!"

The cry shook his chest, speared his rib. Arms tightened behind his back. The firefighter stepped in his way. "Just a minute, sir. She'll need to see the paramedics."

Oh, God. He could have lost her. He still could lose her.

He pulled against the restraining arms, desperate to see, to make sense of the paramedics' frantic activity. Did her arm rise, just for a moment, as they laid her under the blinking orange lights? Dark uniforms swarmed the cot with bags and lines and tubes. That was good, wasn't it? She was alive?

And then he saw her struggle to sit up, her chest heaving, and no power in the world could have kept him from her.

The friendly firefighter protested. ''Sir—''

''Let me see her, damn it.''

He wrenched free.

He shouldered through the medical team and dropped to his knees in the road beside the rolling cot. She was filthy and bloody. Beautiful. Alive. She coughed and twisted and saw him. Above the clear oxygen mask, tears leaked from her red-rimmed eyes. Tears burned in his. Reaching out, he twined his fingers with hers, careful to avoid the line taped and running into the back of her hand.

Her grip tightened. Her other hand reached up and tugged down on her mask.

''Hey.'' She coughed.

His heart swelled. ''Hi.''

Carefully, he replaced her mask, freeing a bedraggled strand of hair from the securing elastic. His fingers trembled slightly as they brushed her gritty cheek. Under the grime, she was white as paper. He could have lost her.

A ponytailed paramedic bumped him impatiently. ''Are you family?''

''No, I—''

''You'll have to excuse us, then.'' She turned to her partner. ''Okay, on three.''

Val's fingers clung and slid from his.

The cop came up on one side, jostling his rib. The firefighter took his arm on the other.

Forced back, Con called to Val as they lifted her into the ambulance. ''I'll be there as soon as I can. I'll be there.''

He didn't know if she heard him or not.

''Hey, buddy, take it easy.'' The police officer sounded unexpectedly sympathetic. ''You'll see your girlfriend again. We've got to get you to the hospital anyway, get your ribs taped or whatever." He shook his head. "I don't know what got into Rob."

The ambulance nudged down the crowded street, orange lights flashing. Con turned his head.

"Call Edward Cutler," he said. "Ask him."

Patrick MacNeill offered Con the foam cup in his hand. Pacing, Con shook his head.

Patrick took a sip himself, his brows drawing together in distaste. "Hospital coffee. It's the pits. I told Kate she should be glad she's pregnant and can't drink it anymore."

Con smiled faintly. He appreciated his older brother's steady presence in the waiting room. But nothing could distract him from the thought of Val lying injured inside, sequestered from him by double doors and hospital curtains and officious personnel.

"Didn't Kate say she'd be out by now?"

"Give her a minute, bro. She's got to introduce herself to Val's doctor, make nice with the locals. This isn't her hospital."

Con acknowledged that with a nod. Patrick had come as soon as Con called, Kate the instant she was paged. Con couldn't ask for more.

Except for Val to be all right.

"I hate not being able to do anything," he confessed quietly.

Patrick got up and laid his hand on his brother's shoulder in a rare gesture of physical support. "Sometimes the best you can do is to be there."

Con set his jaw. "They wouldn't even let me in to see her."

"But you called her folks. She's got her parents with her."

"I'm not sure she'll thank me for that." He swore, his hands balling in his pockets, his gut in knots. Define the problem. *Val was injured.* Solve the problem. *Not a damn thing he could do.*

"I just wish I knew what to do for her, that's all."

"Answer Man. You always did want to solve everything."

"Oh, like you don't," Con retorted.

Their eyes met in rueful recognition, and then Patrick shrugged. "At least you punched out the bastard who did this. You give your statement to the detective?"

"Yeah. Whatever good that will do. She was unconscious when he set the fire."

"It will put him away for a while."

"Not long enough."

"At least they're not going to charge you."

"Yeah, I'm a real hero," Con said bleakly. "Went from aggravated assault to apprehending a suspect in the time it took Cutler to throw his weight around."

Kate MacNeill pushed through the doors, her pregnant belly obvious even under her white lab coat. "Con? You can go in now."

"How is she?"

"She's all right," Kate assured him, her eyes kind. "Smoke inhalation. Bruises and lacerations. A bump on the head."

"Okay." He drew a breath. He was not going in there to carry on over her, to burden her with his terror, rage and relief. He would be strong and reassuring and calm. "Okay."

But when he saw her propped on the emergency room stretcher with a tube running into her arm, her face as white as the surrounding sheets, he almost lost it.

"Holy saints. You look…" He swallowed. "Pretty good, all things considered."

A corner of her mouth moved upward in a smile. He had to jam his hands in his back pockets to keep from grabbing at her. "Well, thanks." Her voice rasped. She coughed. "You don't."

The overwhelmed resident in ER had taped Con's ribs. A sympathetic orderly had liberated a scrub top from the hospital laundry to replace his torn shirt. But even after washing his battered face in the men's room, Con figured he was no soothing sight for an invalid.

"Cross looks worse."

She closed her eyes. "Good."

"He's been arrested, then?" Edward Cutler inquired.

Con pivoted to find him standing just inside the curtains, as if he might slip out at any moment. Typical, Con thought. The guy was clearly concerned and ready to stand in a father's place. He just looked like he'd rather be somewhere, anywhere, else.

Con checked out the thin, well-groomed ash blonde beside him. Val's mother. He wondered if before rushing to her daughter's hospital bed, she'd taken the time to freshen her makeup, to tie that jaunty scarf around her still-firm throat. He tried not to hold her perfect appearance against her. Certain women, he knew, didn't leave their bathrooms in the morning without applying eyeliner. But it left a bad taste in his mouth. Why didn't she touch her daughter? Why the hell wasn't she shaking?

He still was.

He answered Cutler's question. "Detained for questioning. They're still sorting out the charges. The detective said they took your statement."

Edward nodded. "We spoke. I assured him that when you attacked Rob, you were acting on an appropriate suspicion of his misconduct at the bank."

Con was surprised by Cutler's apparent support. "Thanks," he said briefly.

"Of course, you and I both know you still haven't substantiated those suspicions. Until you do, I'm not satisfied you've earned your recommendation."

Like Con gave a rat's ass about Cutler's recommendation at this point. Val was all that mattered. But her father was focused, as always, on his private ledger of personal credits and debits. At least now he was attempting to manipulate Con on Val's behalf.

"I'll give it my best," Con said.

"See that you do," said Edward.

Sylvia Cutler spoke up for the first time. "I think all this business talk could wait till another time. We should leave the two of you alone. Edward, would you show me the coffee shop?"

Con didn't get her at all. Bridget MacNeill would have clawed like a tigress to stay at the bedside of a wounded cub. But he was glad they were leaving.

"Coffee. Yes," Edward said with relief. "We'll speak with the doctor on our way."

Sylvia paused by Val's bedside. Her almond nails hovered a moment over the singed blond braid, never quite touching. Her curtailed gesture of stunted affection struck Con as incredibly poignant. No, pathetic. Couldn't she see her daughter needed her?

"We'll see you again in the morning, darling."

Con stepped back to let them pass before approaching the bed. Despite a cursory wash, Val's face was still streaked with tears and grime. Her pupils were dilated with pain or dope. Her perfect jaw had a lump on one side.

He balled his fists. He wanted to hold her. He was afraid to touch her. He should have insisted Kate give him the full medical rundown on her condition, the way he normally would when he was in control.

He spotted the plastic pan on the tray beside the gurney.

"You nauseous?"

She shook her head.

"Dizzy?"

Her nose wrinkled impatiently.

"How's the head?"

"There's a very good chance—" she coughed again, and he snatched up the water bottle on the tray and guided the straw to her mouth "—I'll live," she finished hoarsely, leaning back against her pillows.

He fought back a grin.

Oh, God, he'd nearly lost her.

Those wide gray eyes saw far too much. The teasing went out of them, and they got all soft and sympathetic, making him feel even more useless.

"You told me I was a survivor," she reminded him gently.

"Yeah." Restless, he turned, paced the two short steps to the curtain and back again. She was so brave. Her strength humbled him. "The fire inspector said you really kept your head. Used the fridge as a fire barrier."

Her fingers plucked the sheet over her legs. "It's not like I had a lot of…options at that point."

She wheezed the last words, choked and coughed. As she leaned forward to spit, another, more violent fit of coughing shook her. His heart rolled over.

"Easy, sweetheart." He moved to the side of the bed, bracing her forehead on his shoulder, supporting her with his arm.

Her lungs rattled as she fought to draw breath. Grabbing the plastic oxygen mask, he held it to her face, helpless to ease her breathing, helpless against the terror that constricted his own chest.

She pushed it impatiently away. "My restaurant…?" She choked and tried again. "My apartment…?"

He heard the rest of her unspoken questions, her unanswered fears. His arms tightened as he steeled himself to reply, to share the things her doctors hadn't known and her parents hadn't seen fit to tell her.

"You sure you want to go into that now?"

Her gaze searched his face. "Gone?"

Hell. "Yeah."

She closed her eyes. He felt the shudder that racked her, saw the tears that slipped beneath her eyelids.

"It's okay," he murmured into her hair. He gathered her closer against his heart. Her grief shook them both, and her tears burned him like cinders, hot and bright. "Sh, sweetheart, it's okay."

He rocked her as she gasped and keened. Her IV bag swung gently on its pole. Her hair was gritty against his cheek and smelled of hospital soap and smoke. He adjusted her mask and held on.

She'd lost everything, he realized. In the space of a single afternoon, her home, her sanctuary, her place of business and her means of independence had all gone up in smoke. The painted tables and butter-hued walls, the stacks of dishes and rows of pots were gone. Her livelihood was gone. The tree of earrings that stood on her dresser, her posters, her pillows, her bed, all gone.

He wanted to make it better. He wanted to make it up to her, and he had no solutions, nothing but the poor shelter of his arms and the poor consolation of his words.

"Dixie." He stroked her back. He kissed her hair, while her sobs softened against his shirt and her breathing eased. "It will be all right."

He wasn't sure how, but he would make it all right.

Her hands clenched the borrowed hospital top convulsively, as if she were afraid he would leave her. Hell, he wasn't going anywhere.

Not without her.

He wondered how she'd adjust to Boston.

With a start, Val woke, bewildered by pain and the flat, hard pillow and steel rail of her bed. And was instantly reassured by Con's presence beside her.

Hospital room. She'd been moved to a private hospital room. Con had stationed himself in the sole recliner, controlled even in sleep, his arms folded against his chest, his raised feet crossed at the ankles. The filtered light revealed his shadowed beard, his compressed mouth, the lines of pain between his brows. A cracked rib, he'd told her, when she pressed. He should have gone home with his brother.

She turned her head to read the digital clock by the bed: six forty-five. White light outlined the heavy curtains. She could hear the lift of nurses' voices and the rattle of a cart outside. They'd be in soon, she guessed, with breakfast. He must have stayed with her all night.

"Dixie? You awake?"

He was watching her, his heavy-lidded eyes concerned. His soft question released a flood inside her. Tears, hot and uncontrollable, leaked from her eyes.

"Hey." He stirred, shifted and sat on the bed beside her. "Hey, now, it's all right."

Once again, he rocked her against his chest, held her as she cried. He was a haven when her haven had been destroyed, wrapping her in the strength of his embrace, in the warmth of his low voice. She burrowed against his solid chest, drawing comfort from the steady beat of his heart under her ear.

"Sorry." She sniffled.

He handed her a tissue. His matter-of-fact thoughtfulness nearly started the tears again.

She blew her nose. "Thank you," she said, her words muffled by the tissue.

The ghost of a smile touched his mouth. "It's nothing."

"Not for the tissue. For everything."

"Forget it."

"I can't forget it. You were there for me, and I'm grateful."

"Maybe I was there, but I sure as hell didn't *do* anything. I didn't protect you."

"You punched out Rob."

"Sunk to his level, don't you mean? Yeah, that was real effective."

She dropped her hands to her lap and sat a moment regarding him. His mouth was compressed, his blue eyes bleak. He believed what he was saying, she realized. He actually believed his championship did nothing for her.

"Look, I'm uncomfortable enough telling you how much I need you," she drawled. "Can't you just say 'you're welcome,' so we can drop the subject?"

That dragged a reluctant laugh from him. But he sat up straighter, shifting away from her on the bed.

"Dixie, I'd love to take your gratitude and anything else you feel like giving away. But the fact is, I haven't earned it. I talked with the police again last night. If all they can charge Rob with is aggravated assault, the guy will walk."

She swallowed a lump of cold dismay. "The arson?"

"They're working on it. If they can prove he set the fire and left you there, they could put him away for attempted murder."

"That's good, then."

"If the lab results are conclusive. And if they can demonstrate motive. If he was stealing from you, that would go a long way in establishing both revenge and cover-up. The problem is I still haven't figured how to prove he was taking your money."

"Is that really your responsibility?"

"I'm making it my responsibility."

She arched her eyebrows. "'Define the problem, solve the problem'?"

He flushed, but he didn't yield. "Yeah."

He was so hard, so uncompromising in his integrity and his support. And right now he was beating himself up because he believed he'd failed her. Something twisted in her chest.

"Maybe you need to redefine the problem," she said.

"And how do you suggest I do that?"

"I don't know." She met his gaze directly, willing him to accept the faith in her eyes. "But I do know you. You'll think of something."

Chapter 18

Con strode up the crumbling walk that led to the women's shelter, a book for Mitchell in his hand and the name of a lawyer for Ann in his pocket. Poor kid. Poor woman. He'd promised Val he'd stop by to see how they were dealing with Rob's arrest.

It was something he could do.

He gave his name through the door and waited while the gaunt Hispanic woman sitting guard checked it against her list of approved visitors and took his driver's license. The door chain rattled as she handed it back.

"Just a moment," she told him.

He tucked his hands in his back pockets and waited some more. He was glad Ann had this measure of protection. Val wouldn't. Last night, Con had called Boston, canceling his dinner with Grandison and postponing his flight to the six-forty-five tomorrow morning. But he had interviews scheduled at Ventucom all tomorrow afternoon. If Rob were released by then...

The thought made Con sweat.

But if he could establish felony larceny, the police would hold Cross for another seventy-two hours. The detective in charge of the case had said so.

Con paced the porch. Lack of proof was the problem. Without a paper trail, he needed someone to finger Rob. Too bad Donna Winston spent her breaks hiding out from Val in the ladies' room.

What had the teller said? *I don't even like seeing her face, all right? She had him, and I want him.*

And just like that, the penny dropped.

He stopped, staring at the closed door while his mind reeled. Ann and Val. Impossible to confuse them. No two women could appear more different. And yet they shared something. Two things: Rob and Wild Thymes.

She had him, and I want him.

Con had assumed the teller was referring to Rob's broken engagement to Val. But what if she'd been talking about his failed marriage to Ann all along?

Redefine the problem, Val urged inside his head.

All this time, he'd been trying to figure how the money could disappear from the bank without leaving a trail, how Rob could remove cash from the teller's desk without being caught. What if he'd gone at it wrong? What if the money disappeared before it ever reached the bank counter?

The door cracked open on its six-inch chain, and Ann stood framed by the shadows of the hall.

"Con? What are you doing here?"

Could he really believe this thin, quiet woman with her swollen face had helped defraud her best friend of almost twenty thousand dollars?

"I brought Mitchell a book," he said, holding it out. "And I hoped we could talk."

"What about?" she asked.

"Could I have a minute?"

Her clear green eyes, amazingly sane in her crazy quilt of

a face, inspected him through the opening in the door. And then her shoulders slumped, and she nodded.

"Yes. All right." The crack narrowed as she undid the chain. She stepped out on the porch. "How is Val?"

"Better."

"Thank the Lord. I... Well, I'm glad."

"Yeah, my sister-in-law says they'll probably release her tomorrow." He watched her closely as she sat on the low, square balustrade of the porch. "Same as Rob, I guess."

She looked up, her distress evident and real. "Oh, surely not? He attacked her."

Gently, he said, "He's been hitting you for years. Why should this be any different?"

"Val's not his wife," Ann said with a simplicity that made Con wince.

Never mind. So, he was a jerk. Solve the problem, MacNeill. "Well, according to the detective, once Rob posts bond, he's still free until the case goes to trial. Or unless..."

"Unless what?"

"Unless he could be charged with something else. If the charge was serious enough, he'd have to appear before the magistrate again."

She hugged her elbows. "How serious?"

"Embezzlement?" Con suggested.

Ann closed her eyes. He had her. The thought brought him no pleasure at all.

"Val told me you operated the cash register," he continued evenly. "Seated the customers, typed the menus. Ran errands, she said. Ann... Did you ever take the daily deposits to the bank for her?"

"Yes," she whispered.

"And what did you do with them?"

"I brought them to Rob. It started...I was there, I was his wife. I thought it looked strange not to stop in to say hello?" She opened her eyes, looking at him as if anxious to see if he understood.

Con didn't understand at all. But he nodded.

"'Leave it with me,' he'd say. 'I'll get it deposited.' I didn't see why not. Only then…Val started to worry so about money, and I wondered…"

A weight like a sackful of quarters rolled off Con's shoulders. "You didn't take the money yourself?"

"Oh, no. No. I feel so *stupid,*" she cried. "But by the time I suspected what Rob was doing, it didn't matter."

"Did he threaten you? Hurt you?"

"Oh." She shrugged. Her matter-of-fact acceptance was more chilling than a blow-by-blow account. "It wasn't that. He told me the police would never believe me. He said he'd tell Chief Palmer it was me, that I took the money. And after that, he made me watch and then take the deposit bag to Cheryl myself. That made me an accomplice, at least. I'd go to jail, and Mitchell…I couldn't leave Mitchell alone in that house with him."

"No," Con agreed quietly. "You couldn't do that."

"I guess I hoped…I thought once I left he might stop."

"Instead of which, he probably worried you'd confess and decided to burn down Val's restaurant."

Ann flinched. "Yes." She let her hands lie in her lap, palms up, empty like her eyes. "What happens now?"

"Will you go with me to the police? If they can establish motive, it might make the arson easier to prove. Rob could go away for a long, long time."

"I can't. I can't risk losing Mitchell."

"Val is your friend."

"And Mitchell is my son," she said fiercely.

"Ann, your best chance of being there for him is getting your story to the police. The court will look at your record. You won't do time for this."

She looked out over the dusty yard and then back at him. "You'll go with me?"

"Yes."

"And be there for Mitchell, if…if I have to stay?"

"You won't have to stay."

"But if I do?"

Val had told him not to get involved unless he was prepared to deal with the consequences.

"Yes," he promised.

"All right. I can't let my husband hurt Val anymore. She deserves better."

He covered one of her thin, cold hands with his. "So do you. I'll talk with the detective. You'll probably get off with probation."

"Wouldn't that be nice," she said with a sarcasm that took him aback. But her fingers closed on his.

"Thank you," she said. "I am so very sick of lying."

Val adjusted the cant of her hospital bed and the droop of her hospital gown and the thin, clear tubing that still ran into the back of her hand. She lifted the steel cover on her dinner tray without much hope or interest.

Macaroni and cheese. The rising steam, thick with gluten and processed cheddar, conjured up the meal she'd shared with Con that last night in her apartment. Her heart squeezed with loss and loneliness.

He hadn't been to see her all day. In the morning, the detective came with his notebook and questions. Her mother visited, bringing a tasteful arrangement of chrysanthemums and two new magazines, and sat with her for an uncomfortable half hour. Kate MacNeill showed up in the afternoon to look at her chart and listen to her lungs and share the news that Rob Cross had been charged with arson and attempted murder. Which explained, Val supposed, why Ann had not dropped by.

And still Con did not come.

Her need for him shamed her.

She coughed and turned on the wall TV for company. As two stiff-haired, smiling newscasters discussed the hot temperatures and the Mudcats' chances against the Kings, she ate tasteless iceberg lettuce that scraped her throat and pale wedges of tomato with dressing that came in a foil packet.

She was going to eat all of her square of chocolate cake. She felt very sorry for herself.

A smoking ruin with the news station's logo blazoned in the corner jumped on the screen.

"And after the break," the female anchor promised, "scenes from a restaurant fire in Cutler where the police suspect foul play."

The macaroni and cheese stuck in Val's throat. She turned off the TV and closed her eyes.

She would deal with it tomorrow, she resolved. Tomorrow she would assess the damage, begin the cleanup and figure how to get on with her life.

"Me and Scarlett O'Hara," she muttered.

"What's that?" Con's deep voice asked from somewhere beyond the foot of her bed.

Squelching her instinctive leap of joy, she opened her eyes. "Tomorrow is another day."

"Yeah. Sure." He strolled forward, bending to kiss her as naturally as a husband at the end of a long day. Her breath came short. "How are you doing?"

Lousy. Her painkillers made her groggy. She was smoke-sick and heartsick from the fire and moping because she hadn't seen him all day.

"Fine. Kate says the airway trauma will take a while to heal. Blood gases are better. She told me Rob was being charged with setting the fire and—" trying to kill me, she thought "—everything."

"Yeah." Con folded himself into the recliner where he'd spent last night.

"I don't know how you did it, but...thank you."

"I just redefined the problem, like you said. Your friend Ann did the rest."

"Ann?"

He hesitated, his sharp blue gaze assessing.

"Tell me," Val insisted.

So she had no one but herself to blame when he did. She understood Ann's motives and her anguish. She forgave her friend's betrayal. But it was another blow when Val was already on her knees, another reminder that she had no one to rely on but herself.

"Ann said she was sorry," Con repeated. "She never meant to hurt you. She wanted me to ask if she could come see you tomorrow."

"Of course she can come," Val said automatically. "But—"

The door to the hall edged open.

"Knock, knock," a cheerful masculine voice called.

A dozen deep red roses poked into the room, followed by Sean MacNeill, his dark hair tied back and his stunning face concerned.

"Hiya, beautiful. How are you doing?"

His breezy entrance provoked her chuckle. She coughed. Silently, Con handed her the water bottle on the bedside table.

"Better," she croaked.

"How did you get in here?" Con asked.

Sean waggled his eyebrows. "It's visiting hours, bro. Besides, I know one of the doctors. Here, these are for—" He caught Con's eye, changed direction and continued smoothly. "The boy genius, here."

He surrendered the bouquet to Con.

Con took them, frowning. "I can buy my own flowers."

Sean shrugged. "So, I just saved you a trip."

"Fine. I owe you."

"Damn straight you do. Sixty bucks."

"Sixty?"

"Flowers and commission," Sean explained promptly.

Val laughed. It hurt her throat.

"Saved me, my butt," Con said. "Thanks. Now, get out

of here before you upset the nurses and get us both kicked out.''

Sean grinned. ''Oh, they wouldn't do that.'' He bent, and his warm lips brushed Val's cheek before he stepped back. ''I told 'em I was family,'' he whispered loudly.

The door closed behind him.

''Hell.'' Con looked embarrassed.

His obvious discomfort eased her own. ''That was nice of him.''

''Sean specializes in nice. I come by it secondhand.'' Con slid the cellophane-wrapped flowers toward her, along the bedside table. ''Here.''

Beneath the dry humor, she sensed his tension. Did he think because they were lovers, because, she admitted to herself, she loved him, that she expected pretty words to go with his pretty flowers?

''Thank you. They're beautiful.''

''I can do better.'' He pulled an envelope from his breast pocket and handed it to her.

She recognized the red and blue printing from the bank, and the pale tomatoes and acid dressing lurched in her stomach. ''What's this?''

''My bonus check. From your father. I want you to have it.''

''Why?''

He shrugged. ''You did as much as I did to earn it.''

''And you made the bargain with my father. No.''

''He's already given me what I wanted. References, recommendations…I'm Edward Cutler's new fair-haired boy. Take the check. It will help you rebuild.''

''I have insurance for that. I won't take money from my father.''

''It's not your father's money. It's mine.''

She was shaking. ''And what do you want for it?''

''Nothing. No strings, Dixie.''

He knew her too well. ''I don't want it. I don't need it.''

Con went very still. "You mean, you don't need me."

"I mean, I won't be bought by some grand sacrifice on your part. I won't be the unequal partner in this relationship."

His eyes narrowed. "It seems to me the real inequality here is that I'm ready to make a commitment and you're not."

She waved the envelope at him, suddenly furious. "This isn't a commitment. This is a payoff. 'I'm leaving for Boston, but I don't want to worry about you, so here's a check.'"

"You could go with me."

The temptation he offered terrified her. "What?"

"You have to start over anyway. Start over with me, in Boston."

He didn't know her at all. She couldn't give up everything she knew and thought she wanted to live with him in a strange city and be dependent on him for every need.

"And do what?" she demanded. "Live in your apartment, entertain your friends, fit my business in around your schedule?"

She choked and coughed. Grim-faced, he handed her the water bottle and waited until the fit subsided. Her dependence on him while she was so weak and he was so cold was an almost unbearable indignity. If he'd even once told her he loved her...

But he didn't.

"I'm not into playing the available, compliant female," she rasped. "And I've tried the big-city routine on my own already. It's no good, MacNeill."

His face was white, his nostrils pinched. "And that says it all, doesn't it? You're so damned afraid of being taken over, everything's your way or no way at all. Well, you've taught me that doesn't work in consulting, Dixie, and I can tell you it doesn't work for me, either."

He stood, enormous in the tiny hospital room, frustration

rolling from him in waves. "I've got an early flight tomorrow morning. Keep the check. Spend it or burn it or give it back to your daddy…I don't care."

The door swung and bumped behind him. Val sat upright in her hospital bed, grief weighing on her chest and burning at the back of her eyes like smoke.

The sky was heavy with humidity, the dawn a gray promise along the horizon. The lit sign for Beyer's Motel gleamed ghostly above the metal rail that guarded I-40.

Val reached forward to touch the cabbie's shoulder. "There."

"I see it. I know Beyer's Motel." He pulled off the highway. In the silence, Val could hear the roll of the cab's tires and the rush of a passing car traveling west. Her driver glanced in the rearview mirror, his dark eyes alight with small-town curiosity and kindness. "You sure you going to be all right, miss?"

She flushed. "Yes, thank you."

"I mean, you just getting out of hospital and all."

She peered down the row of units to Con's room. The heavy lined curtains were rimmed with light. So he hadn't checked out yet. She wasn't too late.

Her heart hammered. "I'll be fine. Down there. Number twenty."

She handed her fare and an extra ten over the cracked vinyl seat back.

"You want I should wait?" asked the driver.

She took a deep breath and almost coughed. Either she was risking it all, or she wasn't. "No, thank you."

But the cab sat idling anyway, its taillights gleaming like the lions' eyes above her desk, until she gathered her courage to knock on Con's door.

It opened, and she was staring at his broad, hard torso in a buttoned-down blue shirt. She forced her gaze up and made herself smile.

Con's face was impassive. "What are you doing here?"

"I discharged myself. It took a call to Kate, but I did it. May I come in?"

He stepped back to admit her to the run-down hotel room, uninspiringly decorated in shades of beige. "That explains why you're here. Why are you...*here?*"

She recognized her own emphasis from their first morning-after. Here in my space, he meant. Here with me. He wasn't making this easy for her. But then, maybe she didn't need him to.

"I came to make you a deal," she said.

"Now, where have I heard that before?"

The dry humor in his voice gave her hope. "So, I'm my father's daughter."

He crossed his arms against his chest. "I'm listening."

She reached to finger an earring, but her earrings were gone, lost in the fire or taken from her in the ER. She let her hand fall and squared her shoulders.

"You told me I was a survivor," she said. "But last night I let my fear control my choices. I acted like a victim."

He uncrossed his arms. "Dixie—"

"Let me finish. I figured all this out, and I practiced it on the drive over here, and if I don't get it said now, before you leave, I may never say it."

He froze into a pillar of marble, leaning against the dresser.

Her palms were clammy, her heartbeat too fast. Panic seared her breathing. But she wasn't chickening out now. "My aunt Naomi would be proud of me. I have goals and means and independence. When the insurance check comes through, I'll have money. I have control of my life. But I don't have the two things that make everything else worthwhile."

His eyes were brilliant as gemstones in his still face. "What two things?"

She risked it all. "Love. You."

He was silent. And she thought, Oh, my God, I blew it, and something inside her squirmed and bled.

"Where did you think I was going?" he asked at last, very quietly.

"To the airport. To Boston."

"I was coming back to the hospital to talk to you." He turned and opened a dresser drawer. "See? Unpacked. I was throwing things into a suitcase last night when it occurred to me that everything I wanted was right here."

Her heart pounded and sang. "And you always get what you want."

His smile showed he remembered. "Usually." He moved away from the dresser and crossed the room to her and took her hands in his, holding them palm to palm between his own. "But in your case, I'm prepared to wait. You've got reasons not to trust me yet. But I'd be a fool not to trust how I feel for you. How you make me feel. I'm not letting you throw me out of your life, Dixie."

He gathered her to him carefully, mindful of her burns and bruises. They kissed, long and sweetly, until his arms trembled and her head spun.

"So, what's this deal you're prepared to offer me?" he asked, tender laughter in his voice.

She moistened her lips. "I want the bonus my father paid you. On one condition."

His expression shuttered. "You want me to sign something? Fine."

"No. Oh, no. I trust you."

"What, then?"

"I don't believe you're bargaining for a share in my business. I know you're not angling for a role in my life. But I want you in both. I'll take the money on the condition that you become my partner in my new restaurant."

Well, she'd surprised him, at least. His handsome face went blank.

"Are you buying my involvement, Dixie?"

She laughed shakily. "I don't know. I don't think so. I mean, I should know better than anyone it doesn't work that way. But I want you in my life. As my partner, as my lover, as anything you want to be."

There. She'd said it. She'd offered him everything.

Con appeared to consider. "These long-distance partnerships...generally, they don't work."

She'd swallowed her pride. Now she nearly choked on her disappointment. "It doesn't have to be long-distance. I can open anywhere."

"No. No, I don't think so." The wry note in his voice dragged her gaze up to his. And the light she found there ignited a hope inside her that spiraled and glowed like a sparkler on the Fourth of July.

"I love you," Con said deliberately. "I want to be involved with you in every way there is. I want to be your partner. I want to be your lover. I want to be your husband. So, if running a restaurant in North Carolina is part of the deal, I'd say I've found a bargain."

Her heart did a slow roll in her chest, making her dizzy.

"Husband?"

His dark brows lifted. "It's the logical solution. But, like I said, I can wait if you need time to get used to the idea."

Rising joy wrestled with doubt. "What about your big comeback?"

"I'd rather come home. To you."

"What about Boston?"

"What did you call it? Doing work I don't care about among people I dislike?" He shook his head with the quick decisiveness that was so much a part of him. "I'd rather be my own man."

The man she loved, she thought. Competent and certain, straightforward in his thinking, honest in his dealings, a little irritating in his Yankee confidence.

She stood on tiptoe to touch her lips to his chin. "How about being mine?"

He drew a sharp breath. His chest expanded. Her heart swelled with love. He framed her face in his big hands, making her feel infinitely precious, and kissed her again with hunger and tenderness and love.

Her fingers curled into his shirt. The ache in her throat owed as much to joy as swallowed smoke. She coughed slightly, to relieve it. "Will it be enough for you, being a consultant?"

"Yeah, it will. I like the work. And it will leave me more time for us."

"And a family." She liked the idea, liked the thought of re-creating the scene on his brother's porch with more babies, more laughter, more MacNeills. "I better warn you. I think I might like a large family."

"Yeah?" His fingers grazed her cheek, his touch impossibly tender. "And what do you expect me to do about that?"

Love welled inside her, rose as laughter to her eyes and spilled as challenge in her smile. She tossed her head, making her braid fly over her shoulder. "I've already defined the problem for you, MacNeill. I'll leave it to you to solve it."

* * * * *

THE
FORTUNES
OF TEXAS™

*Membership in this family has its
privileges…and its price. But what a fortune
can't buy, a true-bred Texas love is sure to bring!*

On sale in February 2000…

The Sheikh's Secret Son

by

KASEY MICHAELS

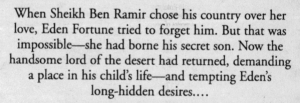

When Sheikh Ben Ramir chose his country over her
love, Eden Fortune tried to forget him. But that was
impossible—she had borne his secret son. Now the
handsome lord of the desert had returned, demanding
a place in his child's life—and tempting Eden's
long-hidden desires.…

THE FORTUNES OF TEXAS continues with
THE HEIRESS AND THE SHERIFF
by Stella Bagwell, available in March
from Silhouette Books.

Silhouette®

Where love comes alive™

Available at your favorite retail outlet.

SILHOUETTE'S 20TH ANNIVERSARY CONTEST
OFFICIAL RULES
NO PURCHASE NECESSARY TO ENTER

1. To enter, follow directions published in the offer to which you are responding. Contest begins 1/1/00 and ends on 8/24/00 (the "Promotion Period"). Method of entry may vary. Mailed entries must be postmarked by 8/24/00, and received by 8/31/00.

2. During the Promotion Period, the Contest may be presented via the Internet. Entry via the Internet may be restricted to residents of certain geographic areas that are disclosed on the Web site. To enter via the Internet, if you are a resident of a geographic area in which Internet entry is permissible, follow the directions displayed on-line, including typing your essay of 100 words or fewer telling us "Where In The World Your Love Will Come Alive." On-line entries must be received by 11:59 p.m. Eastern Standard time on 8/24/00. Limit one e-mail entry per person, household and e-mail address per day, per presentation. If you are a resident of a geographic area in which entry via the Internet is permissible, you may, in lieu of submitting an entry on-line, enter by mail, by hand-printing your name, address, telephone number and contest number/name on an 8"x 11" plain piece of paper and telling us in 100 words or fewer "Where In The World Your Love Will Come Alive," and mailing via first-class mail to: Silhouette 20th Anniversary Contest, (in the U.S.) P.O. Box 9069, Buffalo, NY 14269-9069; (In Canada) P.O. Box 637, Fort Erie, Ontario, Canada L2A 5X3. Limit one 8"x 11" mailed entry per person, household and e-mail address per day. On-line and/or 8"x 11" mailed entries received from persons residing in geographic areas in which Internet entry is not permissible will be disqualified. No liability is assumed for lost, late, incomplete, inaccurate, nondelivered or misdirected mail, or misdirected e-mail, for technical, hardware or software failures of any kind, lost or unavailable network connection, or failed, incomplete, garbled or delayed computer transmission or any human error which may occur in the receipt or processing of the entries in the contest.

3. Essays will be judged by a panel of members of the Silhouette editorial and marketing staff based on the following criteria:

> Sincerity (believability, credibility)—50%
> Originality (freshness, creativity)—30%
> Aptness (appropriateness to contest ideas)—20%

Purchase or acceptance of a product offer does not improve your chances of winning. In the event of a tie, duplicate prizes will be awarded.

4. All entries become the property of Harlequin Enterprises Ltd., and will not be returned. Winner will be determined no later than 10/31/00 and will be notified by mail. Grand Prize winner will be required to sign and return Affidavit of Eligibility within 15 days of receipt of notification. Noncompliance within the time period may result in disqualification and an alternative winner may be selected. All municipal, provincial, federal, state and local laws and regulations apply. Contest open only to residents of the U.S. and Canada who are 18 years of age or older, and is void wherever prohibited by law. Internet entry is restricted solely to residents of those geographical areas in which Internet entry is permissible. Employees of Torstar Corp., their affiliates, agents and members of their immediate families are not eligible. Taxes on the prizes are the sole responsibility of winners. Entry and acceptance of any prize offered constitutes permission to use winner's name, photograph or other likeness for the purposes of advertising, trade and promotion on behalf of Torstar Corp. without further compensation to the winner, unless prohibited by law. Torstar Corp and D.L. Blair Inc., their parents, affiliates and subsidiaries, are not responsible for errors in printing or electronic presentation of contest or entries. In the event of printing or other errors which may result in unintended prize values or duplication of prizes, all affected contest materials or entries shall be null and void. If for any reason the Internet portion of the contest is not capable of running as planned, including infection by computer virus, bugs, tampering, unauthorized intervention, fraud, technical failures, or any other causes beyond the control of Torstar Corp. which corrupt or affect the administration, secrecy, fairness, integrity or proper conduct of the contest, Torstar Corp. reserves the right, at its sole discretion, to disqualify any individual who tampers with the entry process and to cancel, terminate, modify or suspend the contest or the Internet portion thereof. In the event of a dispute regarding an on-line entry, the entry will be deemed submitted by the authorized holder of the e-mail account submitted at the time of entry. Authorized account holder is defined as the natural person who is assigned to an e-mail address by an Internet access provider, on-line service provider or other organization that is responsible for arranging an e-mail address for the domain associated with the submitted e-mail address.

5. Prizes: Grand Prize—a $10,000 vacation to anywhere in the world. Travelers (at least one must be 18 years of age or older) or parent or guardian if one traveler is a minor, must sign and return a Release of Liability prior to departure. Travel must be completed by December 31, 2001, and is subject to space and accommodations availability. Two hundred (200) Second Prizes—a two-book limited edition autographed collector set from one of the Silhouette Anniversary authors: Nora Roberts, Diana Palmer, Linda Howard or Annette Broadrick (value $10.00 each set). All prizes are valued in U.S. dollars.

6. For a list of winners (available after 10/31/00), send a self-addressed, stamped envelope to: Harlequin Silhouette 20th Anniversary Winners, P.O. Box 4200, Blair, NE 68009-4200.

Contest sponsored by Torstar Corp., P.O. Box 9042, Buffalo, NY 14269-9042.

PS20RULES

ENTER FOR
A CHANCE TO WIN*

Silhouette's 20ᵗʰ Anniversary Contest

Tell Us Where in the World
You Would Like *Your* Love To Come Alive...
And We'll Send the Lucky Winner There!

Silhouette wants to take you wherever
your happy ending can come true.

Here's how to enter: Tell us, in 100 words or less,
where you want to go to make your love come alive!

In addition to the grand prize, there will be 200
runner-up prizes, collector's-edition book sets
autographed by one of the Silhouette anniversary
authors: **Nora Roberts, Diana Palmer,
Linda Howard** or **Annette Broadrick**.

DON'T MISS YOUR CHANCE TO WIN!
ENTER NOW! No Purchase Necessary

Silhouette®
Where love comes alive™

Name:

Address:

City: State/Province:

Zip/Postal Code:

Mail to Harlequin Books: **In the U.S.**: P.O. Box 9069, Buffalo, NY
14269-9069; **In Canada**: P.O. Box 637, Fort Erie, Ontario, L4A 5X3

PS20CON_R